VESTA - PAINWORLD

by

JENNIFER JANE POPE

Published by **CHIMERA**
ISBN 9781780806389

This work is sold subject to the condition that it shall not, by way of trade or otherwise, be lent, resold, hired out or otherwise circulated without the publisher's prior written consent in any form of binding or cover other than that in which it is published, and without a similar condition being imposed on the subsequent purchaser. The author asserts that all characters depicted in this work of fiction are eighteen years of age or older, and that all characters and situations are entirely imaginary and bear no relation to any real person or actual happening.

Copyright Jennifer Jane Pope. The right of Jennifer Jane Pope to be identified as author of this book has been asserted in accordance with section 77 and 78 of the Copyrights Designs and Patents Act 1988.

This novel is fiction - in real life practice safe sex.

The masked man was close now and she could hear his laboured breathing, the air hissing in and out of the narrow apertures in his tight fitting leather hood, but in the near total darkness Nadia could see nothing. He, on the other hand, she knew, would know exactly where she was, for her white latex bodysuit would appear almost luminous, while the black leather which covered him from head to toe gave him an unfair advantage.

She stopped, turning slowly, facing the approaching sound, crouching ready for the expected onslaught.

'Okay, clever fucker,' she growled. 'Come get me if you're man enough.'

Her only answer was an ear-splitting crack, as the bullwhip coiled itself around her right ankle, the sudden jerk overbalancing her so that she fell backwards, cracking her head against the unforgiving stone floor and momentarily losing consciousness. It was all her opponent needed and, by the time her head had even halfway cleared, he was on Nadia, grasping her wrists and twisting them cruelly behind her, snapping steel cuffs around them and rendering further resistance all but impossible.

She heard the faint clicking sound of switches being thrown and then, as the dim overhead tubes flickered into life, got her first glimpse of the creature who had been stalking her through these catacombs for the past half hour. Nadia's heartbeat moved up yet another notch as she saw the huge leather pouch hanging down from his groin and the quick release buckles that held it attached to the rest of the suit. Unless some of that was padding...

They were in a long chamber, one wall of which was lined with heavy wooden chests, the other wall beset with racks, from which dripped a lifetime's collection of whips, crops, straps, chains, gags and masks. The bastard had let her lead him here, she realised now, awaiting his moment until they were in the one place he had prepared for her. Her darting eyes took in the cramped cages, the stocks, pillory, whipping post and X-shaped timber cross-bolted into the centre of the floor. How she had managed to move through this minefield without falling over something, she had no idea. Nor had she smelled the heavy aromas of leather and latex that now assailed her nostrils.

'Damn you, Marlon,' she muttered, under her breath. 'That's bloody well cheating.' She slowed her breathing and stared defiantly as her captor walked nonchalantly back towards her.

'Very nice,' he sneered, his pupils bright through the eye slits. His gloved right hand dropped to the pouch and he massaged it, the message obvious. 'The bitch mistress herself,' he went on, standing over her, savouring his triumph. 'The bitch mistress who is about to become the grovelling slave girl.'

'Never!' Nadia cried and spat at him, but the saliva sprayed harmlessly wide of her target as the brute side-stepped with an agile grace his huge build denied. The leather sheathed frame rocked with laughter.

'Never say never,' he gloated, and kicked idly at her high heeled booted foot. 'From where I'm standing, I'd say it was going to be very soon and, quite possibly, forever. Now, let's have you up, bitch queen!' He reached down and hauled her effortlessly to her feet, proof of his strength if proof were needed, for Nadia was not a small woman. However, even in her steepling heels she felt dwarfed by him.

Resistance was futile, but she still struggled as he dragged her across to the pillory. With her hands cuffed at her back only the neck stock was required and, seizing her hair, he bent her forward and slammed the heavy timber board into place. In a trice he had returned, having selected a wicked looking multi-thonged whip, heavy knots at the end of each of its strands. Nadia swallowed hard, for she knew what sort of havoc such an implement could wreak.

'Please,' she wailed, 'not with that. *Please.*'

He laughed and ran the stock of the whip along her rubber-covered spine. 'You'd rather I used the bullwhip, would you?'

Nadia gasped. 'No - no, that's not what I meant!'

'Then it's this, my arrogant bitch,' he snapped. 'What makes you think a slave has the right to select her punishment anyway?'

'But I'm not...' Nadia began, but stopped, realising the futility of further argument. Of course she wasn't a slave, not out there, not in the real world... but here? Here she was in the role of escapee slave girl, caught and about to be punished by her master, a creature whose face she had never seen. The man chuckled, a deep, throaty sound without real humour.

'Not what?' he said. 'Not a cock-sucking little whore who deserves a sound thrashing for her arrogance? Not a hungry-cunted slut who should beg for a man's meat?' He reversed his grip on the whip and brought the handle up between Nadia's thighs. The butt slid easily into her wet quim and he allowed seven or eight inches to penetrate her before stopping. 'Hah!' he exclaimed triumphantly, pushing his face close to hers. 'Even the anticipation of the whip's kiss is betrayed. Well, I'll not keep you waiting.'

The handle slipped from her and Nadia tensed. The wide neck stock prevented her from seeing anything to the side or behind her, but she heard the sound of his boots shuffling on the stone and knew he was carefully adjusting his stance and position for the maximum efficiency. She barely heard the whistling of the braided thongs before the lashes exploded across the middle of her back, but she screamed, unashamedly, as the agonising fire seared through her every fibre.

'Count, bitch!' he roared. Nadia knew the rules.

'One!' she managed to gasp, between sobs. The whip whistled again, and again her shriek echoed around the unsympathetic walls.

'T-t-twooo!'

Whistle.

Crack!

'Dreeeeeeeeee!'

Nadia's world started to turn a deep purple...

James Naylor screwed up his hawk-like features in concentration, as his eyes scanned the crowded VDU screen in front of him. His right hand moved automatically on the mouse, zooming in on different segments of the pages as he browsed them for the second time.

'There!' he said at last, finger jabbing at the relevant menu. 'That's the bitch, even

3

though the site address is different. I'd know her turn of phrase anywhere.' Behind and slightly to one side of him, Christina Fredrickson stirred her powerful body inside its black leather shell and leaned forward for a closer view.

'Virtual reality,' she murmured. 'I wonder exactly how far they've got with it?' Her voice was slightly accented, betraying her Danish origins, but her English was otherwise flawless.

'A lot further than we suspected, judging by this,' Naylor rasped. 'Marlon Vincent may be slightly crazy, but he's an absolute genius. That's why I tried to get the bastard to work for me in the first place.'

'Perhaps you should have offered him more money,' Christina mused. 'He did say that the figures you were talking about wouldn't be enough to fund his research at the level he needed.'

'Bollocks!' Naylor snapped. 'The little bastard was just being plain greedy. I even offered him a percentage deal once we went on the market.'

'Which was no damned good to him if he didn't have the up-front cash to fund the project,' Christina persisted. Of all Naylor's employees, she was the only one, male or female, who would ever dare to disagree with him, but then Christina was an unusual person in more ways than one. At nearly six and a half feet tall and weighing in at a fraction under seventeen stone of fabulously sculpted muscle, she would have been quite capable of flooring Naylor with a single blow. In addition, Naylor knew only too well, the amazonian blonde possessed a cruel streak that exceeded even his own.

She was also extremely inventive and was constantly developing new refinements to practise on their almost willing volunteers, and not-so-willing and steadily growing collection of slaves, most of whom they had tricked into servitude with a mixture of extortion, blackmail and bribery. Christina rose from her seat and walked slowly across to the open window of Naylor's study, her cropped head narrowly missing the light fitting, due to the towering heels she invariably wore. There was only the slightest hint of a limp now, but the broken leg and the way in which it had been inflicted on her would never be forgotten.

That little bitch Lianne and her sissy boyfriend had a lot to answer for in Christina's book, and she was determined that both accounts would be settled before too much longer. She already had plans for the pair of them and frequently lay awake at nights conjuring up ever more evil schemes and scenarios. Her private cellar, deep beneath Naylor's house, already contained the 'trophy pole', upon which Christina planned to mount Lianne Connolly, impaled by the monstrous dildo fixed into the centre of the narrow, curved saddle bar.

As for Paul Dean, Christina had not yet made up her mind, but she did know one thing for sure. When she dressed the little bastard in a rubber maid's uniform this time, there would be no need to strap his male organs out of the way. With the help of a particular doctor of her acquaintance whose gambling habits ensured he was forever in need of large sums of cash, Paul Dean would not just play the part of a woman, she would make sure he became one.

'If Muirhead gets anything like a start on us, we might as well give up altogether,' Christina said, speaking over her shoulder. 'Jurgen Koenig seems to be spending his days with his thumb stuck up his arse. Hasn't he made any sort of progress this last month?'

'Some,' Naylor said, 'but not enough. He's having trouble capturing the visual images in a way that can be regenerated realistically.'

'He's not a patch on Vincent,' Christina said, 'but then we knew that before he even started. I told you that you should have let me deal with little Marlon. A couple of days downstairs with me and the girls and he would have been begging to work for nothing. Then he'd have had plenty of spare funds for the research side.'

'Maybe you're right,' Naylor conceded, grudgingly, 'but it's too fucking late to cry over spilt milk at this stage.'

'Perhaps,' Christina mused. 'And then again, perhaps not.'

'What are you getting at?' Naylor demanded. 'It's certainly too late to get at Marlon now. My sources tell me he hasn't set a foot outside Nadia's place in over three months, except when he's had to go to London and then she sends at least three minders with him. And she won't risk losing him at this late stage, you can be sure.

'She'll know I approached him originally and she'll also have a good idea how fucking useless the Kraut is, so she won't have to be a genius to know that my only hope is in getting Marlon from her. It'd be like trying to kidnap the President of the United fucking States.'

'Not necessarily,' Christina said, turning back to face into the room. The sunlight behind her glinted off the black leather catsuit and created a halo effect around her stubbly blonde skull. 'Marlon Vincent may be safe inside Muirhead's personal Fort Knox, but the rest of the world most certainly isn't.'

'What are you driving at?'

'Well, I always thought you were trying to handle Marlon the wrong way,' Christina began, leaning back against the window frame. 'Money was never going to convince him, except that he needed large sums to fund the development work itself. People like Marlon don't care about money for themselves, which was why I tried to tell you that you should have agreed to his terms originally.

'Marlon Vincent is a borderline fruitcake, like most geniuses. He'd work for nothing, just so long as he could keep on with his compulsion to achieve perfection...'

'Okay, okay!' Naylor interrupted, his features clouding angrily. 'So you were right and I was wrong; there's no need to keep ramming it down my throat. Tell me something I don't already know!'

A slow smile spread across Christina's square features. 'I intend to,' she said, quietly. 'I've made it my business to investigate friend Marlon's background and I've found an Achilles heel, I think.'

'You think?' Naylor echoed, testily. 'Well, madam, for your information, I had Marlon checked out pretty thoroughly myself and all the usual avenues are useless. He was orphaned at the age of five, raised in a home, has never had a girlfriend and has no living relatives we can use as leverage.'

'Except his half sister,' Christina replied, smoothly. Naylor opened his mouth, but no words came out. Christina's mouth twitched crookedly. 'Surprised?' she challenged. At last, Naylor found his tongue.

'I don't believe you,' he growled. 'I had the orphanage records checked out thoroughly and there was no sister mentioned anywhere. If there had been, she would have been taken into care along with him, because there were no uncles or aunts on either side of the family.'

'I said half sister,' Christina pointed out. 'Marlon's father left his first wife while she was expecting their first child and took up with Marlon's mother, whom he'd obviously been screwing on the side for some time, seeing as Marlon was actually born a month before the girl. When Marlon's parents were killed, the first wife refused to have anything to do with what she called the "little bastard". She had already remarried an Australian businessman and moved to Melbourne and she refused to even consider adoption.'

'So why would a half sister, who Marlon has never seen, be a lever?' Naylor demanded.

'I never said he hadn't seen her,' Christina retorted. 'Actually, when he was eighteen, Marlon started tracing his family tree, or what little there was of it, and he made contact with the girl through some agency. His parents had left him well provided for, financially at least, so he took off down under to meet the sister he never had. By all accounts, they hit it off really well.

'The slightly mad genius streak must come from the father's side, because the sister is about as crazy as Marlon. She's made quite a name for herself as a sculptor, though it's not what I'd call art. She welds just about anything and everything together and gives her pieces titles like "Fall of Woman" and "Checkpoint Infinity". Idiots with more money than taste pay hundreds of thousands for her work.' Naylor's jaw dropped even lower than it had upon learning of the existence of a relative in the first place.

'You're talking about Clarissa Beaumont!' he exclaimed, a note of awe tingeing his voice. 'She's the cookie Aussie bird...'

'With the bloody great exhibition in Birmingham at the moment,' Christina finished the sentence for him. 'Which is where she's staying at present. I have the hotel and the room number.'

'But we can't kidnap someone as famous as Clarissa Beaumont,' Naylor almost shouted. 'There'd be a fucking uproar they'd hear all the way back to Australia!' Christina was shaking her head.

'I doubt it,' she said. 'And so would you, if you knew as much about dear Clarissa as I've found out. She has a history of just taking off into the blue and then resurfacing in places like Nepal or Peru weeks, sometimes months later.'

'But not in the middle of an exhibition,' Naylor persisted.

'No? She disappeared for three months halfway through an exhibition in Los Angeles only last year, and halfway through a reception being given in her honour by her home town, she just upped and walked out. Everyone assumed she'd gone to the ladies, but the next they heard of her was when she appeared in New York with a load of scrap iron she called "The Feast of the Vampire King". She said she'd been inspired halfway through the main course and just had to follow her muse.'

'I seem to remember reading something along those lines,' Naylor admitted, thoughtfully. 'The press call her the Iron Butterfly.'

'Something to do with bats would be more appropriate,' Christina snapped back. 'But at least it would work to our advantage. If Miss Scrap Iron melted away overnight, everyone would assume she was off communing with her arc welding kit and just sit back and wait for her to show up again in Outer Mongolia.'

'I reckon you could be right,' Naylor said. He was smiling broadly now. 'Perhaps it might be an idea if you had a couple of the team scout around Clarissa's hotel and see what can be worked out.'

'Already done,' Christina smirked. 'The hotel's not such a hot idea, but I've already set another plan in motion. We'll have ourselves a sculptress-in-residence in about forty-eight hours from now, unless I'm much mistaken.'

'That was unbelievable!' Nadia gasped, opening her eyes and struggling to focus on the figure leaning over her. Marlon Vincent grinned, his balding pate reddening with pleasure as he began carefully detaching the tiny electrodes from the depths of Nadia's luxuriant mane of hair. The headband that ran around her forehead felt heavy when she tried to move her head and Marlon tut-tutted his disapproval.

'Don't be so impatient,' he said. 'These little filaments are extremely delicate and it takes forever to solder them back if they break. I'm working on an improved model, but it isn't finished yet.

'Just lie back and relax. Apart from anything else, you'll feel a bit weak and dizzy for the next five minutes.' Nadia willed her muscles to go limp and lay, staring up at the ceiling, while Marlon fussed over her. Finally, he seemed satisfied and lifted the electronic coronet clear of her.

'You can sit up now,' he said, placing the web of gadgetry carefully on the wheeled trolley beside the narrow bed upon which Nadia was lying. 'But do it slowly, and don't panic if you suddenly feel nauseous.'

Gingerly, Nadia eased herself up onto her elbows and immediately retched. Her ears buzzed and the room wobbled before her eyes, but she refused to give in to it. She screwed her eyes shut again and shook her head, immediately regretting the action, for her stomach lurched violently and, for several seconds, she was certain she was going to be sick.

'Steady now.' She felt Marlon's hands under her shoulders, supporting her and lifting her into a proper sitting position. Slowly, the nausea subsided and Nadia risked opening her eyes again. In front of her, the banks of myriad little lights danced their crazy patterns across the various screens and panels.

'Bloody amazing!' she breathed. 'Absolutely bloody amazing! I didn't think it would be at all like that. It was so realistic, it was just as though I was really there and it was really happening to me.'

'In a way, you were - and it was,' Marlon said, the pride in his voice impossible to mistake. 'After all, in the real world your body sends the impulses and the data your brain translates to enable you to experience the physical reality of your situation. VESTIBULE merely replaces the real world stimuli with the equivalent that she generates to order.

'Therefore, my dear Nadia, you experience events in VESTIBULE's world exactly as you would experience events in your - and dare I use the word - normal world.' Nadia took in a deep breath, held it for a few seconds and then exhaled in a long sigh.

'But I still can't quite believe how I felt,' she said. 'I mean, not only was he so real, but so were the cuffs and chains, the rubber catsuit, and as for the whip...' She did not complete the sentence, simply shaking her head slowly. Marlon chuckled.

'I know,' he said. 'And I'll bet you can't wait to check in the mirror to make sure you aren't marked. Well, I can assure you you're not. You can't even feel the pain any more, can you?'

'No, you're right,' Nadia said. The fact had not occurred to her, but it was true. One minute she had been there, bound and pilloried, her whole being a mass of pain, the hooded man's lashes cutting her back to ribbons and then - wham! Apart from the initial dizziness and sickness, nothing.

Tentatively, she swung her long legs over the side of the bed and lowered her stiletto heeled feet to the carpeted floor. She half expected her knees to buckle when she transferred her weight onto them, but surprisingly they held firm and she stood upright with no difficulty. She turned and looked back at the machine.

'Why do you call this box of tricks VESTIBULE?' she asked. 'Today is the first time I've heard you use that name.' Marlon looked slightly abashed.

'Well, I only just thought it up,' he admitted. 'It stands for Virtual Experience of Sexuality Targeted into Bondage Unusual Longings and Erotica. It's not that good, I know, but it was the best I could come up with.' He grinned. 'Actually, I usually just call her VESTA for short.'

'VESTA?' Nadia pursed her lips. 'And why her? Why is she female?'

Marlon let out a little snort and turned to place a fatherly hand on his invention's gleaming stainless superstructure. 'You don't think a male mind could handle all the things VESTA does, do you?' he chuckled. Nadia laughed herself. Marlon, she had to admit, probably had a good point there. But now came the serious part.

'How many people did you say could use VESTA at the same time?' she asked.

Marlon turned back to face her and gave a shrug. 'How long's a piece of string?' he countered. 'She's got four passive terminals and two active ones at the moment, but that's just limited through financial pressures. As far as I know, theoretically there's no limit, although the physical factor of available space for the terminals themselves would come into it. But, if you had a large enough place, you could have a couple of dozen of both types of terminal.'

Nadia looked thoughtful. 'Tell me again,' she said, slowly, 'what's the difference between active and passive terminals?' She settled herself back to perch on the edge of the bed as Marlon explained.

'Well, you were hooked up to a passive terminal, which means you have no control over the scenarios you experience, other than to react how you would in real life. Those scenarios are largely created and controlled by VESTA herself, but, if someone wants to hook into an active terminal, they can introduce elements at will. They can either participate in the events actively, or else they can just view everything, as though through a monitor.

'As you know, my tests so far have been confined to the two young ladies you so generously assigned to me, plus my own semi-active participation. I daren't experience the passive side personally, at least not yet, just in case something were to go wrong and I couldn't retrieve myself, but it's safe enough on the active terminals. There's a failsafe password I can use and it shuts everything down immediately.'

'Interesting.' Lydia stroked her chin with one elegantly manicured fingernail. 'So, on a passive port you're at the mercy of the machine or someone on an active port, but on an active port you either just observe and tinker with things, or actually take part, but with the ability to change any developments which don't immediately take your fancy?'

Marlon nodded enthusiastically. 'That about sums it up,' he agreed. 'So, what do you think?'

Lydia wrinkled her nose. 'I'll tell you what I think,' she said. 'I think you're a genius.' Marlon's face and head were turning an even deeper hue now.

'Thank you, fair lady,' he said. Lydia slowly stood up again and walked over to stand in front of VESTA.

'Very Exciting Set of Toys for All,' she whispered, stroking the gleaming metal. 'That's what you are, VESTA.' She looked over her shoulder at Marlon, and smiled.

'Tell me,' she asked, 'how long before you could have VESTA kitted out with a dozen of each terminal?'

'It depends on how much money is available,' Marlon said.

'How much would twelve of each cost?' Marlon thought for a few seconds and gave her a figure. Nadia nodded. 'So, how long?'

Marlon grinned. 'Six weeks?'

'Four.'

'Okay, you got it.'

Clarissa Beaumont may have inherited her genius and streak of occasional near insanity from the late father she shared in common with Marlon Vincent, but her looks had come, most definitely, from her maternal side.

Of above average height, she was slim, but with a sensational figure that would have ensured her a career in a completely different walk of life had she not been such a success in her chosen field. A wild mane of deep red hair framed her soft oval features, and her large green eyes and wide mouth had featured in the dreams of thousands of men the world over. Not that Clarissa had even considered the possibility of this, for, although she had lost her virginity in her teens and had not exactly starved herself of sexual activity, sex to her was just something to be enjoyed when the mood took her, in much the same way as she might enjoy a game of tennis when she fancied some fresh air and exercise. Had anyone intimated that Clarissa Beaumont might be the object of carnal desire, she would have stared at them wide-eyed and then giggled with disbelief.

Clarissa was an incurable giggler, though her laughter had a sort of musical beauty about it that ensured no one ever found her habit at all grating. In fact, everything about her endeared her to everybody she met, apart, that was, from her propensity to drop off the planet for weeks at a time, which caused her agent, George Mallory, to consider whether his best course might not be to chain her down somewhere and keep her on a leash whenever she ventured outdoors. He had ventured such an opinion to Clarissa herself, who had found the idea most amusing. In fact, her next piece featured a giant pair of handcuffs and a scold's bridle and was entitled "Fixed Point in a Changing World".

Quite what the significance was of the three bicycle wheels, the two pram handles and the supermarket trolley cut in half along its length, no one was ever quite sure, but the Austrian merchant banker who handed over a cheque for ninety thousand pounds to George kept assuring everyone that he had acquired an absolute bargain.

He did not mention that he would have paid ten times that amount to possess the sculptress herself, possibly aware of her reputation for mixing bar-room language with bar-room physicality if she took exception to certain people and circumstances.

The Asian girl now sitting across the restaurant table from Clarissa was a little overdressed for the Australian girl's taste, preferring herself to spend most of her days in baggy jeans and ex-navy work-shirt, and usually wearing more formal blouses and pleated skirts only when she had to, or when good manners and a certain degree of lip service to convention dictated the polite alternative.

Her dusky dinner companion looked as if she had been poured into the tight satin sheath dress, and as if certain parts of her were trying to pour themselves back out again. About her throat she wore a wide choker of glittering rubies, and her fingers were laden with expensive rings. When she had first entered the room Clarissa found it hard to believe that anyone could stand, let alone walk, in the steepling, needle sharp heels she wore, but the woman had moved with an effortless grace, every male eye in the place riveted to the expanse of nylon clad thigh that the brief hem of her dress left on display.

'I don't usually do commissions,' Clarissa said, her antipodean twang now muted by a few years of globe-trotting, 'but your offer definitely intrigues me. Tell me more about it.'

'There's not much I can tell you at this stage,' the other woman said. 'It's my husband's idea really, and all I am is the messenger. He felt you might be more sympathetic to a fellow female.' Her accent was impeccable, every word betraying an expensive education and Clarissa, although pecuniary considerations had never yet swayed her decisions, imagined that the husband in question would be a very wealthy man indeed.

'All I know is that Stanley has purchased this island in the Caribbean, a remote and very barren little place, which comprises one mountain, one very small village and a landing stage,' the woman continued. 'Stanley seems to think that his mountain would be the ideal place for one of your works, and he sent me to sound you out.'

'And exactly just what does Stanley envisage this work being?' Clarissa probed.

The dark girl smiled, revealing a perfect set of small, brilliantly white teeth.

'I don't think Stanley has the faintest idea,' she confessed. 'Stanley is, shall we say, somewhat different from most men in his position. His grandfather and father made all the money and Stanley became something of a rebel. He had artistic leanings himself, but they were stifled by his family and, although I would never dream of suggesting so to him, he was not quite as talented as he might have liked to believe.' She spread her hands in an effusive gesture.

'I hope you don't think I'm being disloyal in saying that,' she smiled. 'I love Stanley very dearly and would never dream of doing anything to hurt him, but I think you're entitled to know the truth. Stanley is and always has been, a dreamer, a man of visions and ambitions, who seeks to better the lot of his fellow man. He has given millions of dollars to poor countries and invested three art galleries on three different continents, although always anonymously.'

'He sounds like a thoroughly decent guy,' Clarissa murmured. The dark head bobbed enthusiastically.

'Oh, he is,' the woman agreed, readily. 'An absolutely darling man. You really must meet him and see for yourself.' Now it was Clarissa who was nodding.

'I reckon you're right,' she said. She reached for the wine list, noting the bottle between them was nearly empty. 'I'm sorry,' she said, peering over the leather-bound card, 'you'll have to excuse me, but I can't remember your first name, Mrs Brooke-Read.' The woman inclined her head slightly to one side, her smile as brilliant as ever.

'So like Stanley,' she sighed. 'But please, I take no offence. It's Marika, and I'm so glad you agreed to see me.'

Lianne Connolly stood in front of the tall mirror and preened herself, revelling in the dull sheen of her rubber covered body, the neck-to-toe catsuit and the stiff over-corset, laced until her already attractive figure had taken on the sexy hourglass shape that so many of their readers and surfers found impossible to resist.

She breathed deeply - as deeply as the corset would allow, anyway - savouring the heady aroma of warm latex, and smiled at her reflected self. If anyone had told her, only a few months earlier, that she would find the mere act of dressing herself into one of these exotic costumes a sexually stimulating experience, she would have laughed them out of the room, but that was then and this was now.

Now she could assume the role of Mary Lou, inept rubber-clad sidekick of the slightly scatty private detective, Della de Linkwent, on a daily basis, get paid a handsome salary for her exertions and enjoy some of the best sex she never imagined could exist. Her hand dropped slyly to her crotch, her gloved fingers stroking the velcro-sealed opening, closed to cover the slight bulge made by the flanged base of the vibrator that lay embedded deep inside her, silent and motionless at the moment, but ready to burst into tempestuous life at the touch of its button.

'Stop playing with yourself and help me lace up this bloody suit, will you?' Ellen Sanderson's brunette head bobbed into view behind Lianne's left shoulder, her brightly carmined lips parted in a broad smile. Ellen had been the one to introduce Lianne to Nadia Muirhead's operation, when another model had been taken unexpectedly ill. Nadia was head of the Darius Publishing Company, owned the estate and huge old house that served as the base for all their creative activities and was, according to Ellen, fabulously wealthy.

'Anything you say, Miss Della,' Lianne said, adopting the Southern Belle accent she had taken up when the animated version of their cartoon strip adventures had been launched into cyberspace. A natural mimic, Lianne dubbed on the voices for several of the series' other female characters, though Ellen, with her chirpy cockneyesque accent, provided her own voice for Della de Linkwent. Ellen grinned and turned her back to her friend.

'Sometimes I wish they'd find a way to make this catsuit easier to get into,' she said. 'I mean, your rubber outfits simply zip up the back and, at a push, you can get into it by yourself.'

'I don't know what you're moaning about,' Lianne laughed. 'It's me that has to fart around with all the laces.' Ellen's catsuit was fashioned from gleaming white leather, the legs ending in boots, the arms in gloves and a high collar enclosing her throat when it was finally in place. However, because the leggings/boots had to be laced the full length of their backs, the sleeves the full length of the outside of each arm and the back laced from the top of Ellen's buttocks to the neck, it did indeed require a lot of patience to fit and could not be managed without assistance.

For a real life private eye, the suit's design would have been impractical in the extreme, for once all the laces had been fully closed it restricted Ellen's movements and reduced her to little more than a stiff-legged marionette, but then the readers and viewers had no way of knowing that. All they saw was a beautiful leather queen, an obvious dominant, except that Della usually found herself trapped into the submissive role by a series of nasty and increasingly more inventive villains and villainesses.

And that worried Ellen about as much as it worried Lianne, who regularly found herself sharing her 'boss's' plights and, more often than not, was on the receiving end of even worse treatments.

'You know,' Lianne murmured, stooping awkwardly to begin at the bottom of Ellen's left leg, 'if this gizmo of Marlon's works the way it seems to so far and if Nadia brings off this idea of coupling it to the internet, all this will be a thing of the past.'

'How d'you mean?'

'Well, there'll be no need for us to go through all this rigmarole, will there?' Lianne pointed out. 'The whole thing will be done electronically, or by silicon chips, or whatever.'

'You sound disappointed,' Ellen replied. Lianne sighed.

'Well, yes, I suppose I am,' she admitted. 'I've just about got into really enjoying all this, and then...'

'Along comes Marlon and deprives you of your favourite fetish,' Ellen said. 'Yeah, I know what you mean, but then there'll still be the ordinary cartoon strip to pose for.'

'I doubt it. From what Marlon said, his precious VESTA can produce hard copy from the various sessions, and even better than either Sonia or Naylor.' Sonia Hughes was the dark haired artist who had taken over the job of producing the finished artwork from Nadia's original artist, the treacherous and vicious James Naylor. She was also a born masochist and passionate bondage freak, often joining in and playing one of the roles she would eventually depict on paper.

'That's as maybe,' Ellen said, 'but no machine can reproduce what a true artist can convey. Even Jimmy bloody Naylor had the right feel, arsehole or no arsehole, and Sonia's a mile better.'

'We'll see,' Lianne said, turning her attention to Ellen's other leg. 'All I know is that if Marlon's machine can convince me I'm really being strung up and having my lights screwed, it shouldn't have much trouble turning out a cartoon strip.'

'Very nice indeed,' James Naylor whistled appreciatively, staring down at the naked form on the bed. 'I've only ever seen her in magazine photographs before, and she always struck me as a scruffy little sort.'

'She wasn't exactly an advert for Harpers and Queen,' Christina grunted. 'The bloody dress she was wearing when Marika brought her in looked as though she'd bought it from the local Oxfam shop, and I doubt whether she even owns a makeup kit.'

'The basic material's pretty good, though,' Naylor asserted. Clarissa Beaumont's deep red mane was spread out about her head, the matching red bush between her thighs seemingly glowing against her pale skin. 'I think I might enjoy keeping her from getting bored during her little stay with us.' His lips, visible beneath the leather mask that now covered the top half of his head, twisted into a salacious leer, but Christina ignored this.

'First we need to get her ready for her little screen test,' she said, levelly. 'I've put a little something together which will show her off to the best advantage, so, if you wouldn't mind excusing me, I've got work to do.'

Reluctantly, Naylor retreated towards the door, fingers loosening the laces at the back of his mask. It seemed unlikely that Clarissa would regain consciousness for some while yet, but he believed in being cautious. Unfortunately, more especially so since he'd seen the sculptress in the flesh literally, she would have to be released ultimately, though he consoled himself with the thought that, by then, they would at least have access to a virtual Clarissa.

Left alone with her prisoner, Christina lost no time in getting down to her task. She began with a small pair of sharp scissors, clipping away the little bush of pubic hair and slipping it into a plain white envelope. Then, with practised fingers, she used a small spatula to coat the shorn area with a depilatory cream. Ten minutes later the recumbent girl's mound was as smooth as a billiard ball. Christina grunted and fingered the tangle of head hair.

'I'll have that off you, too, before you leave here,' she promised her unhearing victim. 'By the time I'm through with you, the world really will think you're mad; you'll be babbling like a lunatic and incapable of stringing two coherent sentences together. After that, who knows, we might even get you back again. No one will miss just one more crackpot arty-farty.'

She reached down and fingered the narrow cleft beneath the freshly shaven area. The labia seemed thin and tightly pressed together, but Christina persisted, prising the lips apart to reveal the dark pink mouth behind them.

'We'll find plenty to keep this full,' she whispered. 'Give me a month and you'll be able to accommodate a gorilla up there - or my biggest dildo. I reckon you'll look perfect, squirming on the end of Christina's largest cock, sweetie.' With an effort, Christina dragged herself back to the task in hand.

She unfastened the heavy trunk in the corner of the room and lifted the lid back, standing stooped over for several seconds examining the contents, before deciding upon her first move. When she straightened up again, in her hands she held something that resembled a narrow-waisted corset, from the top of the back of which extended a wide, curved plate. However, unlike the leather and rubber garments that were the norm in this place, this creation had been moulded from a thick, rigid perspex, and was completely transparent.

'Perfect,' she whispered to herself. 'Just perfect.' She stooped again and detached the strange key tool from where it had been taped to the underside of the lid, and then turned to study her intended victim. 'Just about the ideal size.' She smiled down at the unconscious Clarissa.

Christina rapidly released the five catches that ran down either side, separating the two halves of the corset. Then, discarding the front piece temporarily, she eased the other beneath the limp Clarissa, adjusting its position until she was satisfied it was exactly right. The curve of the design, added to the curve of the extension plate, lifted Clarissa's lower back several inches clear of the hard mattress and left her upper back and head lying at a downward angle, supported by the perspex extension, which ended at the nape of her neck.

Now, taking the front section, Christina lowered it down, mating it with the first and drawing Clarissa's ample breasts through the two rigid cut-outs, settling them against the near half cup sections that would hold up the helpless girl's bust when she finally returned to an upright position. It then required simple strength, of which Christina had plenty, to force the two halves tightly together and compress Clarissa's waist into the hourglass shape into which the perspex had been sculpted. A few seconds additional work with the key and the corset was locked in place, immovable by its wearer, or anyone else, as Christina held the only key.

Returning to the trunk, the powerful Dane selected the next pieces to the intricate jigsaw, laying them out on the bed alongside the still motionless Clarissa. She took the hinged collar first, wrapping it around the artist's neck and clicking it into the locking mechanism at the top of the extension plate. Now, when Clarissa finally did come around and get to her feet, she would be forced to walk with her spine bent cruelly backwards, the sharp raised point at the front of the collar ensuring that she had to keep her chin well elevated as well.

Two more hinged sections formed rigid gloves, encasing the arms from fingertips to armpit, six more tiny locks holding them to the arms and two larger catches snapping into retaining locks on either side of the back half of the corset. The effect was to hold the arms slightly bent, the elbows pulled back, the strain on

14

the shoulders serving as an ever present reminder to Clarissa, once she regained her senses, that Christina had made her into her helpless slave.

The boots were truly superb, Christina decided, holding the feet as would a normal - if seven inch heels could be described as normal - pair of high heeled boots. But their bases had been shaped so that sole and heel were as one and shaped to the contours of a horse's hoof. There was another pair with the outfit, which could be substituted for these at Christina's discretion, but their rapier thin heels would require practice before Clarissa would be able to balance in them, though at least their rigid construction would prevent any broken ankles. Not that Christina had any great problems with slaves suffering fractures, but only when they were inflicted at her own instigation.

Next, Christina turned to the makeup box on the small dressing table in the window, applying long false eyelashes over Christina's own and thickening them with black mascara. Black eyeliner and dark blue eye-shadow followed, as she turned the normally fresh-faced beauty into a parody of a showgirl.

Deep blusher and vivid carmine lip-gloss emphasised the effect dramatically and, as Christina worked skilfully, the showgirl image became that of an extremely over-the-top whore. When she finally stepped back and scrutinised her efforts, the powerful dominatrix permitted herself a slow smile of satisfaction.

'Your own mother would disown you, looking like that,' she addressed the uncaring form. 'Always supposing she even recognised you.' She leaned forward again and deftly removed the single gold stud from each of Clarissa's earlobes, tossing them into the makeup box with disdain.

The skullcap, which Christina took out next, was moulded to fit perfectly over the upper half of the head, with a locking chinstrap to prevent the wearer from dislodging it. At the crown, a clear tube about nine inches long projected straight up. Taking up a brush, Christina propped her subject up in the bedside chair, legs splayed stiffly before her, and began brushing her wild hair up into a high ponytail.

Initially fixing it in position with a red band, Christina then twisted it temporarily into a long rope, which she painstakingly fed into the tube, drawing it out the other end and sliding the skullcap helmet carefully onto Clarissa's head. Locking the chinstrap, she then proceeded to brush the red mane out again, allowing it to cascade down from the top of the tube like a glorious, auburn fountain.

'My, but aren't we a pretty sight?' Christina laughed, mockingly. 'All locked up tightly, but everything on show. Now then, what's next?'

Next, in fact, came the earrings, two huge prisms of the same clear perspex, the helmet having been designed so that there was a small opening over the lower half of each ear, allowing easy access for the supporting studs to be threaded through the piercings in Clarissa's lobes. There were matching pendants for the girl's nipples, too, but first there was the matter of how to affix them.

Generally, Christina liked to pierce her slaves' nipples, male and female alike, but she wanted this crazy Australian bitch to be wide awake when that time came. Now, as a temporary measure, she took out two specially designed clamps, again in the clear perspex; two flat discs with a hole at the centre, each hole lined with wickedly sharp serrations. The two halves could be opened, the nipple teased into the aperture and then snapped shut again, holding the unfortunate teat in its painful bite until Christina chose to use her key again.

At the bottom edge of each clamp, a tiny hole had been drilled in the perspex and through each of these Christina now threaded the wires that held the pendants. She stepped back and gave each of them an experimental tap, setting them swinging gently to and fro, their weight causing the nipples to distend from side to side as they moved.

'Beautiful,' Christina breathed. 'The artist as a work of art. Now then, let's plug that dear little arse and stretch that other hole like it's never been stretched before.'

Five minutes later, the job was done, the greased dildos thrust crudely into their respective orifices and kept there by means of a curved perspex crotch strap that locked to the front and back of the lower edge of the corset, the transparent material permitting an unobstructed view of the two implements and the degree to which they were stretching both openings.

As she viewed the finished article Christina squeezed her own thighs together, conscious of the growing warmth and of the dampness inside the leather covering her crotch. After they had completed the necessary filming, she promised herself, she was going to enjoy the uninterrupted company of this bizarre little plastic doll she had created. She wondered what the doll herself would make of it.

She had a pretty shrewd idea!

'Looks like you'll be making me redundant before long,' Simon Prescott said, easing his gangling frame into a more comfortable position. Nadia uncrossed her legs, shaking her head.

'No way,' she assured him. 'We were - are, sorry - all part of the team that started this and I happen to be a great believer in a little commodity called loyalty. Besides,' she went on, 'everyone's assuming that VESTA will be able to take over everything, and that's just not so. We'll still need a photographer and we'll still need our cast to produce fresh ideas and input. VESTA may be a wizard lady, but even computers can go stale.'

'So how exactly do you see this progressing?' Simon asked. In his late thirties, he was a few years younger than Nadia, though in truth he looked a lot older. During the years he had worked for her, as photographer, lighting technician, adviser, script consultant and general support worker, a special bond had grown up between them, though it was a bond of a platonic nature only. Nadia scratched her chin, a sure sign that she was still undecided and merely throwing ideas into the ring.

'I thought,' she began, 'that for the moment we'd continue with the normal stuff just the way we've always done it. After all, if it ain't broke, don't mend it. VESTA is completely untried as yet, even if Marlon is confident there won't be any problems. We can try a few experimental lifts and compare the finished article with the stuff we get via you and Sonia, and see what we all think.

'Meanwhile, once Marlon has VESTA up and running, we can offer trial runs to a few selected contacts and see what they think. I've already placed a subtle little piece in one of the VIP websites, just to test the water.

'However, before we do, I think we have to give her a proper field trial. So far Marlon's used Lianne and Ellen and a few other paid volunteers I've recruited for him these past months, but mainly for inputting and only a few output experiences. Apart from that I've tried it as a passive subject, but that was just me on my own, with Marlon tweaking the auto-programming wherever he thought it might help.

'What we don't know - what we can't know, until he's got all the other terminals up and running - is how VESTA will perform under multi-participant status. Therefore, I reckon we have to give her a thorough field test, all of us if necessary. That's you, me, Paul, Lianne and Ellen, Suzy, Carla, Hazel, Gavin and Sonia.

'I make that nine of us, which is a pretty reasonable test, but I could always recruit three or four more, just to push VESTA a bit harder.'

'Well, you're the boss lady,' Simon said. 'Though I'm not sure whether you should include me in all this. Hardly my type of thing. I'm strictly a behind the camera man.' Nadia smiled, seductively.

'You mean you'd pass up the chance of screwing the delectable Lianne?' she teased. 'I've seen the way you look at her, so don't try to pretend otherwise. Or maybe your tastes lay elsewhere?' she continued. 'Maybe there's someone else you'd like to strap down and take advantage of?'

In an attempt to cover his confusion and embarrassment, Simon Prescott stood up and walked across to the drinks cabinet. Nadia smiled to herself. Simon would be in on the trial run, whether he liked it or not, and it would be interesting to see just how he performed, even if it was only as a cybernetic extension of the real him.

'Plenty of tonic in mine, please Simon,' she called over her shoulder. 'I've got some serious thinking to do this afternoon.'

Clarissa, having been shown her reflection in the huge mirror, felt as though she wanted to curl up into a little ball and die of embarrassment, but the strictures of her outfit made that one of many alternatives now denied her. Precariously, she turned, stiff-legged, to stare at the massive blonde woman.

'What the fucking hell d'you think you're doing?' she croaked, her Australian twang far more noticeable than it usually was. 'Are you some kind of crazy bitch!'

By way of reply, the giantess seized the curved spine brace and hurled Clarissa across the carpeted floor, to land face down across the width of the bed. The crop appeared in her hand as if by magic, and two stinging cuts landed, one on each unprotected buttock, bringing screams of agony from the helpless girl's throat.

'Scream all you want, slut,' the blonde snarled, 'but don't ever call me names again, understand? Until we finally decide it's time for you to go, you're nothing but a slave, a worthless piece of shit. Slaves don't speak without permission, or they get more of this.' To emphasise her intent, she dealt another savage blow across Clarissa's exposed left shoulder, drawing an agonised shriek from the pathetic, perspex-wrapped figure.

'Now,' Christina said, casting aside the crop and hauling Clarissa back into a standing position, 'understand this, too. What happens to you depends upon the actions of that goofy half-brother of yours.'

'Marlon?' Clarissa tried to focus through her tear-filled eyes and wished she could raise a hand to wipe them clear. 'What's Marlon got to do with all this?'

'Plenty,' Christina assured her. 'At least, he will have. We want him to work for us and he seems to prefer being somewhere else, which doesn't suit our plans at all. However, once he's had a good look at how his darling sister has been treated, I reckon he might just have second thoughts.

'Now, everything that's happened in this room since you were brought here has been videoed, but now we need to add a few refinements. Then, you're going to make a phone call to Marlon and tell him just exactly how he can see for himself that we mean business.'

'And if I don't phone him?' Clarissa demanded defiantly. Christina gathered up the crop again and held it up to Clarissa's face.

'Do you really need to ask?' she purred. 'Believe me, I don't ever need much of an excuse to thrash a sexy little behind like yours. By the time I've finished with you, my little whore-in-training, you'll be begging me to let you suck my cunt.'

'Never!' Clarissa gasped, but the cold fist that was knotting itself into her entrails told her a different story.

'So, is it really that lifelike?' Paul asked. He was standing in the centre of the bedroom, dressed only in a rubber suspender belt and latex stockings, his limp organ dangling apologetically between his thighs. Lianne, the shapeless rubber helmet still in her hands, turned back from the dressing table and shrugged.

'I thought you'd already tried it out for yourself,' she said. 'You had an entire day's session with Marlon a couple of weeks back, didn't you?'

'Well, yes, but that was just Marlon measuring responses, while I watched a load of our old video footage. I haven't tried the real thing as yet.'

'Then you're in for a very interesting experience,' Lianne assured him. 'I was totally gobsmacked, I can tell you. To be honest, it's quite spooky at first. I mean, you know it's not real, but there's no way you can tell that. It really, really is like being there.

'The spookiest bit of all was when he tried one scene with Ellen and me together, rather than have one of his library characters doing the bit. We were able to talk to each other and act together exactly as we would do in the real world. We even discussed how crazy it all was, just as if we were in the same room together in the normal way of things. God knows how Marlon does it, but it really does work.'

'It's all a bit sci-fi if you ask me,' Paul said. 'But then I suppose that's the world we live in nowadays. Things are happening at a faster and faster rate. Before long humans will be bloody redundant, and I find that more than a little bit worrying.'

Swaying seductively on her high heels, Lianne closed in on him, her fingers encircling his flaccid penis. She felt his back stiffen at the intimate contact and could not suppress a small giggle.

'As long as we don't let this little beauty get redundant,' she cooed, 'I don't care about the rest. And don't you think it's about time you got your uniform on, Pauline?' she added, trying to inject a note of sternness into her voice. 'I've been expecting a decent maid service for the past half hour, and all you can do is chatter away like a silly schoolgirl!'

The room was three floors down from the bedroom in which Clarissa had first awoken, but the problem of navigating the stairs in the awful boots was overcome by Christina picking her up under one arm, as easily as if she had really been a doll, and carrying her down bodily.

If Clarissa's return to consciousness had been traumatic, at least, she thought, she had been spared the initial shock of coming round in this hell hole. The bedroom upstairs had retained an air of normality, even if the costumed puppet that had confronted her in the mirror had not.

The cellar room had been designed for one purpose and one purpose only, to convey an air of menace, evil and sheer terror. The chamber was a pastiche of every horror film, every historical engraving and every nightmare Clarissa could remember. The walls and ceiling were black, bare stone blocks, alleviated only by the various wooden racks, from which hung collections of leather and metal devices whose purpose she could only guess at, and prayed fervently she would never have to find out.

Stumbling awkwardly in the fearsome heels, her back arched cruelly, Clarissa felt as though she was completely stuffed by the two dildos, every shambling step emphasising their invasive presence, and she sobbed with shame as Christina thrust her into the centre of the room.

'Now then, Ginger,' the big woman grinned, backing her captive against an upright post that ran from floor to ceiling, 'let's add a few more touches to your outfit. I do so like my slaves to look really submissive, and you don't quite look submissive enough yet.'

Clarissa stared at her, eyes wide with terror. 'What are you going to do with me now?' she wailed, as Christina began tethering her to the post, threading a strong cord through a ring at the back of her corset and winding it around the timber until Clarissa was drawn hard up against it. To either side of her feet, two heavy ring bolts had been set into the stone and now Christina used more cord to drag Clarissa's legs wide and tie her ankles to them, preventing her from closing her lower limbs together again.

'Please,' Clarissa begged, 'haven't you done enough to me already?' By way of reply, Christina brought the back of her hand down hard against the outside of the helpless girl's left breast, drawing another squeal of pain from her.

'I've already told you once, slut,' she growled. 'Slaves speak only when spoken to.' She stood back, hands on her broad hips, her expression mocking. 'And as for whether I've done enough to you already, I can assure you I've hardly started. I'm as much an artist in my field as you are - or were - in yours, though I use a lot less metal.' She reached out a hand and fingered one of Clarissa's distended nipples.

To her utter astonishment, Clarissa felt a little electric charge run up her spine and she closed her eyes, unwilling to meet the bigger woman's challenging stare.

'You have very pretty tits, slut,' Christina said, very matter of fact in her tone. 'They deserve to be properly ornamented. The clamps are all very well, but I prefer something more... permanent.' She turned away and crossed to a small metal wall cabinet, opening the door and sorting through its contents. A few minutes later she was back at Clarissa's side, carrying a small chrome-plated dish, upon which lay a number of small objects that the terrified girl could not at first identify.

However, their purpose soon became apparent, as Christina picked up the plier-like instrument in one hand and seized Clarissa's left nipple between finger and thumb with the other.

'No-o-o-ooooo!' Clarissa shrieked, but there was no escape. A bolt of ice fire shot through her breast and straight to the base of her brain, as the jaws closed and the sharp needle pierced the tender flesh. A gurgling sound erupted from Clarissa's throat, saliva drooling from her slack lips, and she would have sagged helplessly had her rigid costume and bondage not been supporting her.

Through the red mist that swam before her, the poor girl peered downwards, unable to believe what she saw as her tormentor threaded the heavy steel ring through the punctured teat. Seconds later another spear of agony, and the other nipple was treated in identical fashion.

'Much better,' Christina nodded. 'And don't even think about removing them, even when you get the use of your hands back. The two halves interlock and there's no way of separating them without cutting through the steel. When I ring a pair of tits, they stay ringed until I decide otherwise.'

There was worse to come, and the pain now was too great for Clarissa to bear. Mercifully, she passed out into a semi-coma, barely aware of the agonising piercings that were added to her labia and clitoris. But Christina wasted no time in reviving her when she had finished, releasing the binding cords and thrusting her in front of the long mirror which hung from the end wall. Every step was agony and, when Clarissa peered into the glass, she saw the reason why.

Clips had been attached to the labial rings and fastened to tiny half rings set at the top of the inside of each boot, so that the act of walking forced the mouth of her sex to gape open and move with every movement of her legs, exposing the third ring and the elongated shape of the normally hidden bud through which it had been set. With her brain almost numb from the shock, Clarissa thought, stupidly it seemed, that she could not even remember Christina removing the fat dildo from her sex, though the one at the rear was still only too obviously in place.

'Very provocative, wouldn't you agree?' Christina sneered. 'A slut on display, just begging to be fucked. Well, I'm afraid there'll be no real cock for you just yet, though I do have a nice substitute lined up for later on. But first, I nearly forgot with all the excitement. Get back over to the post.'

She dragged the sobbing girl across the room and quickly re-secured her to the upright, although this time she ignored the ankle restraints. Clarissa soon discovered why, for it seemed that Christina was finished with the area between her legs and was intent only on the addition of a sixth and final ring. When she stepped back, the steel oval drooped from Clarissa's septum, resting lightly against the soft flesh just above her top lip.

'And if you don't do exactly as I tell you and phone your brother with the correct instructions,' Christina said, flicking the steel loop with her forefinger, 'I'll pierce your lip and use the ring to keep your mouth permanently open!'

Completely disoriented, pain raging from a million different nerve ends, Clarissa could only stare at her, tears running down between her cheeks and the hard perspex that covered them, a thin trickle of urine worming its insidious passage down the inside of each thigh, between flesh and boot, as Christina replaced the original crotch strap with another that was thin enough to pass over her gaping sex lips, but pass between the two labial rings.

'And now,' the amazon announced, straightening up, 'it's time to take some pretty pictures and show off my latest work of art.'

'I'm still not sure I'm happy about Nadia's mass tryout,' Lianne said. She and Ellen were sitting sipping cold cola between scenes. So far the afternoon's shoot had been a doddle, just a few background bondage positions and Gavin lightly whipping the two 'prisoners' as they spun slowly, strapped back-to-back in an intricate leather harness, a double-ended dildo adding an extra element of togetherness.

'What's your problem?' Ellen asked, leaning forward amidst a symphony of creaking leather. Lianne looked furtively from side to side before answering. Seeing that they were some distance from the rest of the cast and crew, she continued, though in a harsh whisper.

'Well, it's one thing to be chained up and fucked by an illusionary character,' she said, 'something that VESTA's created out of all this random data-feed Marlon keeps on about, but this time it'll be real people. I mean, I know they're not real *real* and they're only images inside our heads, but they'll seem real at the time. And, well, Simon's going to be in on it.'

'Aha, I see,' Ellen nodded, although with some difficulty, for the leather collar kept her head permanently held high. 'Don't fancy the idea of being our Simon's helpless little slave girl, eh?'

'To be honest, no, I don't,' Lianne admitted. 'Oh, he's perfectly sweet and I like him a lot, but, well, I just couldn't fancy him.'

'Does that matter?' Ellen retorted. 'After all, it's not like it's the real him or the real you. Besides, Marlon reckons VESTA can do a bit of form shifting, alter the perceptions of the bodies involved, or something. He tried to explain, but you know Marlon.'

'Swallowed the science lab at school and never got over it,' Lianne agreed. She furrowed her brow in thought. 'So, what you're saying is that Marlon could drop Simon into VESTA's world and make him look like a real hunk?'

'Apparently,' Ellen nodded. 'Well, I think that's what he said.'

Marlon Vincent sat staring in sheer disbelief at the freeze-frame on the VDU before him. He had played the download four times in less than an hour, yet still he could not believe the evidence before his eyes.

'You've got to access the following website,' Clarissa had insisted, and had repeated the internet details twice, her voice sounding strangely detached. She had then given him a password, without which, she had assured him, no one else would be able to view what was on the site. Marlon had tried to press her for details, reasons, but she cut him short. 'Just do it, Marlon,' she had almost shrieked. 'Please!'

And there she had been, his only recently discovered half sister, crudely naked, but for the cruel see-through bondage, fresh whip marks showing when the camera panned around her, rings and pendants dragging on newly pierced flesh, her face a distorted mask of pain beneath the disguising layers of cosmetics. If there had not been footage showing her transformation, Marlon could easily have convinced himself that the poor little puppet on the screen was not Clarissa at all. But the narrator's voice, combined with the carefully edited clips, left him no room for doubt.

It was definitely his half sister, perched astride that awful pole, her vagina distended and distorted by whatever it was that thrust upwards from the centre of the painfully narrow seat that threatened to split her asunder. The strangely heeled transparent boots hung a few inches clear of the floor, but even had they not, there was no chance of the poor creature lifting herself off the impaling phallus, for both ankles were strapped to the pole with broad leather cuffs.

Marlon brushed a tear of frustration from the corner of his eye and focused on the tiny rectangle in the bottom right hand corner of the screen. The type was small, but still easily readable and gave him precise instructions what to do, once he had fully assimilated and understood the scenarios that had been given to him...

Lianne emerged from the en suite bathroom, wrapped in one towel and vigorously drying her hair with another, to find Paul Dean sprawled across the huge double bed they now regularly shared. As it was still a warm afternoon, she should not have been surprised to find him clad only in a thin pair of shorts and indeed she wasn't, for she had long ago abandoned the idea of being surprised by anything he might appear in.

As a writer, Paul was in the top division, but as a creator of the story lines they all acted out, he was in a league of his own. Lianne and he had become an item since their shared captivity and brutal treatment at the hands of James Naylor and his warped cronies. But even though that torrid episode was now many months in the past, Lianne still understood very little of what went on in her strange lover's even stranger head.

She knew that he regularly enjoyed dressing up in the female versions of the many costumes the organisation had accumulated, many of them designed by Paul himself, and she joined in the charades with eager enthusiasm, forcing him to be her maid and to endure the sorts of indignities and trials that were normally her lot 'on set'. The results were phenomenal, for once in character, Paul was an inexhaustible lover, ready on demand, whenever his 'mistress' decreed.

'You look tired,' she commented, crossing the room and sitting on the stool in front of the antique dressing table. 'What have you been up to?'

'Letting Marlon siphon my innermost thoughts,' Paul sighed. 'He's had me lying there, hooked up to his electronic girlfriend, imagining scenes in my head and then making me explain, down to the tiniest detail, anything that hadn't registered properly in his box of tricks. I didn't realise that having wet daydreams could be so exhausting.'

Lianne looked shocked. 'You didn't!' she gasped, accusingly. Paul grinned.

'What, come my load in front of our tame boffin? Hardly, though my imagination was running riot long before the end of our session and I felt really embarrassed whenever he looked at me. Not that he seemed to notice anything except for those bloody screens of his. I tried to see what was on them, but all I could see was a load of gibberish.'

'No good asking me,' Lianne retorted. 'I gave up trying to understand all this after the first ten seconds. You wait till you actually go under with that thing, though. That'll really blow your mind.'

'It really is that realistic?' Paul narrowed his eyes and Lianne could tell that he still did not believe what she and Ellen had told those of the crew who had not yet had the chance to experience VESTA's magic at first hand. She nodded.

'And it's getting even better,' she replied. 'According to Marlon, every little extra titbit of data that VESTA consumes is adding to its ability to create a world that's totally indistinguishable from the real one.'

'I thought you said it could do that already?'

Lianne looked thoughtful. 'In a way, it can,' she agreed, 'but there are little odd things that let it down. Too many instant scene shifts, for example, and characters appearing out of thin air. One minute you're on your own, the next there are people all over you with whips and dildos and everything. I did point that flaw out to Marlon and he said he can sort it in a little while.

'Apparently he still needs to run in some background material, but he's working on it day and night. And he's also got this new programme he's about to add. I didn't understand a word of the technicalities, but he reckons it's got some sort of artificial intelligence. Throw in enough basic data and it'll merrily write all the other stuff in all on its own, updating and improving all the time.'

'Sounds impressive,' Paul yawned. Lianne shrugged.

'Sounds too bloody complicated,' she said. 'And I've been starting to wonder if it's really such a good idea, putting ourselves at the mercy of a load of wires and valves.'

'Hardly valves these days,' Paul pointed out. 'Though I do take your point. But I shouldn't worry. I've spoken to Marlon at some length and it's all quite safe. There's a safety shutdown feature, so if anything should go wrong, VESTA switches herself off after a few hours.'

'Having first fried our brains?'

'No, don't be silly. We'd just be stuck in VESTA's little world for a bit longer than intended, that's all. And don't forget, everything that happens there is just an illusion. No real harm can come to any of us.'

Marlon adjusted the throat microphone, studied the twin screens immediately in front of him, and addressed the occupants of the twelve perspex-domed cubicles that stretched away from VESTA in two rows of six.

In her cubicle, Lianne lay flat on her back, trying to calm her thoughts, but already warm and clammy inside the black latex bodysuit and helmet. It had been

Marlon's idea that they should all 'go under' in character, but it had provided him with a lot of extra work, cutting tiny slits in the helmets of those who wore them in order to secure the sticky little electrodes. Lianne gazed along her body, at her wrists shackled to the rings on either side of her corset and at the heavy hobble chain dangling between her ankles, and wondered if that had been totally necessary.

Marlon's voice boomed out of the tiny speaker above her head. 'What I'm going to do is allow VESTA to take an almost random decision as to who'll be going in as passive and who'll be active, apart from the three of you who I think would prefer to play your usual submissive roles.

'The original idea was to have separate active and passive stations, but a few simple alterations have enabled me to construct units that will do either. That saves us having units left empty when we're top heavy on demand for one type or the other. You'll go in at different times and you'll be involved in separate scenarios, at least to start with. It may even be that you don't see all the others while you're there, but don't worry.

'The main thing to remember is that whatever happens, it ain't real, but don't hold on to that thought too firmly, else you won't enjoy yourselves half as much. Okay then, here we go. *Bon voyage*, everybody.'

Bon frigging *voyage* to you too, Lianne thought.

And then everything went black.

She was in a field and it was sunny, but the day could not have been too warm, for Lianne felt quite comfortable, even though she was still encased in her latex bodysuit. The helmet mask still covered her head and face, though the wires to the electrodes seemed to have disappeared, as if by magic.

She was in a field.

And she was on a horse. A grey thoroughbred. With a saddle. A saddle with a difference and the difference was the massive phallus fixed to it that was currently stretching her vaginal muscles to their capacity.

The horse was trotting in a slow circle, a long rein attached to a post keeping it to its same path. Peering down, Lianne could just see her booted feet, strapped into the specially adapted stirrups, and the straps that secured her upper thighs to either side of the saddle. Secured her, but did not hold her rigidly enough to prevent her bouncing up and down in time to the grey's staccato progress, so that the dildo was reaming her with every step the horse took.

She could feel that she was already very wet, and she could also feel the now familiar heat beginning to build deep inside her. She looked around to see who was controlling the horse, but there was no one; the creature simply continued round and around, oblivious to its jockey, or to what was happening to her.

Biting hard into the ball gag that had somehow appeared between her teeth, Lianne fought desperately to keep herself under control, determined to take proper stock of her new surroundings before the sensual stimulation made coherent thought impossible. She seemed to be wearing the same outfit as when she had been strapped into the VESTA capsule, except that now she was gagged and her arms were secured tightly together behind her back by means of a laced single sleeve. And she could feel a butt plug moving inside her, which definitely hadn't been there earlier.

All very clever stuff, she thought, but there was something missing, something wrong with this simulation. Almost immediately she put her finger on it. There had been no build up, no ritual, no slow gathering of the senses as she was rendered progressively more helpless by the strict bondage. It was that, as much as anything else, which she found so alluring; the gradual heightening of tension, the growing awareness of committing herself into the control of another and the knowledge that her actions were no longer hers to decide.

Still, she reasoned, that could probably be sorted out, once she'd had a chance to speak to Marlon about it. During the experimental runs and when she and Ellen had been scanned for input data, all Marlon had been interested in was establishing the basis for as many options as possible and recording the reactions in their brainwaves. Quite how it all worked was beyond Lianne, but work it certainly did, and now needed nothing more than a few refining touches here and there.

The two men appeared out of nowhere, which was very disconcerting. One minute the field was empty, apart from Lianne on her phallic mount, and then they were there, both blond giants, both wearing tight leather breeches and cutaway leather tops, and both wearing Dick Turpin style leather masks. They could have been twins and, when Lianne peered closer, she saw that that was, in effect, what they were. Marlon's database was still relatively restricted and Lianne guessed that he had used the same set of peripherals for both men.

They were physically based loosely upon Gavin, who generally played the role of brutal master in their 'real life' scenes, but there was also a hint of something else, for their features were sharper and more threatening than Gavin's. The first twin stepped forward, seized the horse's bridle and brought it to a halt. He looked up at Lianne and bared his teeth in a wolverine grimace.

'Nothing like a nice brisk trot in the open air to prepare a slave for proper use,' he said, and his companion laughed, mirthlessly. The first man raised his right hand and inserted his fingers roughly between the saddle and Lianne's cleft, nodding knowingly. 'Just about simmering, I should say,' he sneered. 'Well, let's have the little slut down and bring her to the boil properly.'

The high timber frame also seemed to have materialised out of thin air. It most certainly had not been in the field when Lianne first arrived, but it was definitely there now, two sturdy uprights supporting a horizontal beam about ten feet from the ground. A thick rope had been thrown over the upright, its two ends dangling ready for use, and there were further ropes knotted about the base of each support post.

The powerful men hoisted Lianne clear of her saddle with effortless ease and half dragged, half carried her under the beam. Working in perfect unison, each grasped one of her ankles, dragging her legs wide apart and securing them with the lower ropes. Satisfied that she was correctly straddled, they then knotted one end of the hanging rope to the steel ring at the end of her arm sleeve and pulled on the other, so that Lianne's arms were dragged cruelly up and away from her body, forcing her head forward and down, until she was held with her spine parallel to the ground.

Both men now had long canes in their hands, taking up positions behind and to either side of their helpless victim, and she tensed, knowing exactly what was coming. During the earlier runs she had been astonished at how realistic VESTA's artificial world could be and, although she knew the imminent beating could not harm her real body, it was definitely going to hurt whatever she was in now.

The first stroke swished in from her right and she screeched into the gag as it landed squarely across her buttocks. Hardly had the searing pain registered, when the second stroke came in from the opposite side. Lianne swayed forward, her full weight falling on her contorted arms, and she felt her bladder lose control in the same instant. The thin hot stream of liquid hissed onto the muddy grass, bring a raucous shout from her two torturers.

'Filthy little whore!' the one to the left exclaimed. 'Look at her piss, man; look at her go.' Deeply ashamed, Lianne fought desperately to halt the cascade, but two more rapid cuts destroyed all attempts at disciplined concentration. Only when her bladder had finally emptied itself did the torrent become a trickle and the trickle a few final, humiliating drips.

The beating continued, a beating more ferocious than anything Lianne had ever known before, and she felt sure she must pass out. Through the red haze that now enveloped her, she could hear her stifled sobs and squeals, even these growing less as the pain diminished her every sense.

At last they threw aside the canes, but they were far from finished with her yet. A hand was once again cupping her sex, fingers exploring, working in and out of her sodden love tunnel, other fingers working at the base of her butt plug. From the front, more hands cupped her hanging breasts, kneading her swollen teats through the thin rubber, moulding her firm globes with a rough carelessness.

Lianne groaned, but this time it was not from the pain, for the heat from her ravaged buttocks was slowly beginning to give way to another, fiercer and far more intense heat that was building from inside. And, when the ball gag was suddenly pulled from between her lips, she gratefully sucked in the rampant penis offered in its stead. Scarcely had she drawn it deep into her throat than its twin was thrusting into her from behind.

She gasped, her saliva trickling down over the first twin's heavy testicles, her love juices soaking those of his fellow, and she knew the moment of release was close. Sure enough, seconds later her head exploded in a massive spasm of gratification and, as it did, twin jets of semen filled her throat and her womb in perfect, salty unison.

And, once again, her world went black.

Ellen found herself in a predicament as far removed from Lianne's as she could have conceived, had she known Lianne's situation, which she did not. Not that she currently could have given much time to considering anyone but herself and her immediate environs, for this scenario had been quite deliberately designed to hold one hundred percent of her attention.

The long boots that were laced up her legs, virtually to her naked and shaven crotch, were fashioned in such a way that they forced Ellen to walk on the very tips of her toes, *en pointe* as the world of ballet would have described it. And unlike a similar pair of boots she had worn before, out in the 'real' world, there were no heels upon which to distribute any of her weight.

Around the ankles the boots seemed to have been reinforced with either metal, or with some sort of rigid and extremely strong synthetic, for try as she would, there was no way Ellen could lower herself into a normal standing position. In any case, such a move would have been rendered near impossible by the way in which she had been positioned in this bizarre *corps de ballet*.

The far wall of the long room was one huge mirror, and in this she could see not only her own reflection, but also the reflections of the four other fetishistic ballerinas, of whom Ellen was the centre one. All five were identically dressed and presented a very erotic spectacle indeed.

In addition to the boots, each girl wore what could just about be described as a tutu, although it was really a very stringent corset of leather - white to match the boots - with a series of stiff net skirts sticking out at right angles and with the tiny quarter cups designed to lift and support the breasts. But not to cover them in any way, so that the firm high mounds were presented on open display, huge gold nipple rings and bells dangling grotesquely from them and jangling at the slightest movement.

The girls' arms - each entwined through that of its neighbour and the wrist secured to the hip of the corset tutu by means of a cuff and single link - were encased to the shoulder in tightly laced leather gloves. A high posture collar forced the dancer to hold her head stiffly erect, also covering the lower edge of the thin rubber mask that had been pulled over each set of features, presenting a bland, identical face upon each and every girl and holding some sort of padded gag within her mouth.

The masks had a sort of wig attached to them; black hair scraped up into a chignon, the rubber cheeks coloured bright pink, the rubber lips unmoving, unspeaking lines of bright carmine. Only the eyes were animated, where they peered through apertures that clung to the features so closely that only a close inspection revealed that the girls were masked at all.

'Ah, I see my little swans are ready for me!' The man had appeared as if by magic, standing in front and slightly to the left of the line, dressed in flesh-coloured rubber tights and a bright green rubber leotard of sorts, and clutching a long switch in his right hand. Ellen guessed he was in his late twenties and her keen eye did not miss the well muscled legs and the light way in which he moved about on the balls of his feet.

Well, she thought, VESTA couldn't have chosen better, for the blond newcomer, his unkempt tresses giving him something of a swashbuckling air, was Ellen's epitome of a sexy male. And though she could not move her hands to investigate properly, she could certainly feel the heat rising in her sex and knew she must already be very wet down there. Despite the anonymity of her mask and despite the fact that she knew none of her companions were real, she felt herself blushing.

She was brought quickly back to reality - or at least VESTA's version of it - when the tip of the switch caught her exposed sex lips with a sharp slapping sensation. A high-pitched squeak burst past the gag and her instinctive reaction set the entire line tottering from side to side, five pairs of nipple bells jingling merrily.

'Pay attention, swan number three,' the man snapped, stepping closer to her. 'Pay attention, or we shan't give your hungry little twot its dinner, shall we?' He strutted up and down the line, the switch flicking at this girl and that, darting between open thighs one moment and clipping engorged nipples the next.

'Now,' he said, casting the weapon aside and reaching for some sort of fastener over his crotch. 'Who shall we dance with first?'

This time Lianne was in a small cell and the rubber outfit had been replaced by a simple shift of a rough woven fabric that stopped several inches short of her bare knees. Her hands were secured behind her back, presumably by cuffs of stout leather, and her head was encased in a harness made of thinner straps of the same material; a harness which held immovably in place a ball of yet more leather, foul tasting as it wedged between her teeth, pressing on her tongue and rendering speech impossible.

Suddenly the heavy timber door banged open and the doorway was filled by a huge figure, a man dressed in close fitting black leather breeches, heavy boots, a hangman style hood and wearing studded gauntlets which glinted in the sunlight from the 'world' outside. Instinctively, Lianne shrank back, eliciting a loud guffaw from her latest adversary.

'Yes, you should cower, witch!' he bellowed, his voice almost deafening in the confines of the room. 'Your time has come to atone for your devilish sins!' He strode forward, grasped her by the arm and dragged her easily across the few feet separating her from whatever fate next lay in store for her.

Outside there appeared to be quite a crowd gathered, though their appearance was somewhat nebulous and every time Lianne tried to focus on any individual, or particular knot of individuals, their outline became indistinct and only the mass of people behind them seemed to exist. She assumed VESTA was not yet quite capable of projecting a scene as complicated as this one seemed to be, but she was left with little time to ponder the subject.

The platform to which her captor dragged her looked far more solid than the crowd, as did the little group of figures who stood around the top of the rough hewn steps leading up to the top of it. There were four of them in total, two men dressed similarly to the giant who had hold of her, although their masks covered only the top halves of their features. The other two were robed as priests of some sort, black cassocks, monkish hoods thrown back over their shoulders, and vestments of white, gold and red draped about their necks.

Despite herself and the gag which filled her mouth, Lianne almost laughed out loud, for the features of the latter two had clearly been derived from any one of a hundred Hollywood B movies; lantern jaws, deep set dark eyes, hawkish noses and hollow, cadaverous cheeks. However, the fierce pressure of the big man's huge hands on the soft flesh of her upper arm seemed real enough, and she winced with pain as he all but threw her up the rustic stairway.

Lianne stared about her, eyes darting from side to side. Above, a thick hemp rope, stereotypical hangman's noose at its lower end, dangled limply in the airless afternoon. To the side a shorter post supported a cross member, from each end of which hung an open manacle of thick leather. On a bench beside this lay a selection of whips, tiny steel teeth glinting in the woven fibres of each.

It's not real! she screamed to herself silently. It's just part of the script. This isn't really happening to you - none of it is!

Yet the splinters which dug into her bare feet seemed only too real, as the two assistants grasped her and hauled her across to the whipping frame. A small box had been positioned before it and very quickly Lianne was lifted onto this, her fetters unlocked and her arms stretched high and wide for her wrists to be re-secured in the waiting straps. Another strap was buckled about her ankles, pressing her legs close together, and then the box was unceremoniously dragged from beneath her, leaving her dangling helplessly, toes agonising inches from the decking.

She groaned as her weight fell upon her protesting shoulders and only the greatest effort of willpower managed to prevent her from screaming into the gag. Her eyes rolled wildly and her breath hissed through her nostrils. Her common sense kept telling her that none of this was really happening to her, yet every nerve ending, every brain cell, screamed out that it was real enough.

'Strip her, executioner!' This was from one of the priests. The hooded giant nodded to his two assistants, who stepped forward once again and ripped the crude shift from Lianne, tossing the ragged cloth into the crowd and bringing forth a bay of anticipation. Her face pressed against the upright, Lianne hung and waited. She did not have to wait for long.

Into her vision swum the haunting features of the first priest, his lips bared to reveal rotted teeth and a deep crimson tongue. Curiously, despite the pain that was threatening to overwhelm her, Lianne realised the man ought to have terribly fetid breath, and yet she could smell nothing.

The corners of his mouth twitched cruelly, as he took from within his robes a roll of parchment of some kind, unrolling it with slow deliberation and holding it at arms length.

'The witch Griselda has been tried by the rightful church and found guilty as charged,' he intoned. 'She is guilty of heresy, blasphemy, consulting with the dark forces and of murder, upon which all charges she has been sentenced to death. She has further been sentenced, upon the charges of witchcraft and heresy, to be scourged, that she may be received into the next world with her soul cleansed of her mortal sins.' He allowed the parchment to roll itself up again and stepped back.

'Executioner, do your duty!' he cried. 'And may the gods have mercy on her soul.'

The whip landed across Lianne's unprotected back with a sound like a pistol shot, and a spear of red-hot pain shot through her. She bucked and writhed, high-pitched mewling sounds forcing their way past the leather gag, and kicked her bound legs helplessly.

The second lash cut across the tops of her thighs, red, purple and green lights exploding in front of her eyes. Dimly, she was aware of a huge cheer behind her; the crowd, however nebulous they had appeared to her earlier, was clearly programmed to enjoy such sport. By the time the sixth lash scored a vivid line across the tops of Lianne's shoulders, the noise had risen to a cacophonous crescendo, but she could scarcely hear it through the haze of pain that now engulfed her.

'Enough!' The priest stepped forward once again and held up a hand, the executioner staying his wrist just as he was about to snap out the snakelike coils for the seventh time. 'Let her hang there for a short while,' the cleric instructed. 'She must not lose consciousness, for her evil master lays wait to claim her in the dreamworld beyond.'

Can I actually pass out here? Lianne had no idea, other than that there was no way she should have been able to endure such a vicious beating under normal circumstances. Marlon's wizardry was still mostly beyond her ability to comprehend, but she understood enough to know that the pain she was experiencing was being transmitted straight to the appropriate part of her brain.

She remembered an accident she'd had at school, during a games session, when she had badly torn a tendon in her ankle. The pain had been excruciating and she fainted; apparently it was the brain's way of saving its owner from things when they became too bad. Vaguely, she wondered if the priest's intervention was Marlon's way - VESTA's way - of achieving the same effect. Certainly she'd felt herself on the verge of losing consciousness after the last lash.

Amazingly, the burning sensation in her supposedly ravaged flesh began to subside almost immediately the whipping ceased. Closing her eyes, Lianne concentrated for all she was worth, repeating to herself over and over again that the whole experience was illusory and that the pain was not real pain at all. It worked, and not only did the pain in her back, shoulders and buttocks evaporate, but she realised that even her arms and wrists no longer hurt. However, the respite was short-lived.

'Begin again!' the priest ordered and, as the lash cracked across her skin again, even the utmost concentration could not stop the fresh pain. True, it did seem to hurt less than the first onslaught, but it still hurt, and Lianne was quickly bucking and writhing under the leather braid's wicked kiss.

Ten times the whipping was ended temporarily, only to begin again after a few minutes' respite, and now Lianne was beginning to fear that something had gone wrong. Maybe VESTA had become locked into an automatic cycle, but then common sense told her that Marlon would be sure to sense an error of that kind and bring her out of this cruel scenario.

Fighting to re-establish mastery of her senses, Lianne hung panting through her nose, little rivulets of saliva escaping at either side of the gag and trickling down over her jaw to drip onto her heaving breasts as they were pressed out to each side of the upright support pole. She felt a hand probing between her buttocks, forcing the tops of her thighs apart to permit a finger to explore inwards and trace a line along the lips of her sex, and she realised she was very wet there.

Surely that could not have been simply as a result of the whipping? Yes, it was true she could get off on bondage and rubber, and even a spanking or strapping as well, but the physical pain thing was not her particular bag. Ellen had told her of girls who did get turned on by being whipped, but Lianne didn't consider herself as being among their number. No, she reasoned, VESTA had to be applying some extra stimulus somewhere.

The two assistants were reaching to free her wrists now and the box was pushed back beneath her feet, but she was not left unfettered for more than a second or two. Her arms were forced cruelly behind her once more and fastened there, presumably with the leather cuffs she'd originally worn in the cell. A second set of cuffs locked about her ankles as soon as the strap that had bound them together was removed. These cuffs were joined by a stout chain of no more than seven or eight inches, preventing her from taking anything other than very tiny steps. The reason for this quickly became apparent.

Looking down, Lianne saw the crowd had divided into two, leaving a narrow avenue between them, the front row of which now comprised figures that looked far more solid than those in the main body. There were men and women, she saw, all dressed in archaic costumes that she guessed were either sixteenth or seventeenth century, and each one now clutched a long cane.

A gauntlet line, she realised, and a whimper forced its way past the gag, for at its far end, where there should have been the cell building from which she'd been led to this scaffold, there now stood another raised platform, from the centre of which rose a blackened stake and about the base of which was heaped bundles of kindling wood and twisted sections of either large branches or thin tree trunks. It was, Lianne understood, a pyre - a pyre designed for one purpose only, that of burning a witch.

Her.

Clarissa had never believed it was possible to feel so wretched as she did now, perched astride the horrendous display pole, the thick dildo filling her vagina and stretching it to an impossible extent, the plug in her anal passage all but forgotten in comparison to this monstrous invasion. How long it had been since the massive blonde had mounted her so lewdly, she had no idea, but there had been several visitors since to admire Christina's handiwork.

Thanks to the rubber ball gag the Dane had forced between her teeth, the wretched captive could do nothing but stare back at the procession of strangely garbed voyeurs, trying vainly to shut her ears to their mocking comments.

'Hang a couple of lights on those tits and she'd make a great standard lamp,' one woman had laughed. 'I'll have to ask Christina if we can have her up in our suite for tomorrow night's party.'

'Might as well use her for furniture,' her male companion had sneered. 'By the time she's spent a few more hours like that, her cunt will be too slack to be of much use.'

'Maybe for you,' the woman mocked, 'but I know one or two who could still really make her yelp. Maybe I'll make a couple of phone calls tonight. She'd look a treat, wriggling on the end of Max's cock.'

Clarissa felt her face burning with shame and she would have closed her eyes, shutting out their leering faces, but the ice cold drops Christina had put in her eyes seemed to have frozen the muscles that controlled her eyelids, so that she was forced to endure the maximum humiliation.

'Still here then?' Christina said, when she finally reappeared. Her gloved fingers toyed with the clitoral ring, which she had carefully ensured had been pulled into full view when she mounted her trophy earlier. 'What do you think of my slut stand then, eh? I had it specially made, though not for you. There's a certain little whore who's going to spend most of what's left of her miserable life where you are now.

'Actually, I might have a few more made and then I can mount you as a pair,' she mused. 'And the sissy writer bastard, too. Yes, that would be a nice touch, I think. Three unwise monkeys - two cunts and a cock - speak no evil, see all evil, suffer all evil.

'Well, Miss Clever Bitch,' she went on, her mood changing in an instant, 'your dear brother knows the situation exactly, now. He should be getting in contact within the next half hour and, if he does, I've agreed to take you down from there.' She laughed, harshly.

'Of course, whether I really do or not depends on my mood at the time. And on your attitude,' she added.

'Ready to suck my cunt yet, are you?'

Clarissa stared down at her, grunting through the gag, and shook her head as vigorously as the stiff perspex collar would permit. The thought of doing what the amazon was suggesting revolted her and, in any case, she suspected any relief earned by co-operating with her would be short-lived indeed.

Christina shook her own head, smiling crookedly. 'Suit yourself, sweetmeat,' she said. 'You've only had a couple of hours up there so far. I'll ask again in another two.'

Two hours! Clarissa couldn't believe what she was hearing. She had to have been on the stand for far longer than that. Ten hours must be more like it. Christina seemed to sense her disbelief.

'Yes, it seems like a lot longer, doesn't it?' she growled. 'Well I can assure you, by the time I've finished with you, you'll feel like you've lived another complete lifetime.'

'It's still not quite right,' Ellen said, relaxing back into the deep armchair. 'I mean, the action's all very convincing at the time, but those blackouts between scenes are a bit off-putting.'

'Yeah,' Lianne agreed, nodding. 'It's all too much like isolated video clips. There's no proper build up.'

Marlon stood up from where he had been perching on the arm of Nadia's long sofa and paced across to the huge fireplace. He turned and faced his waiting audience and eight pairs of eager eyes sparkled back at him. 'I understand what you're telling me,' he said, 'and I guessed it was coming, but it's just a matter of time now.'

'How much time?' Nadia asked, crossing her long legs and smiling encouragingly. Marlon gave a small shrug.

'A day - two at most,' he replied. 'As you will all doubtless appreciate, my energies initially have been concentrated on setting up the hardware itself and then developing a software package powerful enough to handle what amounts to an entire new world. VESTA is so far in advance of anything else in her field and now has the capacity required, as well as the necessary processing speed, but as you so rightly say, she does not have all the necessary background resources.

'To date, I have managed to programme her with sufficient data to create quite a variety of scenarios, but this all takes time. Now I have to concentrate on getting enough additional data into place to enable VESTA's world to become continuous, without breaks and with all the subtleties of build-up and apprehension that the real world contains.'

'Sounds like a huge undertaking,' Paul said. 'I'm no computer buff, but I understand enough to know that what you're talking about is no one or two day job.'

Marlon nodded. 'Ordinarily,' he said, 'you'd be perfectly correct in that assumption.' He made a wry face and a touch of red appeared in his cheeks. 'However,' he went on, 'I long ago gave up on the concept of "ordinary".

'The idea of a realistic virtual world is not a new one and I have been working on various aspects for quite some while now, even before I first met Nadia and she agreed to finance the project to a conclusion. Of course, with my own limited resources the big stumbling block was always constructing the hardware, without which I could only ever test out the main software programme in theory.

'However, I was always well aware of the fact that, once the main system was in place and working, realism would require that VESTA digested a massive amount of background material, the sort of amount, as Paul suggests, that would require hundreds, if not thousands, of man hours work. However, computers should save labour, not create it, and so I used much of my then spare time in developing a little programme ready to cope with that.

'I shan't baffle you with the intricacies of what I perfected. Just suffice it to say that this little wizard will not only accept material from a variety of sources, it will actually go out and actively seek, evaluate, dissemble and repackage anything it finds that fits within a certain set of parameters I've given it. It is also capable of making comparisons and adjustments to those parameters, altering its predestined agenda as it goes.'

'That's artificial intelligence!' Simon Prescott exclaimed, his gaunt frame suddenly tensing with excitement. 'Good grief, man, you could write your own ticket in the world with that!'

Marlon shook his head. 'Not quite yet,' he said. 'Intelligence suggests an ability to think and react to any given situation, no matter how new and how unexpected. VESTA can't do that, not as such. She still is bound within certain confines and only rewrites within the spectrum I have created for her. It's a wide spectrum, it's true, but it nevertheless has limitations. Fortunately, for our purposes, those limitations are far more than adequate.'

'So, where does VESTA search for all this...?' Lianne began, but a light suddenly dawned in her eyes. 'Ah, I get it!' she cried, clapping her hands together with a loud crack of rubber on rubber. 'The Internet! You've got VESTA surfing the Internet!'

'Indeed I have,' Marlon confirmed. 'But I've also got her scanning pages and pages of every magazine and book I could lay my hands on. The recognition software was a bugger to get right, but I made it in the end.'

'So right now VESTA is going through a huge pile of pornography?' Nadia grinned. Marlon looked aggrieved.

'Not just pornography,' he protested. 'There's all manner of stuff she needs to assimilate, everything from Shakespeare to... to...'

'The Marquis de Sade?' Paul suggested, and there was a general ripple of laughter around the room.

'Your dear brother is trying my patience,' Christina snarled up at the hapless redhead. 'If he thinks delaying tactics will help you, he's very wrong - very wrong indeed.'

Clarissa scarcely heard what the big blonde was saying. Time had long since ceased to have any meaning for her and her entire body had become numbed. Her entire body, that was, apart from her vagina, which seemed to have acquired a life of its own, throbbing and pulsing in response to the sporadic attentions of the vibrating mechanism within the dildo that filled and stretched it.

'Perhaps I should send him an update,' Christina sneered. 'You're definitely beginning to look a bit jaded up there, slut. Or perhaps I should hang you up and give you a good flogging, take that gag out and let him listen to you screaming for mercy.' She walked slowly round her immobile captive, apparently considering her options.

'One more hour,' she said finally, reaching up a gloved finger and stroking the shaven mound just where the cleft began and just above where the huge phallus had entered it. Clarissa felt a new series of tremors beginning, but she no longer had the will, nor the energy, to try to fight them back down. The cruel amazon could now make her climax with the simplest of touches and they both knew it.

'One more hour,' Christina repeated. 'Then we'll have to start work on you properly, beginning with that hair of yours.' Clarissa's eyes betrayed a total lack of comprehension, but Christina quickly removed any doubts as to what she intended.

'Yes,' she went on, 'that lovely red hair of yours; we'll shave it all off and polish your skull until it gleams. And we'll have the eyebrows off, too.

'There's a lot we can do with that body of yours, just to fill in the time. You're not the only artist around here, I can assure you!'

Marlon banged down on the return key in frustration and pushed his chair back from the desk on unresisting casters, staring at the VDU screen with a mixture of annoyance and disbelief.

'Clever bastard,' he said, speaking as if to his unseen adversary. 'Very clever indeed.' He sighed, stood, and walked up and down the narrow room for a minute or two, his muscles, cramped from so long being in the same position, complaining at every step. He stopped, turned, went to the desk and opened the top drawer, taking out the packet that had lain there unused for three months; three months during which he had not once lit up a cigarette.

'Deep layered, triple encryption, double firewall and at least three proxy connections,' he intoned to himself, taking out a cigarette and rolling it between his fingers. 'You know your stuff, my friend, whoever you are.'

After the initial shock of seeing Clarissa's tormented situation, Marlon had quickly re-gathered his senses, for he was nothing if not practical, at least when it came to something he understood and loved. The bastards who were holding his half sister were relying on the gargantuan anonymity of the Internet to protect and hide their identities and location, but huge as the web was, there were always ways of following a trail.

Or so Marlon had thought.

Until now.

Whoever had put up this particular website was good, there was no doubting that. Using his own unique talents, Marlon had quickly penetrated the first couple of layers of defences, convinced that it was only a matter of time before he came up with something that would give him a clue as to where these people were based, but there was nothing. Every avenue he explored led to a dead end and even the phone number that had been used to post the site onto the net turned out to have been registered to a district nurse in the highlands of Scotland.

Marlon had even tried dialling the number and the woman had answered it herself on the third ring, excusing herself to pull her car over onto a verge before continuing with the conversation. No, she hadn't lent her phone to anyone and no, it had been neither lost nor stolen and she's had it for nearly two years now. Where had she bought it? A telephone shop in Fort William and aye, they were a very reputable company and why did he want to know anyway?

Marlon mumbled something about consumer research and an article about organised gangs cloning, or ripping-off people's mobile phones for fraudulent use, and then broke the connection as quickly as he could without arousing any further suspicions. He cursed out loud, for he had been so sure of himself to begin with.

Random cloning, that had to be the answer. Not easy - in fact the phone companies claimed it was impossible to do, though Marlon knew different - and no good for continuous use. But for someone who just wanted to make a handful of calls over a period of one or two days, it was an ideal barrier against being tracked down.

'Damn!' Marlon thrust the cigarette angrily between his lips and scrabbled in the cluttered drawer for a lighter. Already his fertile brain was heading off at an entirely different angle, but he needed time and time was something he did not appear to have very much of.

'You've been a bit quiet since the big run,' Ellen said. Lianne looked up from her book, her expression temporarily blank. 'And it's not like you to just slop around the place in a robe, even if it is silk. You've hardly been out of something rubber in all the months you've been coming here.'

'Except in VESTA's little world,' Lianne muttered.

Ellen raised her eyebrows. 'Oh?' she invited. 'Only you still haven't told me what happened. I told you about my little experiences, but you've said nothing and that's not like the usual you.' Lianne gently closed the book and set it onto the table beside her armchair.

'To be honest,' she said, 'it's all a bit confused now. Oh, I can remember the main stuff, but lots of the details are a bit hazy.'

'Or you don't want to remember them,' Ellen suggested. She knelt down in front of her friend and peered up into her face. 'Maybe it wasn't quite what you were expecting?' she prompted. Lianne pursed her lips.

'Something like that,' she admitted, grudgingly. 'I think VESTA's been searching some very peculiar places for backgrounds and stuff,' she said, after a long pause. 'Either that or Marlon - or somebody else around here - has some bloody weird fantasies; weirder than what passes for normal even in this place, at any rate.'

'Want to tell me about it?' Ellen said, very gently, placing a hand on Lianne's knee.

'Not really,' Lianne said. 'But seeing as I'm unlikely to get any peace around you until I do, I suppose I'd better.'

Jurgen Koenig had little about him to suggest the archetypal German; at a little over five feet seven, he was below average height, slightly built, with stooping rounded shoulders and a shock of unruly near-black hair. He viewed the world through a pair of spectacles that could have done duty as wine bottle bottoms and, despite his best attentions, the apologetic attempt at a moustache refused to take on anything other than a poor replica of a sooty toothbrush.

His English, however, was flawless, without the slightest trace of an accent and only his perfect grammar betrayed the fact that it was not his native language. That and his occasional idiosyncratic misuse of certain idiomatic and slang expressions.

'As I have told you, on more than enough occasions, Mr Naylor,' he said, peering hard across the desk at his current employer, 'it has only been your inability to provide this project with sufficient funds that has prevented me from taking my research into a productive practical stage.

'If our friend Vincent has actually succeeded in building a working model, no matter how advanced a stage it is now at, I can assure you that a few hours application will enable me to assume control of it, my dear bean. Allow me uninterrupted access to this brainbaby of his and I will hand it back to you, pig and poke, fully operational for whatever use you wish to make of it.'

'For someone who has spent a great deal of time and a whole lot of my money,' Naylor said, 'you had better be right. Of course, we could always "persuade" Marlon Vincent to operate the system himself, but then that would be a risky undertaking, seeing as none of us would have the first idea what he was up to.'

'Child's games, Mr Naylor,' Koenig said. 'The Muirhead woman's funding may have permitted him to progress far beyond what we have achieved, but I am as well versed in the theory as any person alive and kicking. As I say, a few hours dissecting his programming and I shall be able to guarantee complete control. I may even be able to improve on what he has done.'

Koenig removed his thick spectacles, breathed on each of the lenses in turn and began to polish them furiously on his shirtfront.

'Do we know exactly how far he has progressed?' he asked, without looking up. Naylor sniffed.

'Not exactly,' he admitted, 'but we are pretty sure he has constructed at least a working prototype. There have been whispers.'

'And you have your ear very much to the wall,' Koenig said. 'Ah well, then we must get ourselves a look-say at this set-up, the sooner the better.'

'That we must,' Naylor agreed. 'The matter is already in hand.'

'It would also help,' Koenig said, mildly, 'if I could see any notes he has made. Every software engineer has his own little quirks and anomalies and there will be many different codes involved, put in to prevent unwanted interference.'

'I had assumed that myself,' Naylor snapped, 'otherwise I should no longer require your services.'

'That is a rash assumption to make, Mr Naylor,' Koenig countered, totally unmoved. 'I have spent a lifetime in this match and even I will not find this a piece of pudding, believe me. There will be several failsafes built in, for a start, and I shall need to identify these and either remove them or re-code them to recognise my instructions. If I do not, the consequences could be disastrous for you.'

Naylor's eyebrows rose in alarm. 'In what way?' he demanded.

'For a start,' Koenig replied, 'it would be unsafe to risk a direct link with a system that could be aborted, or worse, by the use of a simple password. As I understand it, you will be hooking up yourself and several of your associates to this network, becoming a part of it as much as the subjects you intend it to control.'

'True, but then you yourself told me that there will be passive links and active links. We shall all be connected via active links, thus giving us complete control.'

'Except that a simple "safe" word might be used to take that control away from you,' Koenig said, replacing his glasses once more. 'Your "active" links could be disarmed, or even converted to passive status as simply as someone saying Jack in the Beanstalk, I promise you.'

'And you've waited until now to tell me this?' Naylor roared, the colour rising in his cheeks.

Koenig tilted his head to one side. 'Until now,' he said, 'the premise was that we should be using a system of my own design, not taking control of someone else's work. Of course, I could be mistaken, but I don't think so. If the boot were on the other shoe, I know I would build in safeguards against anyone else using my creation against me.

'However, what goes down must come out, as the saying goes. Whatever Mr Vincent can put into his programming, I can trace and remove, replacing it, if necessary, with a different set of passwords.'

'You're absolutely certain of that?'

'Of course. No matter how deeply he may try to bury these things, there are always trails to follow.'

'You'd better be right,' Naylor snorted. 'Because you're going to be connected to this contraption yourself.' He stared across the desk, but if he expected the German to flinch, or to show any reticence, he was disappointed. Koenig simply sat back, a satisfied smile playing across his lips.

'My dear Mr Naylor,' he purred, 'I cannot wait. Ever since your delightful companion showed me the video films of the blonde girl, Lianne, I have been more than eager to meet her in the flesh, even if that flesh is only virtual.'

Naylor clasped his hands together and cracked his knuckles loudly. 'Get this thing to work properly,' he said, 'and you can have her in the flesh for real. I owe Ms Connolly a few, but I can wait a day or two longer.'

'Needs must when the devil plays conkers, eh?' Koenig chuckled, standing up, and behind the thick lenses there was a new gleam in his eyes.

'Okay, so I knew none of it was real,' Lianne finished, 'but it seemed real enough at the time, I promise you. And I kept wondering, what if something goes wrong? Maybe I could burn in here. I tell you, that smoke seemed genuine enough and those flames were getting bloody hot by the time I was pulled out.

'The only thing was,' she went on, 'I couldn't smell the smoke and in the real world, if I'd been tied to a stake with a load of wood burning all around me, I'd have been coughing and spluttering and the tears would have been streaming down my face.'

'Having seen your attempts at making toast when you're pissed,' Ellen retorted, 'I can agree with that.' She shuffled herself back into a more comfortable position on the deep piled bedroom carpet.

'Apparently Marlon's working on the smell part. I asked him if it needed more powerful programming, but he said no, it was a case of getting the sensors on our heads positioned more accurately, or rather adding a couple more to do that.

'Originally, he said he thought the same sensors would work for taste and smell, but apparently he was wrong. Taste and smell are controlled by bits of the brain only millimetres apart, but Marlon reckons there are different frequencies involved. But he has made it work once, with Nadia, so he thinks it should be another of his so-called simple adjustments.'

'It's all Greek to me,' Lianne confessed.

Ellen snorted. 'Hey, I never said I understood any of it,' she said. 'I just happen to have a good memory, so I'm only repeating what our mad boffin told me.'

'Well, apart from the lack of smell and the fact the smoke wasn't affecting my eyes,' Lianne went on, 'everything else was horribly realistic. Those bloody peasants had whipped me raw on the way to the stake. That executioner character put a collar round my neck, with a chain leash. And there was another leash leading back to one of his monkeys, so I couldn't have run even if my ankles hadn't been chained, but I could have got down that line a damn site faster if they'd let me.

'Then the bastard roped me to the pole and fucked me in full view of everyone,' Lianne continued, very affronted.

Ellen laughed. 'But they weren't real people watching,' she pointed out.

Lianne tossed her blonde mane to one side. 'They bloody well seemed real,' she snapped. 'At least, most of them did.'

'So where's your problem?' Ellen asked. 'You've screwed with Paul and with Gavin, on camera and in front of all of us.'

'That's different,' Lianne muttered. 'There were only a few of you and I was masked and suited and everything, not stark bollock naked, and neither was the guy fucking me leering into my face and telling me how he was going to enjoy watching my flesh frizzle and fry in his bloody fire!'

Ellen shuddered visibly. 'Ugh!' she said. 'I see what you mean. I don't reckon I'd have been too keen myself.'

'It makes me wonder just what we all think we're doing here,' Lianne mused. 'This bloody box of tricks Marlon has created might well turn into some sort of Frankenstein's monster, if we're not careful.'

Ellen shook her head. 'I don't think so,' she said. 'After all, Marlon did say it was early days yet, and he's working on getting all the kinks out.'

'More likely getting us kinks in,' Lianne grinned. 'But if he ever puts me into another witch burning scene, I'll fry his balls for real afterwards.'

Clarissa had been barely conscious by the time Christina and her two male assistants finally lifted her from the frame on which she had been mounted, and had scarcely felt the hands that pawed her so roughly as they dragged her away and threw her into the little cell-like room. Left alone on the thin mattress, she had fallen into a deep sleep, during which someone had removed the gag. But when she finally awoke and struggled into a sitting position it was with some considerable difficulty, for she was still locked into the restrictive clear plastic outfit.

Getting to her feet was an act that required a great deal of effort and ingenuity, together with the support of the wall as leverage. But after several unsuccessful attempts, she finally managed to stand and take stock of her surroundings.

Not that there was much to take stock of, for apart from the mattress, the only other furnishings in the room comprised a narrow bench, fixed to the wall just below waist height, offering somewhere to perch without actually sitting, and a stainless steel bin in the corner which, when Clarissa lifted the lid slightly, proved to be some sort of chemical toilet.

There was a narrow window above head height, heavily barred, even though it was out of reach and far too small to permit an average sized person to get through it. But the main illumination was provided by a square fluorescent panel set into the centre of the ceiling. By its light Clarissa examined the heavy steel door, but there was nothing to encourage her there. It was clearly designed to open outwards and there was no handle, nor even any sign of a lock on this side, just a simple spy hole, covered on the outside by yet more steel.

Moving like a marionette, arms and legs rigid inside their plastic casings, she crossed the short distance back to the bench and leaned her weight onto it, realising that its height from the floor was deliberately calculated to enable a prisoner dressed as she was to make use of it; a lower bench would have been very awkward, deprived of the ability to flex her knees as she was.

Fighting back the urge to cry, Clarissa closed her eyes and tried to think.

Obviously her present situation was connected with Marlon, the half brother she had only learned about so recently and was, from what little she had been able to gather from Christina's conversation, to do with his work with computers. She knew very little of what was involved, only that it was extremely advanced stuff and that she, Clarissa, would probably not have understood any of it anyway.

Not that that mattered, she realised, for all she was was a hostage. Christina and whoever it was she was involved with, intended to use her in order to put pressure on Marlon, and it was almost certainly some sort of industrial espionage. Marlon, or his employers, had something Christina and company wanted, and wanted badly enough to kidnap her and put her through a series of horrific ordeals in order to persuade her half brother to give it to them.

On the other hand, she thought, opening her eyes and peering down at the bizarre costume, all this bondage stuff was not directly to do with the Marlon situation; they hadn't created this costume especially for her. Nor, to judge from the cell and from Christina's overall attitude, was this something new to her captors.

'Crazy people,' she whispered aloud. 'Stark, staring bloody crazies.' She closed her eyes again and felt her vaginal muscles twitch at the memory of the huge dildo that had been forced into her, and her stiff fingers moved towards her sex without apparent volition from her brain.

'Bastards!' she hissed. 'Bloody drongos! Just you wait, you dyke, I'll have you over for this little lot.'

'VESTA will be ready for another run in the morning,' Nadia announced, striding into the room. Lianne, Ellen and Gavin looked up from their respective seats around the television. Lianne spoke first.

'No more burning witches,' she said, firmly.

Nadia nodded. 'No, I've had a word with Marlon. Apparently the scenario was supposed to stop short of the actual stake, but his data gathering programme added on the embellishments on its own.'

'That's spooky,' Ellen put in. 'I'm not sure I fancy going back on that machine, not if it's got some sort of mind of its own.'

'It hasn't,' Nadia said. 'Marlon just hadn't got around to putting in the right bits and bobs in the main programme, so he told me, but he's taken care of it now. According to him, if there's anything you really don't fancy just let him know and he'll ensure it can't happen. In any case, none of it's real, is it?'

'That's what I tried telling myself,' Lianne said, 'but it didn't seem to help. I kept wondering what if something had gone wrong? Okay, nothing physical was happening to my real body, but the body my head kept telling me I was in was starting to fry and my virtual bladder, if that's what you'd call it, reacted the same way I reckon my real one would have done if that had happened to me in the real world.' She looked across at Ellen, defiantly sticking out her chin. 'Yes, that's right,' she snapped, 'I bloody well peed myself with fright and, when I came out of VESTA, I realised I'd also done it for real. So what would happen if something even scarier happened in there, eh? I've heard of people dying of fright before now.'

Nadia held up a calming hand. 'Nothing like that will happen again,' she promised. 'I had a very serious word with Marlon and explained a few things to him. Our little mad professor is a genius with his microchips and things, but he apparently didn't quite understand exactly what we were about. To him, being whipped by a sadistic witch hunter or hangman is no different from getting a severe paddling from someone you'd quite fancy screwing afterwards.'

'All I can say,' Lianne said, 'is that it was a good thing I couldn't smell anything. That bastard who was fucking me would have had appalling bad breath, to judge from the state of his teeth!'

'He's agreed to your demands,' Jurgen Koenig announced, brandishing the sheet of paper before him as though it were a sword. 'This is a print-out of his reply.'

James Naylor allowed himself a satisfied smile, but the big blonde did not seem at all impressed.

'Of course he's agreed!' she snapped. 'I have a way of persuading people, as you must surely have realised, and the thought of abandoning his dear sister clearly would never have entered young Mr Vincent's head. The images I sent him were clear enough.'

'I saw them,' Koenig said, letting the paper drop onto Naylor's desk. 'Just a trifle extreme, don't you think?'

Christina gave a loud, derisive snort. 'Extreme?' she sneered. 'I haven't even started with that red-headed bitch yet. And she's a tough one, believe me. Many a girl would have been begging to be let off my little perch within minutes, let alone hours.'

'That gag scarcely allowed much scope for begging,' Koenig pointed out, reasonably enough, but Christina shrugged off the criticism.

'There are ways of begging without the need for speech,' she said. 'I gave her several opportunities, but she refused to crack. However, give her another day or two in my hands and I'll turn her into a perfect little lapdog. She won't be able to please me fast enough.'

'What you do with the girl is neither here nor there,' Naylor interrupted. 'Just so long as you keep her healthy enough to serve the purpose for which we brought her here. Once Vincent's given us what we want, fair enough, she's yours to amuse yourself with, for as long as you want.'

'Oh, I'll amuse myself,' Christina assured him. 'Most certainly I'll amuse myself.'

For the third time in half an hour, Marlon checked that the door to the room was really locked. Not that anyone would have dreamed of interrupting him when the door was simply closed, for it was understood that this was Marlon's inner sanctum, this low-ceilinged, square chamber high in the roof of Nadia's rambling mansion. It was within these four cramped walls that VESTA had gradually come into being, and although the main hardware was now housed in the largest of the cellar chambers, they still contained an access console through which Marlon could control the entire network.

He sat down in front of the screen, his right index finger moving over the touch sensitive pad, rows and columns of numbers and symbols scrolling before his eyes in a jumble that would have been meaningless to just about anyone else. Except, he realised, to whoever had set up that complex website connection. Whoever he - or she - was would soon decipher this little lot; access codes, barring codes, safety codes - everything.

Turning away from the VDU, Marlon picked up the curious helmet which lay on the side table, turning it over slowly in his hands, eyes narrowed in concentration. Time was running out now and this had to be done right, otherwise there was no telling what these bastards might do to Clarissa. The image of her impaled upon that awful stand was burned into his memory forever. And he didn't doubt for a moment when they told him that what they had done to the poor creature so far was nothing compared to the fate that awaited her if he failed to deliver.

Marlon made a final check on the multi-ribbon connector cable, nodded to himself, raised the helmet and slowly lowered it onto his head.

'Time to go walkies, sweetmeat.'

Christina stood framed in the open doorway to Clarissa's cell, high black boots, black waistcoat-styled jacket and black gloves all gleaming in contrast to the pure white silk blouse and leggings she wore. In her right hand she carried a vicious looking riding crop, which she now pointed at Clarissa.

'We've got a bit of time to kill, waiting for your brother to come across,' she said, 'and I have a very low boredom threshold. C'mon, move that fat butt, or do you want me to put a nice red design on it for you?'

'What do you want with me?' Clarissa cringed back, but there was nowhere to retreat to in the tiny room. Christina chuckled, but it was not a very pleasant, nor humorous sound.

'What do I want, indeed?' she replied, stepping into the cell and reaching out to clip a leather thong to the front of Clarissa's collar. 'Well, to start with, it's a very nice day out there and I fancy some fresh air. We're very remote up here and there's some beautiful scenery I like to take in.

'The problem is,' she continued, jerking Clarissa into an upright stance, 'that I don't enjoy walking. There's a nice pony trap I can use, but then keeping and grooming ponies is so time consuming, so I prefer to use a different kind of pony - the two legged variety. You!' she grinned, pulling Christina closer to her and forcing her head back.

'You're going to be my pony for the day.'

'You're bloody mad!' Clarissa squealed, trying to fight for her breath at the same time. For a brief second a dangerous light flared in Christina's eyes, but it faded immediately and she relaxed her grip on her captive slightly.

'That tongue of yours will get you into trouble,' she warned. 'Take care, or I'll have it cut out. Ponies don't need tongues, remember.' She switched the crop into the hand that held the leash and forced her right index finger between Clarissa's lips and teeth, probing deep and causing Clarissa to retch.

'And afterwards, once Naylor's got what he wants from your Marlon,' Christina went on, 'I think I'll keep you as my own personal pony.' The leather-covered digit pressed against Clarissa's upper back molars and Clarissa had to fight the urge to bite down, knowing that if she did the consequences didn't bear thinking about.

'We'll have a couple of teeth out either side, top and bottom,' Christina said. 'Makes it easier to fit your bit, pony girl. And we'll have this pretty little face tattooed. I think you'd make a good palomino, don't you? However, I mustn't damage the goods too much just yet, must I? Have to let dear Marlon think we've taken proper care of you, otherwise he might not play the game.'

Paul Dean had his own private sanctum, also high up in the roof, but at the furthest end of the house from where Marlon worked. His room was also larger than Marlon's, two of the original servants bedrooms knocked into one, for here Paul stored everything he needed for his work, plus copies - hard copies, so unusual in this electronic age - of everything his original outlines had produced.

The rows of filing cabinets contained scripts, prints of photographs, rough sketches and even copies of the final artworks, originally the work of James Naylor before the artist's treacherous greed had driven him to try to betray Nadia's close-knit organisation, and now the creations of the even more talented Sonia Hughes, who had succeeded him just after Paul and Lianne had finally managed to escape Naylor's fiendish clutches and the even more fiendish attentions of his amazonian henchwoman.

With a barely audible sigh Paul opened a drawer at random, picked out the first file his hand encountered and flipped it open. With a grin, he recognised the manuscript as one of the very first he had ever produced for Nadia. The story line had been developed, enacted by a willing cast that included Gavin, Hazel and a couple of other girls who were no longer involved - it would still be another two and a half years before Lianne had become part of the team - photographed from all angles and videoed too, by Simon Prescott, and the final panels produced with meticulous care by Naylor.

The very first Della de Linkwent cartoon strip; probably a collector's piece by now, Paul realised, especially in its original artwork form. Not that he had the original artwork. All of that was kept carefully under lock and key in Nadia's specially constructed vault in the cellar complex; each completed strip, once scanned for printing, sealed in its own fireproof box, inside a fireproof safe, inside a fireproof, bombproof vault of nine inch steel walls and outer jacket of two feet of reinforced concrete.

'This lot will be worth millions, some day,' Nadia had once told him, confidently, but Paul knew such lavish security precautions were not there simply to protect the fruits of their combined creative genius. Nadia was very rich - very rich - and did not trust too much to banks. Not simply because they were liable to be robbed, because the average bank was more than secure enough in that respect nowadays, but because, in common with a lot of other incredibly wealthy people, she preferred not to share too much of her fortune with the taxman. And in that way, unless you kept a numbered account in Switzerland, banks were far less secure.

Paul had occasionally tried to estimate what Nadia was really worth, but had given up the attempt each time, for to call her affairs complicated would have been doing them a grave injustice. He knew she had inherited this huge estate and that it had been in her family since the time of Cromwell, at least, and that there were other properties dotted around the country, including at least two hotels, an international shipping company, several magazines and a company that specialised in manufacturing everything from latex suits to pony girl tack; an astonishingly lucrative enterprise to a one time naive young writer.

Nadia Muirhead was worth millions, and she was also generous to her friends and employees. Della de Linkwent and Mary Lou were a terrific commercial success, but Paul doubted whether the strip and its spin-off videos and Internet episodes made enough to justify the huge salaries that most of them now received.

Of course, he could be wrong in that assumption, he supposed. After all, none of them ever had any dealings with the financial end of things, Nadia preferring to handle everything herself, closeted away with her team of three personal accountants for three or four days in every month. She never mentioned money directly and none of the elite team ever broached the subject themselves. Della de Linkwent and Mary Lou just were, and that was that.

Closing the file, Paul replaced it in the drawer and slid it shut on noiseless, well lubricated runners. He wondered whether he would still be standing here in this room in another ten years time, or even five, for he had a dreadful suspicion that the computerised age was fast beginning to make creative writers redundant.

Marlon's bloody VESTA machine was probably only the tip of the iceberg, crazy though that might seem. Paul could remember his own first computer, a cumbersome black box with two floppy disc drives on the front and a total memory storage and processing ability that an average modern personal computer could now duplicate a thousand-fold, and in probably one hundredth of the time. Technology was racing forward at an ever-increasing rate, a breakneck speed that Paul, a confirmed Luddite in many ways, found utterly alarming.

He hadn't wanted any part of the VESTA experiment, at least not when it came to being one of the test subjects himself, but he felt he owed it to Nadia to at least make a show of it. Life was pretty good here and Paul, along with all the other team members, was paid handsomely for doing something an awful lot of people would have willingly paid to do. And he knew that even were the likes of Marlon and their electronic wizardry to remove the need for human creativity, Nadia would never drop him. She was a great believer in loyalty.

Moving to the desk, Paul produced a small key from his jacket pocket and unlocked the top drawer, lifting out the neat grey cash box and placing it on the top. He closed the drawer, sat down and used a second key to open the box in turn. Inside, the carefully folded statements and accounts lay atop an inch thick wad of Swiss thousand franc notes, each of the notes worth something in excess of four hundred pounds sterling, the bundle numbering six hundred notes at the last count.

There were also three very fine diamond rings, each valued conservatively at around twenty-five thousand pounds. But seventy-five thousand pounds' worth of pressurised carbon and a quarter of a million pounds in cash represented only half of what Paul had managed to squirrel away from his royalties and salary, courtesy

44

of Nadia. Thanks to her nous, he had also invested nearly two hundred thousand pounds over the years, a sum that had all but trebled in the interim.

With two bank accounts and a further account with a very large building society, Paul himself was fast approaching millionaire status. He no longer owned any property; it had seemed stupid keeping on the little mews cottage when he spent virtually all his time here now, and there was always Nadia's two Spanish villas, or the house in Nassau if any of them fancied a break. But he had lately begun to consider the possibilities of buying a new place, for he had every intention of proposing to Lianne in the very near future, and every confidence she would accept.

Life with Nadia was tremendous whirlwind fun, it was true, but the pages of the calendar never went backwards, and there would have to come a time...

The hateful plastic bondage outfit had finally been removed, but what Christina had selected to replace it was, if anything, even worse, and Clarissa's initial attempts to resist the dominatrix had met with a beating so severe that she no longer had any fight left in her. Not that there were any marks left showing; Christina was far too expert for that. But every muscle and nerve in Clarissa's body now seemed to be on fire.

Glaring resentfully, her eyes still tearstained, there was nothing the redheaded artist could do but submit, for the great Dane outweighed her by at least five stone, outreached her by several inches, and carried more muscle than a trained light heavyweight boxer.

First came the rubber helmet, a close fitting latex hood that left only the eyes and mouth showing, two brass ringed apertures permitting air to enter and exit the nostrils. It laced tightly to hug every contour of Clarissa's skull, a high tubular opening at the crown allowing her flaming hair to emerge in a gloriously cascading ponytail that was emphasised starkly against the black rubber and even dwarfed the two long, high-pointed pony ears that were attached at either side.

The body suit was next, more close-fitting rubber in black, brown and white, giving a dappled effect that was not lost on Clarissa, who also noted that, in addition to the strategically placed rear opening, the suit was cut away at the front to leave her shaven sex mound clearly on display, the added pressure from the stretchy fabric forcing her lower lips to protrude and bulge quite grotesquely. Even worse, there were two round openings through which her nipples now stuck out, the pressure around their bases causing them to distend horribly, so that the nipple rings hung on them like hoops on a fairground stall.

It required a certain amount of patience and the application of generous dustings of talcum powder to fit the garment, for it was intended to hug the body like a new skin. Especially over the hands, for the ends of the arms were shaped into rounded mittens, forcing the fingers into clenched fists and rendering them incapable of any dextrous task whatsoever.

'Yes, you'll make a splendid little horsy,' Christina announced, giving Clarissa's generously rounded buttocks a hard slap. 'Nice muscle tone and a good generous rump. We'll have to find you a nice stallion to mate with eventually.' She ran a gloved hand down over Clarissa's latex-covered belly. 'Have to get this filled up with some pretty new foals, I think,' she smirked.

Clarissa recoiled from her touch, but the big blonde just found this amusing.

'Oh yes, my little slut pony, we're going to have such fun with you.' She turned and picked up a complex assembly of leather straps, the centrepiece of which was a broad, corset-like girth piece. This she wrapped about Clarissa's middle, fastening it at the front with a series of five smaller straps and buckles, cinching each until the unfortunate girl felt breathless. However, the adjustments were far from complete, for the two halves of the girth were joined by stout cross lacing in the rear and there remained a gap between them of some three inches, which the powerful blonde now began to reduce in stages, tugging and hauling and seemingly impervious to Clarissa's squeals of protest.

By the time the gap had been eliminated completely, Clarissa felt as though she were being held in a vice, for this was even tighter than the perspex corset had been and every bit as unyielding, for the polished leather was a good quarter of an inch thick. She stood unsteadily, gulping and gasping, trapped and useless fingers scrabbling helplessly in a futile attempt to release the front buckles.

'Better remove temptation,' Christina rasped, and seized Clarissa's right wrist, buckling a wide studded strap about it and securing it to a ring at the hip of her girth by means of a strong snap link. Moments later, the left wrist had been similarly dealt with and, if there had ever been any chance that the hapless girl might have released those straps, there was certainly none now.

'Hooves next, I think,' Christina announced, holding up a pair of curiously shaped knee length boots. Wide-eyed inside her horse's head mask, Clarissa saw they were designed with extremely high heels and a thick platform sole, but that heels and soul had been moulded together and the shape flared out into the profile of a hoof, on the underside of which was a glittering steel horseshoe.

The hoof boots looked heavy, as indeed they were, as Clarissa discovered when Christina had finished lacing her into them. Experimentally, she tried to shift her stance and the weight dragged even out of proportion to what she had expected.

'There are lead inserts in the soles and heels,' Christina smirked. 'I call these training boots, as they help to build up the leg muscles. Very handy if I decide to race you.'

'Race me?' Clarissa echoed, horrified. The blonde's leering grin grew even wider.

'Oh yes,' she said. 'There are plenty of clubs and organisations interested in pony girls, I assure you, and races most weekends. A good thoroughbred can win several thousand pounds if she comes out as overall winner at a meeting.'

'You're a bloody barbarian!' Clarissa shrieked, and immediately wished she'd kept her mouth shut, for the roundhouse kick that landed in her kidneys would have done serious damage, but for the protection the girth corset now afforded them. Even so, the impact sent her sprawling sideways to collapse in an ungainly heap, and it was several seconds before she managed to haul herself unsteadily to her feet again.

'I think we'll definitely have that tongue out of your head before too much longer,' Christina snarled. She moved in on Clarissa and seized the two straps that dangled down from the front of the corset girth, throwing them over Clarissa's shoulders, crossing them at the back and buckling them tightly to the upper edges of the broader band.

A secondary strap hung down from each at about the level of the bottom of the shoulder blade and these she drew around Clarissa's upper arms, cinching tightly so that her shoulders were forced painfully back and holding her in an artificially erect posture, a pose which was further accentuated by the addition of a wide leather collar, the upper front edge of which rose to a sharp point, preventing Clarissa from lowering her chin without a great deal of discomfort.

'And now for your tail,' Christina said, taking up the article in question, a flowing cascade of black and white hairs, real or artificial it was impossible for Clarissa to say. What was most certainly real was the device to which they were attached, and by means of which the tail was intended to be affixed to her, for the long slender dildo was designed for one orifice only.

Without ceremony Christina forced her victim to bend forward, at least as far as her new harness assembly would permit, kicking her booted ankles as far apart as was possible without losing her balance completely. Clarissa tensed her rectal muscles, but there was to be no respite.

'If you fight it,' Christina warned, 'it'll hurt for sure. Just relax and it'll slide in easily. One way or the other, it's going in, even if I have to hammer it home.' With a great effort, Clarissa willed herself to relax, but even so the initial entry was far from pleasant. However, as she stood up again and her captor buckled in place the intricate crotch strap assembly that would prevent her from ejecting the invader, her body was already beginning to acclimatise itself and the discomfort rapidly began to give way to sensations of a different sort; sensations Clarissa was determined not to acknowledge.

Although she could not bend her neck to see down between her legs, Clarissa's other senses were now on full alert and she could tell that the harness, as Christina finished adjusting the final buckle, was designed so that the two front straps divided and passed upwards in a V-shape, so that her sex, distorted and made more prominent by the cloying rubber of her bodysuit, was framed by it and not obscured from view in the slightest. She felt more naked now than if she had truly been so, and could not understand the little shivery fingers that seemed to be dancing up and down her spine.

'Yes, a pretty filly indeed,' Christina murmured. Her eyes were gleaming now, but she did not allow herself more than a few seconds to admire the effect so far, for there was still more to come in Clarissa's humiliating ordeal. There was absolutely nothing the younger girl could do to resist as the heavy bridle assembly was lowered over her head.

She did consider trying to refuse to take the rubber-covered bit into her mouth, but she guessed, correctly, that it would have done her no good. In fact, she was convinced now that any lack of co-operation would bring severe punishment as its reward, not just now, but even worse later. From what Christina had been saying these beasts were capable of just about any extremes, and this was being tempered only by their need to convince Marlon that she would be released to him, safe and unharmed, when he had given them whatever it was they wanted so badly.

Mute now, Clarissa stared stoically straight ahead, only the stiff collar preventing her from bowing her head under this latest burden, for the bit, straps, chains and thick blinkers that were positioned to either side of her eyes combined to make a total weight of several pounds, she guessed. And having ensured that the straps formed a satisfactorily close fit, Christina added even to this, by the addition of several small bells, above her forehead and to either side of the strap that secured the bit itself.

'Wonderful!' Christina said, finally stepping back to take in the overall effect. 'I should have done this for that Connolly bitch. But then,' she added, with a malicious grin, 'if she thinks she's seen the last of me, she's in for a big shock. In fact, I think I'll get her tack ready when we get back from our little trot this afternoon. The two of you would make a very nice racing pair.'

James Naylor stood peering over Jurgen Koenig's shoulder, trying to make some sort of sense of what was on the German's VDU screen. Koenig was nodding his head as he scrolled through the seemingly endless displays of figures, tables and diagrams, but as far as Naylor was concerned, the entire thing could have been written in hieroglyphics.

'What's the verdict?' he demanded, unable to contain his impatience any longer. Koenig scratched his chin before replying.

'What we are looking at, my friend,' he said finally, 'is a perfect example of what can be attained if the resources are made available as and when they are needed.'

Naylor snorted angrily. 'Just stop whining on about money and tell me straight,' he snapped. 'Has he done it, or hasn't he?'

Koenig sniffed, but did not turn away from the screen. 'Whether he has, or whether he hasn't,' he said, deliberately, 'is still a matter for conjecture. What we are looking at is the theory of what friend Vincent has put together, plus engineering drawings of his various hardware developments.'

'And you can't tell me whether they work or not?' This time Koenig did look round, but only to give Naylor a sideways look that bordered on contempt.

'My dear chap,' he said, and the tone of his voice was unmistakable, 'you could point out a car to me and ask me if it works. And I could say yes, it has an engine where an engine should be, it has wheels in all the appropriate places and the drawings show it has brakes, a gear box and so on, but there would be no certain way of knowing that it worked until you placed the key in the ignition, started it up and made it move.'

'We're not talking about bloody cars here!' Naylor snarled, but Koenig remained unmoved.

'Of course we're not,' he answered amiably, 'we're talking about something more complex than a million cars, something far more advanced, even, than the technology they are using to send men into space. You see,' he continued, rising slowly to his feet and turning fully to face Naylor, 'we are not just talking about the most powerful computer programme yet devised, we are also dealing with a processing system even more powerful than that. We are talking about the human brain here, my friend.'

'So,' Naylor sighed, trying to keep his temper in check, 'we're no better off than we were two days ago, is that what you're trying to tell me?'

'Certainly not!' Koenig looked shocked. 'Most certainly not,' he repeated. 'Vincent assured me it does work and I have no reason not to believe him. After all, if he could convince us it did not, why should we want it?'

'Maybe he could be bluffing,' Naylor suggested. 'Maybe his machine is a load of old rubbish after all, or maybe it isn't and what he's sending us isn't the genuine article anyway.'

'Maybe,' Koenig agreed, 'but I think not. You are, after all, holding his sister as hostage and he would not be naive enough to think you would let her go until we had proof of the value of the goods. I myself have made that clear enough to him.'

'So we have to try this out ourselves,' Naylor said. 'How long would it take you to put something together from his data?'

At this, Koenig promptly turned and sat down again, his entire body rocking with laughter. Naylor stared at him in bemusement.

'What's so fucking funny?' he demanded. It took Koenig a few seconds to compose himself, but when he turned again there were still tears in his eyes and he was unable to keep a completely straight face.

'Funny?' he said. 'I'll tell you what's funny Herr Naylor - you are, except it's not a very good joke, is it? You really have not the slightest idea about all this, do you? Let me explain.' He jabbed a finger at the screen.

'In there, as far as I can tell in the short time in which I have had to evaluate it, is all the data necessary to build something that will create a sophisticated, realistic virtual reality experience. And the number of people who can share in it at the same time appears to be limited only by the space required to house the individual pods, or terminals.

'We do have most of the computing power we need to duplicate it, though not all, and we can lift all Vincent's programmes as they are, which will indeed cut out many months of work. I can even add improvements and refinements of my own, given time enough, but such hardware as we currently have at our disposal falls far short of what they have there. And even if you gave me six months I could not guarantee to construct it, not without a great deal of money - money you do not have, or if you do, you have been reluctant to put at my disposal before now.'

'How much money?' Naylor asked.

'How long is a piece of string?' Koenig countered. 'I'm no cost accountant, nor do I wish to become one, but I will give you a guess, if you'd like?'

'Of course I'd like. How much?'

'Six or seven millions - pounds sterling, not marks.'

'You must be joking!' The colour drained immediately from Naylor's cheeks. 'I haven't got that sort of cash.'

'I did not think you had,' Koenig replied, evenly. 'However, the good Fraulein Muirhead evidently has. And she has spent it too, so why bother to reinvent the wheel?'

'What are you saying? You're not suggesting we try to steal their set-up, are you?

My god, I know that place. Don't forget, I was there long enough. There are top-secret government establishments that aren't as well protected as that place is now. It was bad enough anyway, but since my little run-in with her the woman's gone overboard, from what I've been hearing. You couldn't get a brass nut out of there, let alone something the size of what we're talking about. And if you're thinking of trying to get in, you can forget that, too. The place is tighter than a drum.'

'Right now, you are doubtless correct,' Koenig said. 'However, I have considered a different approach, an approach which will not only give you control of their machine, but also of the entire Muirhead estate and all the personnel involved there. I have already transmitted certain demands to Vincent, together with further footage provided by the inestimable Christina. He was not happy with what I suggested, but he really does not have any other viable options.

'Tomorrow, Mr Naylor,' he continued, standing up again and walking across the small room to stand before the open window, 'we shall walk straight into Marlon Vincent's virtual world and assume control of it, at a time when the Muirhead woman and all her minions are inside it and at the mercy of whoever has their hand on the tiller, so to speak.

'The initial entry will be made from this very room, via a telephone link, but that is only a temporary expedient, as the sort of data transfers we are talking about are far too massive to be handled by even a group of ordinary telephone lines. However, just as soon as I have established control of the system, Vincent will admit yourself and however many people you decide to take with you, and you can secure a physical control of the premises.

'Once that is done, I suggest you deal with Vincent before he starts fretting about the beautiful Clarissa. I am assuming you have no intention of releasing her, not if I am to judge by the tremendous amount of fun your Christina currently seems to be deriving from her.'

'I think Christina would break his neck first,' Naylor muttered.

Koenig laughed. 'I am sure she would and I do not doubt she is capable of doing it, but we are not murderers here, are we? Besides, it would be a criminal waste of an excellent resource. No, I suggest the safest way to deal with our Mr Vincent would be to put him safely inside his own virtual world, from where we can control him as easily as we shall control the others.

'Apart from the efficiency of such a plan, I think you might find it all rather amusing. Think of it as one giant toy box, inside which you will find every little goodie you have ever wished for.'

Wherever they were, Clarissa was certain of one thing: Christina had not been exaggerating when she said it was remote and isolated. All around, in every direction, the horizon was dominated by bleak, featureless hills, rising up out of the tangle of moorland and sparse coppices, without a single indication of human habitation other than the big house and its surrounding outbuildings from which they had emerged.

The pony cart itself was not heavy and had been well designed to be pulled by a human equine, balanced perfectly on its single axle, the two huge wheels moving over the less than even ground without hindrance. But the added handicaps of Christina's bulk and the weighted hoof boots made for hard work, and Clarissa was very soon sweating profusely inside her rubber pony skin.

She had been hitched to the twin shafts by means of metal clasps attached to her hips where her wrists had first been secured, and a long rein ran back from either side of her bit strap, enabling her driver to guide her left and right by the simple expedient of tugging on the appropriate trace. Any signs of slacking were quickly rewarded by a savage slash across unprotected buttocks, Christina clearly being well versed in the use of the long carriage whip she employed for this purpose.

Biting fiercely into the bit, eyes screwed up in concentration, Clarissa could do nothing but keep going forward, the jingle-jangle of her harness bells accompanying her every step, ringing loud in her ears and serving to emphasise the humiliation of her position.

There appeared to be a network of trails leading across this wilderness, but they were hardly well defined and Clarissa stumbled several times in her unfamiliar footwear. Fortunately, Christina seemed well enough aware of what she could or could not expect, particularly from a novice such as Clarissa and did not insist on anything above a gentle trot, though even this soon had leg and back muscles protesting and Clarissa was relieved when she was eventually reined in beneath the shade of a small group of straggly looking trees.

However, she soon changed her mind when she saw the contents of the small case Christina had brought with her on the cart. Unable to utter any coherent protest because of the bit, she nevertheless squealed loudly enough when Christina brought the barbarous looking needle up to her right nipple.

'Should have finished this earlier,' the Dane said, 'but I thought we'd break you in a bit first. Now, hold still.' Not that she left Clarissa with much option, for her fingers exerted a vicious grip on the ring that was already through the swollen teat. The point penetrated helpless flesh and the sound that ripped past the bit gag was so much like a frightened whinny that Christina commented upon it.

'Very good sound effects,' she sneered, withdrawing the needle and threading the gold ring through in its place. 'You see, you won't miss that tongue at all when it's gone, will you?' The second nipple was likewise pierced, eliciting still more squeals from its terrified owner, though in truth there was very little pain to what she had been anticipating.

'Now for your extra bells,' Christina said, replacing the needle carefully into its case and withdrawing the two shimmering gold orbs to clip to the nipple rings. She gave each a playful flick with her finger, setting them tinkling merrily in unison with the bells on Clarissa's bridle as she tried to jump back.

'I'll add some more down there soon,' Christina warned, jabbing a finger in the direction of Clarissa's exposed genitalia. 'I do so like my ponies to make pretty music wherever they go. Now,' she went on, moving round and pulling herself up into the driving seat again, 'let's play ourselves some nice little tunes and then we'll see if it might not be worth letting you keep that tongue after all.'

Red-faced, Clarissa was in no doubt as to what the amazon meant; no more than she any longer entertained any doubts that she, Clarissa, supposedly world famous superstar artist, would almost certainly be prepared to go along with whatever she was now told. As she moved forward again, to an accompanying symphony of jingling bells, she reflected on how quickly she had been subjugated and wondered just how many other horrors lay in store for her before she finally got away from this place and these monstrous people.

Always assuming, she thought grimly, picking up pace, that she ever did get away.

'So it's all set for another run in the morning?' Lianne said, stretching herself out on the bed. Seated at the dressing table, Paul Dean was in the process of completing his transformation into his female character of Pauline the rubber maid, in an effort, he hoped, to jolt Lianne out of the lackadaisical mood she had been in since the previous test run of VESTA.

'Does that worry you still?' he replied, fiddling with the fastening of a heavy pendant earring.

Lianne made a petulant face at him. 'It'd worry you if you'd found yourself being burned at the stake,' she said. 'And okay, so I know it wasn't for real, but I've been over all that a million times.'

'Well, Marlon's promised no more witch burning routines,' Paul said, picking up the second earring, 'so there's no need to worry about it.'

'So you say,' Lianne replied. She lifted the hem of her rubber skirt and made a show of adjusting the suspender clip at the top of one of her latex stockings. 'But I'm not so sure. It doesn't seem right, somehow, just laying down in that pod thing, having a load of wires clipped into that weird helmet and then suddenly waking up in a world where you know things are going to happen, even if you don't know what.'

'At least we now have safe words,' Paul/Pauline pointed out. 'Mine's "jasmine" - what's yours?'

'Would you believe "belfry"?' Lianne pouted. 'And don't ask me why.'

'Maybe Marlon thinks you've got bats in it?' Paul suggested. 'Didn't you ask him?'

'No, I had a raging headache at the time.'

'Well, I hope you aren't going to tell me you've got a headache now?' Paul stood up amidst a rustle of rubber skirt and petticoats and teetered across the carpet on steepling heels. Lianne looked up at him and smiled.

'No, Pauline,' she said, reaching under her skirt again and grasping the hem of her rubber panties, 'I most certainly haven't. But you can get straight back over there and cuff your hands behind your back, missy. I've got a little job for you that only requires your tongue, at least for the time being.'

She finished dragging the flimsy latex down to her ankles and kicked the garment to one side, lying back with legs splayed, her naked hairless sex lips gaping invitingly. On the far side of the room two sharp metallic clicks announced that Pauline had dutifully followed her instructions, and now he turned back to her, his tongue flicking in and out, eyes as bright as Lianne's with anticipation and lust.

'You are certain he hasn't hidden any more code words inside this programme?' The clock on the wall above the VDU showed it was past three in the morning and Jurgen Koenig's red-rimmed eyes were evidence of long, unbroken hours of concentrated screen study. He yawned, covering his mouth with the back of one hand, and looked up.

'Absolutely,' he confirmed. 'I have found a whole series of what they call "safe" words, each dedicated to a particular individual, the use of which will, or would, I should say, bring their particular participation in this VESTA to a close. I have constructed a simple programme that will disable them at the press of a single key, when the time is right.

'I have also found four separate master code words, each designed to bring the system to a halt in different ways, the final one instigating a total systems crash and preventing the master programme from being restarted for a minimum of twelve hours. He is indeed very cute, this man Vincent, and was at great pains to hide the whereabouts and existence of these codes. But I think I am more than a match for such trickery.'

'He couldn't have hidden anything else in there, I suppose?' James Naylor persisted. 'I don't profess to know that much about it, but I understand it's quite possible to camouflage these things?'

'Quite possible,' Koenig agreed, 'but there are always trails to follow. For such codes to work they must be able to activate a certain series of pathways; find the pathways and you eventually get back to the codes themselves. Fairly simple,' he added, 'especially if you have a programme which will do it all automatically for you.

'No,' he said, sitting back and stretching cramped shoulder muscles, 'I can assure you that I have combed every line of programming, even in the most remote corners, speaking metaphorically of course, and there is nothing left that he could use to stop VESTA once it is running.'

'Nothing?'

'Nothing. Once he is in there, he will be as helpless as the rest of them and VESTA, the estate, all of it, will be within our control.'

'Excellent,' Naylor nodded. 'You've done well. I shall look forward to tomorrow.'

'I, also,' Koenig said. 'But now, before I finally get some sleep, you must excuse me while I prepare some escape codes for our own use. I am assuming, of course, that you will want to play an active part in this little game?' He raised one quizzical eyebrow. James Naylor gave him a grim smile in return.

'Try stopping me,' he growled.

Hot and exhausted, the sight of the stable outbuilding coming back into view sent an overwhelming wave of relief washing over Clarissa. Every sinew in her tortured body ached from the effort of trotting in the weighted boots and dragging Christina's weight behind her in the pony cart, but if she had expected to be allowed time to recover from her ordeal, she was rapidly disillusioned.

Unhitching her from between the shafts, the big woman removed the driving reins from Clarissa's bridle and replaced them with a short chain leash, which she

53

clipped to the stiff collar, dragging the stumbling girl into a room she had not seen before and which, as she looked around it with staring eyes, she immediately wished she was not seeing now, for the racks of chains, whips, canes and paddles and the various frames and stands which covered the floor space did not need words to explain.

'Knees!' Christina barked. Numbly, Clarissa sank down, too tired and frightened to even think of not obeying instantly. Deftly, Christina passed the leash over her left shoulder and wound it about Clarissa's ankles, preventing her from rising again, and strode across to the nearest wall rack, from which she selected a vicious looking braided whip. She flicked it through the air experimentally, producing a loud crack, and the bound girl flinched.

'Right, pony girl,' Christina drawled, moving up to stand astride, with her silk-covered crotch only inches from her face. 'Let's see how much you've learned in your short time here.' Her free hand moved down, cupping her sex suggestively. 'And let's see if that tongue really is worth keeping. Do you understand what I'm saying?'

Clarissa nodded.

'Excellent. Now, make no mistake, pony girl, I'd be quite happy to whip the hide off you and this little beauty could do that, even with that rubber covering you, though it would be a shame to ruin such craftsmanship, so I'd probably strip you first anyway.

'However, I could just be lenient with you, depending upon how you perform. Understand?' Again, Clarissa nodded, bells jangling to the movement. 'Good. Now, let's see, shall we?'

Christina reached up under the skirt-like hem of her leather bodice, fingers seeking the zip, which hissed downwards in a single whispered movement. In the gap that appeared between the white silk, Clarissa saw a thick bush of pale pubic hair and, as Christina eased the fabric down over her hips, below it appeared a vivid crimson gash, lips already parted in anticipation of what was to come.

'Damn!' Christina cursed and stepped back. For a second or so Clarissa was afraid she had done something to arouse the older woman's ire, but then she saw it was simply a case of her being unable to get the leggings far enough down without trapping her thighs too closely together for what she intended. However, the dilemma did not last long.

Boots clattered across the stone floor, landing untidily against the wall, and then Christina was stepping free of the restrictive garment, tossing it to join her discarded footwear and turning back to her hapless captive. She stepped closer, reached out to unclip and remove Clarissa's bit, and then seized the bridle straps where the blinkers were attached. She glared down at Clarissa's upturned face, a malevolent expression on her own features.

'Now,' she leered, 'let's try that tongue for size. C'mon, pony slut, get it in good and deep.' Clarissa swallowed hard, pursing together lips that had suddenly become dry, and closed her eyes, making no effort to resist as her tormentor slowly drew her mouth towards its gaping target, offering her tongue to the moist yaw, her nostrils filled with the acrid-sweet scent of her mistress's desire.

'Nearly time,' Lianne said quietly, looking across at the bedside clock. She smoothed the sleeves of her black latex catsuit, wriggling her fingers within the attached gloves, making sure the rubber fitted without wrinkling and rippling, as far as was possible. On the end of the bed heavy rubber ankle boots awaited her, boots with almost cripplingly high heels and locking ankle straps, boots she would once have found impossible to believe existed, let alone able to walk in.

By the dressing table Paul was still dressed as Pauline, a surprisingly convincing image from someone who was so undoubtedly masculine beneath the frivolous latex maid's uniform. For the first trial run he had worn rubber also, but that time it had been a male version of the suit that Lianne now wore beneath the tightly cinched corset. Lianne had not commented on the change and she knew none of the others would, for they were all used to seeing Paul in his various female costumes.

'You still worried?' he asked, making final adjustments to the curly blonde wig. Lianne pulled a face.

'Nah,' she muttered. 'Not really. I've had time to think about it and I guess I was being silly, that's all.' She flexed her shoulders, the light dancing off the highly polished surface of her suit. 'No, I'm just going to relax and enjoy it this time,' she went on. 'If all Marlon's little improvements work half as well as he claims they will, this could be a very interesting few hours.'

'Well, he's added a whole load of my original script concepts,' Paul told her. 'I dug out four cases of floppy discs and gave them to him, so VESTA now knows all about Della and Mary Lou, though quite how Marlon does all this is beyond me.'

'Me too,' Lianne admitted. 'But what the hell, let's go get ourselves screwed, eh?'

'About an hour now,' Jurgen Koenig said. He was holding a glass of brandy in one hand and a short cigar in the other, and appeared relaxed and confident as he watched the screen. Naylor had half expected to see pictures there, but instead it was just the usual meaningless jumble of figures and symbols, none of which meant a thing to him.

'What's happening down there at the moment?' he asked. Koenig took a sip from his glass before answering.

'Vincent is hooking them all up to the central unit,' he explained. 'Each participant is fitted into a sort of capsule, or pod, where they are strapped down to prevent unnecessary body movement during the event. Various probes and sensors are attached to them at strategic points, although the most important connection is via the helmets Vincent has designed.

'Those helmets are quite something, my dear bean,' he continued. 'They had a team of four technicians engaged in their manufacture, though apparently none of them was ever told quite what the nature of the final product would be, and each of them has to be worth at least twenty thousand pounds, maybe more.

'They permit electronic stimulation of all relevant parts of the brain, recreating every sensation that would normally be initially received via nerve endings in places such as fingers, lips, breasts and so on. However, our friend has also incorporated more direct stimulation of certain areas for additional intensification. All very thorough.'

'Very,' Naylor concurred. 'So, very shortly all of them except Vincent will be "under", as it were, inside this VESTA world?'

'Correct,' Koenig replied. 'All except Vincent himself, of course. At that point I shall be able to assume some sort of control from here, although really only by way of a monitoring brief, to ensure he does not try anything clever while you are all on your way down there. You have tested the radio link?'

'Several times,' Naylor confirmed. 'And there are backup sets in the chopper, just in case.'

'How long do you estimate it will take you to reach them?'

'About an hour and a half. The four of us will then establish complete control, while the chopper returns for you, Marika, and a couple more personnel. By the time you arrive the backup team should have arrived by road and the perimeter will be secured. They left over an hour ago.'

'Then I suggest you should be on your way also,' Koenig said. 'There is no need to wait longer. I can radio you when all is ready to move in.'

'Yes, you're right,' Naylor agreed, checking his watch. 'I'd better go down and see whether Christina has prepared the beautiful Clarissa for travelling. She's a bit reluctant to interrupt her training, but this has to look good, otherwise friend Marlon won't let us inside the building. Unless he throws the switches, it's no good. Storming it would take hours, and meantime he'd bring the others out of VESTA, so it would be a waste of time and effort anyway. Therefore his dear sister has to look as though she's in reasonably presentable condition when we arrive. The sight of her trotting up to the house in full pony harness would hardly do much to win his confidence.'

This time the emergence into the virtual world was a much smoother experience. Lianne lay still for several seconds, listening, sensing, and then slowly opened her eyes. Above her she could see a high timbered ceiling, traversed by heavy beams. And when she turned her head she saw stone walls that reminded her of the way in which the outhouse buildings were constructed. She flexed her arms and moved her legs, surprised to find she was not restrained, and then sat up, swinging her legs over the side of the bench on which she had been laying.

She looked down at herself and saw she was still dressed as she had been when she'd entered her pod and, for a moment or two, wondered whether she really was back in the virtual world, or whether there had been a last minute change of plan. But on reflection she realised there was nothing particularly familiar about this building, and also that the colours seemed slightly sharp, something she had previously noted as a feature of Marlon and his machine's imaginary environment.

Lianne lowered her feet onto the stone flags and stood up, taking a few paces towards the far end of the barn, where a wide door stood slightly ajar. The sound of her heels echoed convincingly enough and, remembering, she paused, taking a deep breath through her nostrils.

Rubber! The scent of her own suit, plus a strange damp odour of newly mown

56

grass. She smiled to herself. So Marlon really had managed to overcome that one! It was quite incredible. She looked around again, expecting to see at least some sort of indication of what was to come, even if it were just a rack of whips, but the interior of the barn was, with the exception of the wooden bench, totally bare.

'Hello?' she called out tentatively, but only a slight echo of her own voice came back to her. Yes, she thought, this was definitely much more realistic. Whatever was going to happen was going to happen as though it was real life. Whether it lay outside beyond the door, or whether it would come looking for her, Lianne had no idea.

Probably outside, she thought, though she guessed that if she stayed here long enough 'someone' would come looking for her eventually. She wondered how patient VESTA was programmed to be and, heels clacking, she started towards the door.

Paul Dean could hardly believe the evidence of his eyes, much less that produced by his fingers when he probed beneath the hem of the short skirt and inside the elasticated leg of his panties.

'Bloody hell!' he breathed. 'It can't be - this is impossible.'

Anything's possible with VESTA.

He recognised Marlon's voice, but there was no sign of him anywhere within the room, which appeared to be a fairly unremarkable bedroom of the type generally found in cheap hotels and motels throughout the world.

'Marlon?' Paul blinked. 'Where are you?'

Out here, where I've always been. I'm hooked up to an active link, so I can see and hear everything that's going on with all of you. I could materialise a body for myself, but there's not much point. My job is to monitor and evaluate.

'Bully for you!' Paul retorted and gave a start, for he had not realised initially how feminine his voice now sounded. 'Is this your idea of a joke?' He made a gesture with his hands that took in the very feminine looking body that now appeared to be his, from the bubbly blonde hair, the large breasts that were fighting a winning battle with the purple silk blouse, to the long fishnet clad legs that appeared from beneath the scandalously short hem of the black leather skirt.

Don't you like it? Marlon sounded genuinely surprised. *I thought... well, given some of your preferred outfits I've seen you in, well, I just thought you'd like to experience being inside a female body itself, rather than just dressing the role.*

'Well, you could have warned me!' Paul protested. 'In any case, the fact I prefer dressing as a female at times doesn't mean...'

Oh, I see. Silly of me. I'm afraid I'm not terribly good on some of these things. Hang on a bit and I'll get it put right.

'Uh... no, hang on for a bit.' Paul turned around to the dressing table mirror. 'Listen, don't get this wrong, but maybe it would be kind of interesting,' he admitted. 'Just one thing, though.'

Whatever you say.

'Make sure I don't end up getting screwed by some hairy-arsed gorilla. I'm not into sex with men, right?'

Right. A short pause. *Yes, I see... yes, I see I've been guilty of some stupid assumptions, but don't worry. VESTA is light years ahead of me on these things now. She really is a quick learner, you know.*

'Good,' Paul muttered, tight-lipped. 'Because I meant what I said. Female contact only, otherwise I'll take a sledge hammer to VESTA when I get back out of here, quick learner or not!'

The net dropped silently as Lianne stepped out through the barn door, ensnaring her before she had a chance to react, and jerking back into the air again, taking her with it in a helpless, tangled ball, which swung slowly to and fro a few feet clear of the ground.

'Bugger it!' she hissed, half under her breath, for she had started to think she might have a bit of fun trying to evade the virtual captors who were doubtless waiting for her somewhere in here, and she had fallen at the first hurdle. Struggling to ease her cramped position she peered out through the close mesh, scanning the distant line of trees for any sign of movement.

Somewhere overhead a bird chirruped away merrily, but apart from the steady progress of a few fleecy clouds across an otherwise unbroken blue sky, there was nothing. Lianne sighed and hoped she would not have too long to wait...

Ellen's arrival inside VESTA was slightly more dramatic than Lianne's had been. She materialised inside a small clearing in what appeared to be dense woodland, and a quick look down at herself, combined with the distant but closing sound of baying hounds, immediately told her what she was in for.

Her entire body was now clad in some sort of synthetic catsuit, 'cat' being a very appropriate word in this case, for it was spotted and coloured to resemble the skin of a leopard, complete with claw extensions on her fingers. Her feet were clad in awkward boots, high heeled within, but outwardly shaped to resemble large paws, and it took her several seconds to achieve a proper balance in them.

About her waist a narrow leather belt had been cinched tightly, so that her figure resembled the traditional hourglass so beloved of Victorian fashion devotees and late twentieth century fetishists. And there were stout rings set into it, obviously placed in readiness for some sort of restraining straps or chains. Similar though smaller straps had been locked about her wrists and ankles, again with sturdy rings included and, when she felt about her neck, using the back of her hand for fear of damaging herself with the awesome claws, she felt that a similarly equipped collar circled it also.

Her head and face was covered in a tight fitting hood, to which there appeared to be attached ears, though it was difficult to tell with her sense of touch so badly hampered. There were openings for her nostrils, though the front of the mask protruded to form a very catlike contour, but her mouth was covered, holding in place some sort of soft gag, through which all attempts at coherent speech emerged as a cross between a purr and a growl.

'Pussy cat, pussy cat,' she thought, smiling to herself. She turned her head and saw the long tail extending behind her, the pressure within her rectum leaving her in no doubt as to how it was attached. And when she peered down her front, past breasts which seemed a whole lot bigger than those she normally expected to see there, a flash of pale skin revealed that her sex had been left exposed.

So, she thought, now we know what the hunters are after, as if there was ever any doubt. She turned, looking around the clearing, ears alert in an effort to work out from which direction the pursuit was coming. Satisfied, she nodded to herself, weighed up the alternative routes leading off into the trees, made a rapid decision and began padding awkwardly for cover.

'Fairytale One, this is Fairytale Two, do you copy?' The metallic voice burst from the overhead speaker and, not taking his eyes from the screen, Koenig leaned forward and depressed the transmission key on the tabletop microphone alongside it.

'Fairytale Two, I copy you,' he intoned. 'Have you an ETA yet?'

'Touchdown in approximately ten minutes, Fairytale Two.' This time it was Naylor's voice, easily distinguishable, despite the distorting effect of the UHF radio link. 'Everything ready for us down there?'

'Everything proceeding according to plan,' Koenig confirmed. 'You are to land on the large lawn at the rear of the house as agreed, and approach the door at the eastern end of the building. He'll be watching you, Fairytale One, and he almost certainly has some sort of magnifying equipment, so I trust you have seen to things with your passenger?'

'Affirmative,' Naylor returned. 'She looks totally delightful, I assure you. Everything is prepared to deal with our host. How's he doing?'

'He appears to be simply monitoring a random programming sequence. VESTA is working on several scenarios at the same time, some of them apparently intended to overlap at some stage. I have not interfered, but my key programme is ready to drop in the moment you give the word.'

'Roger, Fairytale Two,' Naylor came back, and now Koenig could detect the excitement in his voice. 'We have visual on the target area now. Just circling around to be sure. Keep your eyes glued to that system and hit the alarm at the first sign of anything. I'm leaving this channel open.'

The minutes continued to tick away, but still there was no sign of whoever was supposed to have set the net snare for her, and Lianne was beginning to feel distinctly uncomfortable. A couple of times she tried to squirm around and reach up to where the net was gathered at the bottom of the rope from which it swung. But she soon gave up any hope of freeing it, for the running slipknot was held tight by her own weight and could not be loosened again until she was lowered back to the ground.

'Sod it, Marlon!' she hissed through clenched teeth. 'I know I said things happened too quickly before, but this is ridiculous. I'm beginning to think you've forgotten me.'

She turned to survey the tree line again, and this time she was rewarded by the sight of two figures emerging from the dense undergrowth...

Seated in the back of the circling helicopter, Clarissa was close to shedding tears of frustration. Her short spell as Christina's prisoner had taught her what it was to feel truly helpless, but even the ordeal impaled upon the cruel display perch seemed unimportant compared to her present situation.

Her captors clearly intended to trick Marlon, there was no doubt whatsoever of that, for Christina had already made it clear to Clarissa that she had other plans for her other than handing her over to her half brother. Yet there was no way she could warn him, nor any way that he could see she was even gagged, so cunningly had the task been carried out.

Removing the harness and pony hood, Christina had forced a hard plastic device into Clarissa's mouth, a curved shield, shaped like the skin of an orange segment, which fitted neatly between her teeth and the inside of her mouth, held in place by four tiny screw clamps that now held tightly to her back teeth.

From the inside centre of the shield a tongue-shaped piece projected inwards, forcing her own tongue down and preventing speech, while from the outside, as Christina took great pleasure in showing her in a mirror, her lips were held apart slightly and the outer surface of the plastic was contoured and coloured to reveal what appeared to be a perfect set of gleaming white teeth, the overall image that of a welcoming smile.

Her hoof boots had been replaced - only temporarily, Christina had assured her - by knee length boots with slightly less exaggerated heels, while a full length leather coat, drawn tightly about her waist, hid the fact that she still wore her dappled pony skin underneath. Cunningly concealed cuffs held her hands uselessly inside the pockets of this coat, so she was powerless to do anything to remove the curious heavy pendant that had been hung about her neck, an adornment which although decorative, Clarissa suspected had other more sinister purposes.

The room had, indeed, proved to be part of a hotel, and downstairs the bar area was well patronised by a colourful selection of fellow guests. Poised on the high stilettos, a small bag slung from his shoulder, Pauline swayed into the room, avoided the eyes in those heads that immediately turned, and minced up to the bar, perching on a bar stool that emptied itself as if by magic.

'Martini,' she said, smiling at the barman, who was making no attempt to conceal the fact that he was undressing her with his eyes. 'Make it a large one.' She turned away and surveyed the length of the bar counter.

Most of the patrons at the bar itself were male. But a little way along a raven-haired beauty, clad in a skirt as daringly brief as Pauline's own, sat brooding over a half empty glass of wine, her talon-like red fingernails drumming an erratic and lazy tattoo on the polished surface. Pauline felt sudden urges that were at once familiar and unfamiliar and, as her left hand made to move the small bag to hide her obvious excitement, she suddenly remembered there was currently nothing in her panties to cause any such embarrassment.

'Can you hear me, Marlon?' she said, under her breath, but there was no reply. Slowly, a smile began to spread across Pauline's new features, for as she studied the other woman closer, she realised she was Hazel O'Dee, who had spent the past few years playing the wicked Madame B's sidekick Dolores in the Della strip, and who was, Pauline knew, a confirmed lesbian.

This could be fun, the former artist thought, taking a five-pound note from her bag and passing it across in exchange for the tall glass the barman placed before her.

'Keep the change,' she said aloud, flashing him a wide smile and then, picking up her drink, she slipped elegantly from her perch and began making her way along the bar.

'Too easy,' the first hunter said, thrusting a booted foot against Lianne's balled-up body as it hung trapped in the net, setting her swinging gently to and fro. His companion, whose dark hair was cropped closely to his skull, leaned on his curious spear gun and grinned.

'They always are at first,' he said. 'But it's surprising how quickly they learn, once they get their new skins.' He dropped the bulky sack he was carrying and nodded an unspoken instruction.

The fair-haired man had already set his own gun aside and reached up with a wicked knife, sawing away at the rope just above the point where it had tightened the mouth of the net.

'The skin she's wearing is okay by me,' he leered. 'And she looks to have a pretty good filling for it.'

Lianne sighed. 'Hey, don't mind me guys,' she said. 'Just talk about me like I'm not here, eh?'

'Oh, you're here all right,' the blond hunter laughed. 'Though pretty soon you're going to wish you weren't.'

'Naturally,' Lianne retorted, stifling an urge to giggle. 'And I suppose you just happen to have a whip in that sack, right?' she went on. 'And of course you're going to string me up, possibly to one of those trees over there, and whip this rubber catsuit off my defenceless body, yes?'

'We've got a mouthy bitch here, by the sound of it,' the blond man said, sourly, redoubling his efforts to sever the rope. 'And this bloody knife has no edge to it, Greg. Here, pass me yours.'

Close-crop reached down and withdrew a blade from its sheath at his belt. It looked far less imposing than the one his partner was struggling with, but it evidently had a much keener edge, for with two swift strokes it parted the rope and Lianne was deposited in a bruised and ungainly heap on the hard packed earth.

'Get the net off her, Marcus,' the one called Greg instructed, taking back his knife and turning to the sack. 'And watch she doesn't try anything clever. The bitch seems to fancy herself.'

Marcus certainly was not taking any chances, for he kept a firm grip on the back of Lianne's neck, his powerful fist knotted painfully into her hair, using his free hand to drag the net clear of her with unhurried deliberation.

'She won't be so damned feisty once she's been through the genetic accelerator,' he said, and laughed as he saw the flicker of confusion cross Lianne's face. 'Let her sound off all she wants... while she still can,' he added, and this time his companion joined in with a loud guffaw.

After a surprisingly short time, Ellen found that the high heeled 'paws' into which her feet had been placed did not offer as much a handicap to fairly swift movement as she had initially anticipated. She settled into a curious lope whenever the trees gave way to brief, grassy open spaces, slowing again to negotiate the gradually thickening carpet of undergrowth that lay between the trunks beneath the green canopy overhead.

In the distance the baying hounds seemed closer now, but not worryingly so as yet, and she wondered if the hunt would be protracted deliberately, presumably for her own benefit, unless one of the others was even now part of whatever virtual party was pursuing her. After what she guessed to be the better part of half an hour she stopped, crouching between two dense bushes, and attempted to take stock of her situation again.

The fearsome claws made any attempt to remove even a part of her outfit impossible, always supposing that it would come off, here in this curious, electronically generated world. But at least they did offer her some form of defence, though she shied away from the thought of raking these wicked talons into even a virtual animal. She grimaced and wondered if the computerised pack of hounds would extend such considerations to her in turn, and somehow doubted they would.

Marlon had matters to engage him other than monitoring the progress of the subjects inside VESTA's bizarre world, even though he was aware of the presence of several 'bug' files that were already altering and adding to his original scenarios, and even to those being created by VESTA herself.

Clearly, Jurgen Koenig had not been content to use the telephone link-up simply to monitor VESTA's operation, nor to render inoperative her system of escape passwords. But neither of these facts came as a surprise to Marlon. Watching out of the small window, peering towards the line of hills in the distance, he grimaced, but there was nothing else he could do, not until he was certain that Clarissa was safely back with him and out of the clutches of these hideous monsters. Up to that point, he knew, he was helpless to intervene, and he was also pretty certain that Naylor and his thugs wouldn't simply hand his half sister back to him anyway, not until they had exacted every iota of tribute available to them.

And, with VESTA opened up to their access, that tribute was almost incalculable.

Blissfully unaware of the impending danger, Nadia Muirhead was just beginning to enjoy her latest venture into virtuality, this time as the hunter, rather than the hunted, a stipulation she had made to Marlon very forcibly.

Dressed in a form-fitting leather leotard, thigh boots, gloves and collar, the areas of flesh in between shimmering through the fine mesh of what appeared to be a body stocking, she approached the wall mounted racks and ran a leather-covered hand lovingly over the array of whips, crops and paddles that hung there.

'Very nice,' she murmured. 'Just what the customers will love.' She selected one long-handled paddle and swished it through the air experimentally, letting its broad end smack against the stone wall with an ear-splitting crack. Even Nadia was impressed, for the implement's balance and lightweight handle belied the force it was able to generate in her expert hands.

'Top stuff, Marlon,' she muttered. 'Or is this some of VESTA's own handiwork?' Not that it mattered, Nadia thought, as long as the finished product was as good as this. She looked down at herself and once again a grin of satisfaction spread across her usually impassive features. Everything so far was not just perfect, but absolutely class; the perfect replication of the ultimate fetish experience - a replication for which certain people would be willing to pay handsomely.

Not that Nadia needed the money, but it was a satisfying thought that she could soon begin to recoup a little on her massive financial investment. She replaced the paddle, took out a wicked-looking crop, and turned back towards the door of the long chamber.

Time seemed to be taking on a curiously elasticated quality. The dogs seemed to be little nearer as yet, even though Ellen felt as though she had been trotting through woods and undergrowth for hours. However, judging from the positions of the shadows cast by the trees, it might scarcely have been minutes, for the sun did not seem to have shifted its position in all the time since she'd found herself in the role of hunted cat.

She didn't get it, pausing in the midst of a thick screen of bushes. Okay, so maybe she was over estimating, but it had been more than an hour, so why the bloody delay? Why not just move it up to the final chase stage and have done with it?

Briefly, she wondered if the idea were to exhaust her before bringing the hunt to its climax, but quickly dismissed that theory, for here in VESTA's electronically generated domain there did not seem to be such a thing as fatigue. In the real world, Ellen knew, running, even jogging as she had been, for such a length of time in these extreme boots would have had her panting heavily long before this, her calf and thigh muscles screaming out for oxygen and for any relief from their distorted positions.

She emerged from the bushes, crossed a patch of grassy ground, found a large tree that stood alone and apart from its fellows, and lowered herself to sit with her back against it, eyes darting about the perimeter line of green foliage for any sign of movement.

She let out a long sigh that emerged, via the peculiar device that filled her mouth, as a loud purr, and only the gag itself prevented Ellen from laughing out loud.

'Whatever is this place?' Pauline almost squeaked, as the dark version of Hazel flicked a switch and overhead strips began flickering into life. But she already knew the answer before the bigger woman opened her mouth, the various wooden and metal racks that adorned the end wall and the menacing looking frame that stood in the centre of the floor, picked out by a circle of five spotlights, saying more than any words ever could.

'Just my playroom,' Hazel said and, before Pauline could react, moved behind her and shoved her roughly inside, slamming the door behind them and barring any line of escape as the lock clicked shut with an ominous finality. For a brief instant the old Paul machismo tried to reassert itself - the old Paul could have easily outfought Hazel, big as she was, but the new Pauline had only to look down at herself to understand the futility of such a course.

At very little over five feet tall without the heels and weighing well under a hundred and twenty pounds, poor little feminine Pauline was like a helpless midget beside the dominant, nearly six foot frame of Hazel O'Dee - or Dolores, as she had introduced herself in the bar, reverting to her in-character name. Idly, Pauline realised that both artists, the villainous Naylor originally and now his brilliantly talented female Welsh replacement, had always drawn Dolores as a brunette, rather than as the blonde she was in real life.

But for now there was no chance to dwell on such little idiosyncrasies. Hazel loomed over her, eyes gleaming.

'Time for some fun and games, Susie,' she hissed.

Pauline had selected the name out of thin air, not wanting to give any indication as to his real identity, and conscious of the fact that Hazel would know that Lianne always referred to his male-to-female transformation character as Pauline. She held up her hands in a vain attempt to ward off the closing predator.

'No, listen,' she squeaked, the maddeningly girlish female voice echoing in her head. 'You don't understand, Hazel. Look, I ought to explain - just give me a minute!'

'My name is Dolores,' Hazel grated. 'However, sweetmeat, for the moment you can call me mistress.' Pauline continued to back away, her voice now filled with genuine panic.

'No, listen, Hazel - I mean Dolores... mistress! Oh shit! Please!'

The low building seemed to suddenly appear from nowhere, the dense woods melting away to reveal a small clearing before it. Stumbling along behind the two men, Marcus tugging roughly on the leash that connected to the heavy collar that was now locked about her throat, Lianne was concentrating so fiercely on keeping her footing on the rough ground that she hardly had any time to take in any of the exterior details before they entered by way of a sturdy and businesslike door at one end of the structure.

Lianne's nostrils twitched at the tang of antiseptic that filled the air, and she at last looked around her. Not that there was much to see, for they appeared to be in some sort of foyer, with just a spartan steel-framed desk table and single upright chair behind it as furniture. The white painted walls were bare of any decoration, the only break in their monotonous surface being a second door, apparently leading deeper into whatever place this was.

Marcus turned and began unfastening the leash, but the sturdy cuffs that still held Lianne's wrists close behind her precluded any chance of escaping. Not that any attempt was likely to avail her for long, she guessed, for VESTA was undoubtedly programmed to ensure that she met whatever fate had been ordained for her in this part of the 'game'.

As the neck chain dropped away the inner door swung open and two females emerged, both wearing what was presumably intended as a parody on a nurse's uniform; a brief ensemble in dark blue and white that had clearly been lifted straight from the pages of a fetish magazine. For not only was the hemline at least a foot higher than any normal hospital would have tolerated, but the entire garment was made of thin, clinging rubber.

The women themselves were tall and willowy, though each boasted a bust that appeared to be defying all natural laws of gravity, even the tight latex unable to flatten out the incredible curves. Despite herself, Lianne smiled - she was beginning to learn more of what made Marlon tick, she thought...

Hanging by her wrists, naked, Pauline was afforded a perfect view of her helpless body by the strategically placed mirror on the wall before her, whilst behind her reflection she was able to clearly see 'Dolores', as the grim-faced mistress prepared for action.

Dressed now in high boots and rubber body stocking, she pulled a half mask over her head, adjusting it so that her eyes peered out through the slanted apertures and tightened the back lacing to draw the soft leather tightly about her upper skull. Satisfied that the hood was held firmly in position, she drew on a pair of heavily studded gauntlets, picked up a coiled whip from the bench and stalked menacingly up behind her victim.

'Nice big tits,' she purred, reaching around and squeezing Pauline's left orb, weighing it in the palm of her gloved hand. 'And such big nipples, too.' She pinched the engorged teat and drew it out into a distended shape that brought the breath hissing through Pauline's clenched teeth.

'Perhaps we should ring them?' she suggested, releasing her grip and moving round in front of the hanging female. 'Would you like that, Susie?'

'Please!' Pauline gasped. 'I'm not Susie, I'm Pauline - you know, Paul!'

'You don't look like a Paul to me, sweetie pie,' Dolores grinned. 'Besides, I don't know any Pauls, with or without juicy tits and juicy cunts.' Her right hand slid down Pauline's stomach as she spoke and one leather-sheathed digit probed for the opening they both knew was there.

'But you must know me!' Pauline wailed. 'Look, this is all part of the big game, right?' Dolores' eyes narrowed and she stepped back half a pace.

'Game?' she echoed. 'Yes, I suppose this is a sort of game, except that there's only one winner in my games.' She let the whip uncoil with a lazy flick of her wrist, and the braided leather slapped across the stone floor with a sound that brought a knot to the pit of Pauline's stomach, for suddenly the hapless 'girl' understood.

This wasn't Hazel O'Dee at all, just a character that VESTA had created, doubtless using Hazel's fictitious alter ego as the basic model. And this Dolores had none of Hazel's own character traits, just the worst traits of the character she played and a few more thrown in for good measure.

'Now, let's see where we should begin,' she said, her eyes glittering malignantly.

'Perhaps just a gentle warming up and then I think I'll pierce and ring you with my ownership tags - tit and clit tags, I think.'

'Oh god, no!' Pauline thrashed about in her bonds, but with her ankles held fairly wide apart by the cuffs and chains that fastened to the base of the frame, it was a wasted effort. After a few seconds she fell still, hanging breathless, sweat pouring down her face and breasts, glistening under the harsh spotlamps.

'Please,' she groaned, for the thought of what her torturer was proposing was too terrible to contemplate. Although she had only possessed this female body for what amounted to a few hours, Pauline knew enough to understand that whilst having her nipples pierced and ringed would be bearably painful, the second proposition would bring with it horrendous agony. Dolores, however, seemed more than pleased with the terror her announcement had instilled and appeared to be in no hurry to begin inflicting any physical pain as yet.

'Perhaps, poppet,' she sneered, pushing her face close to Pauline's, 'I should let you try to earn a reprieve?'

'A - a reprieve?' Pauline swallowed and nodded fervently. 'Yes, anything!' she squeaked.

Dolores nodded. 'Strange how a girl can suddenly become so anxious to please,' she hissed. She stepped back further, fingers groping at the crotch of her catsuit, pulling at some hitherto unseen fastener, pulling aside the heavy latex, to reveal...

...An indisputably male organ, already swelling up as it was released from the suit's clinging embrace. Pauline's eyes goggled, but the 'woman' merely chuckled.

'Surprise, Susie?' she leered, taking her stiffening shaft in her right hand, massaging it between leathered fingers to encourage its further growth. Deliberately, she stalked forward again, casting aside the whip and reaching up with her freed hand for Pauline's manacles.

'Now, I'm sure you know exactly what I expect of you, sweetie,' she drawled, snapping open the first cuff. 'I want to see you down on all fours, like a good little bitch doggie, tongue out and panting to show your obedience, savvy?'

Pauline blinked, gulped and nodded, her gaze drawn down to the now massive shaft that was pressing against her stomach.

'Yes - yes, mistress,' she whispered, horrified to hear the words, yet knowing that anything was preferable to the alternative that this creature had planned for her. If sucking that huge phallus was what it took to keep her delicate clitoris in one pristine piece, then so be it, and a few moments later as the swollen head pushed her full lips wider and wider apart, somehow it did not seem such a terrible ordeal after all...

Lianne could not remember whether they had drugged her or not; certainly she had no memory of anything being administered to her, and the last thing she remembered was the two supposed nurses stripping the rubber bodysuit from her, after which...

She opened her eyes, trying to take in her surroundings. She was lying flat on a fairly hard surface, broad straps across her chest preventing her from sitting upright, yet revealing breasts that, even in their present position, were clearly a lot larger now than they had been before. She peered hard along herself, trying to determine if there were any signs of surgery, and then realised there was another change, something far more sinister.

Going nearly cross-eyed from the effort, she stared inwards towards where the tip of her nose would usually have been just visible, only to find something else there instead, something she could not identify, other than to say it was far larger than her usual pert proboscis.

'She's awake.' The sound of the female voice made Lianne start and interrupted her effort to see what had been placed on her face. She turned her head to one side and immediately felt something wrong, something about the weight distribution that caused her head to loll far further over than she had intended.

'Get her up and let her see herself.' This time it was a male voice and, as the speaker moved into view, Lianne saw a tall gaunt figure, wearing rimless spectacles and with a small goatee beard and receding hairline. Marlon's - or VESTA's - idea of a mad doctor, perhaps.

As the straps were unbuckled and the two nurses helped her to stand, Lianne expected to feel unsteady, and was surprised to find she was not, indeed, suffering from the usual after-effects of anaesthesia. Of course, there was no reason why VESTA should waste time on human weaknesses when she could cut to the chase, Lianne realised.

They were in some sort of recovery room, except that one end of it was tiled with flagstones and the far end wall was covered by a large wooden rack, from which dangled a bewildering array of leather straps and harnesses. There was little doubt in Lianne's mind that some of them were intended for her, but first they guided her towards the large wall mirror that sat halfway down the room.

Except that it surely could not be a mirror at all, for the figure she saw apparently reflected in it could in no way be herself... only it could, she knew, and indeed it was. Blinking back tears of disbelief and horror, she stepped closer, peering at the glass for a better look, her head shaking slowly as she struggled to take in what she was seeing.

The feet - how come she hadn't seen or felt them until now? - the feet were no longer human feet, but hooves, and as she dragged her gaze from the mirror to stare down at them through the valley between her huge breasts, try as she might she could see no signs of any joins that would indicate artificiality. Appalled, she looked back to the mirror again, only now beginning to fully comprehend the modifications that had been made to her body.

Her hugely inflated breasts - double G at the very least, she guessed - were made to look even larger by the impossibly tiny waist, which in turn was made to look even more extreme by the flaring hips and long, exaggerated thighs. Slowly, she raised the now useless hands, staring at the curious mitten-like appendages, oval pads where once there had been fingers and thumbs, until they reached her face.

Only it was no longer her face.

She tried to speak, but the only sound that escaped from the widened mouth in the elongated jaw was a low whinnying. Tears flowed from the almond-shaped eyes that sat between the elongated equine ears beneath the fantastic mane of bright pink that ran from the crown of her otherwise bald head to cascade down her naked back, a back which now, she guessed, like the rest of her body, was cloaked in a shining skin of dappled brown, black and white.

'She seems a little bit confused,' the darker of the two nurses said. Her companion, whose hair was a more reddish brown, chuckled.

'They always do at this stage,' she said. 'Mind you, hardly surprising, is it? You'd be a bit shocked to wake up and find yourself transformed into a human pony girl.'

Slowly, the initial horror was abating for Lianne, as she realised that what she was seeing was no more real than anything she might encounter in a bad dream, even if there was no likelihood of her waking from it in the immediate future. Taking a deep breath, she turned away from the mirror and confronted her captors, thrusting out her immense breasts in a gesture of defiance.

'Promising,' the second nurse murmured. 'Very promising indeed. Better get her out to the handlers and see how she shapes up.'

Marlon peered into the security monitor, his features screwed into a mask of concentration as he studied the party that approached across the broad expanse of lawn from where the helicopter still sat, rotors beating steadily through the low whine of its idling engine.

He did not recognise the three escorts personally, although the massive blonde had to be the Danish sadist Lianne had told him so much about. There was also the hatchet-faced male, which was probably Naylor, and another fellow, a real heavyweight, probably some sort of minder. For the moment, however, Marlon's attention was focused almost exclusively on the fourth member of the party, the unmistakable auburn-haired figure of his half sister, Clarissa.

She appeared to be unharmed, no visible signs of mistreatment, and she was walking unaided, albeit with some difficulty, which when he zoomed the camera in on the height of her footwear, Marlon scarcely found surprising. Moreover, she appeared to be unhampered by any sign of bondage, although the hands in the pockets, he was astute enough to realise, were as likely as not camouflaging something a little more subtle than a simple pair of handcuffs.

Marlon reached for the switch on the microphone, depressed it and spoke, the sound of his voice amplified through the speakers above the rear entrance bringing an instant response.

'That's far enough!' he ordered. The four figures, acting as one, came to an immediate halt. 'Clarissa walks on ahead,' Marlon continued. 'When I'm satisfied she's okay, I'll admit the rest of you. Now, which of you is Naylor?'

'I am.' Hatchet face stepped forward, peering up in the general direction of Marlon's voice, looking straight into the concealed camera. 'And how do we know you'll keep your word? You could grab the girl inside, lock the door and try to summon help, maybe even bring your friends out of the machine.'

'How do you know I haven't done that already?' Marlon retorted. He saw Naylor's mouth twist into a sardonic smile. 'But of course, you have Herr Koenig monitoring VESTA, I'd almost forgotten,' he lied.

'And he now has control of all the failsafe keys,' Naylor reminded him, though

Marlon needed no reminder. Three hours of frenzied activity had failed to produce anything that the German would not recognise as being an electronic trick.

'Which is why you know that, once I have Clarissa back and we are allowed to leave unharmed, I will allow you access to VESTA directly,' Marlon countered. 'Your continental friend will confirm that even if I were to try to double-cross you, it would take at least an hour for me to take back control, during which time he could inflict permanent damage on any or all of VESTA's current subjects.'

'And during that same time we could force an entry anyway,' Naylor snapped. 'However, there is just one small matter.' He turned to the bodyguard and whispered something to him. The big man nodded and scuttled heavily away out of range of the camera.

'Frank has gone around to cut your telephone lines,' Naylor explained. 'Of course, you have the radio phone, but that is now under the direct control of VESTA and Koenig, and the helicopter back there houses a small jamming device which will prevent anything operating on the normal mobile phone frequencies within three or four hundred yards radius.'

'I told you,' Marlon snapped. 'All I'm interested in is getting Clarissa back. No phones, no radios. You can have everything else that's here.'

'A commendable attitude,' the blonde said, speaking for the first time. She reached out and pushed Clarissa gently between the shoulder blades. 'Here, take your sister. You'll see she has suffered no permanent damage. But you will then have ten minutes in which to open the doors again, otherwise we shall instruct friend Koenig to begin frying the brains of all your little friends, starting with Ms Muirhead herself.'

The woods, or forest, seemed to be unending, though Ellen realised she could easily have been moving around in circles. More likely, she thought, the computer itself was operating on some sort of circular loop. She knew little enough about such things, but she had heard Marlon trying to explain something to Nadia the day before, telling her that the basic data was used like a sort of backing track, taking samples from a vast library to build the random scenes, but also setting up basic patterns upon which everything else was built later.

But why the delay? Did the absence of any real action signify a problem? Maybe VESTA had picked up a fault, some sort of bug that had jammed her own particular scenario on 'repeat' - except there was nothing to repeat, not unless you counted trees, trees and more bloody trees.

And then, quite suddenly, he was upon her, exploding from the undergrowth in a blur of black and yellow, knocking Ellen sideways into a sprawling heap, paws and claws thrashing in the air, the breath forced from her lungs by the impact.

Rolling onto her side she lifted her head, turning to find her assailant crouching, snarling, poised to await her next move, a leopard boy, face hidden within a mask that must be mirroring her own, eyes twinkling from behind the tiny slits that allowed what little vision the outfits permitted.

Shaking her head, Ellen pulled herself up onto all fours, keeping the leopard boy fixed firmly in her gaze, and then slowly rose upright once again. The boy growled and began to circle. Crouching slightly she extended her arms, claws curled menacingly, and growled back.

The stable block that VESTA had created was archetypal Victoriana; rough brickwork, heavy timber stall partitions and bare stone flags under foot, or in Lianne's case now, under hooves, which clattered on the unsympathetic surface as the youth led her to her latest fate.

Appearing in the 'hospital' in answer to the nurses' summons, he was perhaps seventeen or eighteen years old, with fair tousled hair, freckled face and a lightly tanned complexion, which extended to arms and legs left bare by the simple leather singlet and shorts he wore. He had arrived prepared for his charge; a tangle of straps draped over one arm, a tangle he quickly shook out to reveal a specially made bridle - specially made for human ponies.

With an easy grace borne, it appeared, of long practice, he threw the harness over Lianne's head, tugging the straps into position and buckling them snugly about her horsy features, then slipping a simple metal bit between her teeth and clipping it to rings situated to either side of her mouth. He made one final check of all the buckles, then clipped a lead rein to one side of the bit and gave it a sharp tug.

'C'mon, horsy girl.' His tone was not harsh, rather that of someone who was used to being obeyed by his charges and who would encourage, rather than mistreat. But in many ways Lianne found this far worse. From the neck down, apart from her hooves, she was quite utterly human, albeit with considerably enlarged feminine attributes, yet this youth obviously regarded her as the equine her new features pronounced her to be.

She tried to speak again, but once more only the pathetic little whinny escaped her widened lips and the distorting bit, bringing a smile to her handler's face.

'Steady, girl,' he soothed, turning to pat her flank. 'This is just your new stable. You'll soon get used to it. Now, let's get you into a proper harness and then over to the smithy.'

The 'proper harness' turned out to be a very intricate assemblage of heavy leather, the whole made even heavier by the fabulous display of horse brasses with which it was adorned. And once it had been buckled into place, Lianne felt as though she would hardly be able to walk a step in it.

The girth strap, as the stable lad called it, was in reality a leather corset, which encircled Lianne's already tiny waist and drew it in to even more fantastic proportions. Above it her breasts were left bare, though supported and lifted in part by two stiffened platforms of hide, and pushed forward by a curious circular harness that ran up from the top of the girth, adjusted tightly around each orb and then passed over the shoulders to buckle to the main corset at the rear.

Two further straps passed from the lower front hem, forming a V-shape which framed her naked sex, then joining and separating again so they in fact formed an X, the rear V buckling once more at the back and drawn tightly up so that Lianne's nether lips were compressed and thrust into prominence. Her rear orifice was also left unimpeded by the whole arrangement.

Next came two sleeves, terminating in stiff mittens, which laced the entire length of her arms, preventing all but the slightest movement at the elbow. And even that was then denied, when short straps on the inside of either forearm were drawn firmly through strategically placed rings at either hip of the corset girth.

Stepping back, the lad looked Lianne up and down appreciatively, nodding as he did so.

'An excellent filly,' he murmured. 'Good muscle tone, long legs and a fine chest - racing and show material, that's for certain. Now, let's get you shod and see to your ornamentations.'

Despite herself, Lianne felt a thrill course through her body at the way he looked at her, and the heat rising between her thighs meant only one thing. One brief look from the youth and he would see the first signs of the wetness that would surely only get worse, for the inner Lianne was loose again and the familiar sensations that always stemmed from being so helpless would not, nor could not be denied.

Standing well to one side of the door, Marlon peered out through the heavy security glass, beyond his sister, to where Naylor and the Danish woman still stood on the grass, a good eighty yards away from the house. Of the heavy, Frank, there was no sign, but the smaller windows to either side of the rear entrance afforded a clear view in both directions, so there was little chance of him sneaking up when Marlon opened up to bring Clarissa inside.

Besides, Marlon reflected grimly, his hand pressing against the bulge inside his jacket before moving inside to grasp the heavy butt, the old .38 calibre was a little less sophisticated than some modern weapons, but it was capable of blowing a big hole in anything it was fired at. Not that Marlon was a violent man, nor at all conversant with firearms in the normal course of events. But these events were about as far removed from the norm as he could conceive, and where Clarissa's well being and safety were concerned, he knew he would be capable of almost anything.

With one final look to either side, he reached out with his free hand and turned the heavy security lock. The door swung open and, gun now brandished in full view, Marlon stepped forward, grabbed Clarissa and unceremoniously hauled her inside the house, having to almost carry her as she overbalanced on those ridiculous heels. Gasping from the effort he steadied himself and kicked the door shut, the locking mechanism engaging automatically with a satisfying clunk.

'Oh jeez!' he wheezed, letting the .38 clatter to the floor and wrapping his arms protectively around the tottering Clarissa. 'Oh jeez, what have they done to you? Are you all right? Can you use your hands? Have they chained you?'

He stepped back, holding her at arm length and stared at her, worried, disturbed by her silence. Perhaps it was something to do with the shock, he thought fleetingly, but the sudden volley of grunts and squeaks and the way in which she was trying to curl back her lips to show him left no doubt as to the real reason.

Desperately, Marlon tried to prise Clarissa's lips apart, seeking to remove whatever it was that was preventing her from speaking, but she seemed determined to stop him, drawing back, shaking her head furiously and letting loose with another burst of what could only be construed as protests.

'Clarissa!' he cried. 'It's me, Marlon! You're safe now. I'm not going to hurt you, I just want to get that thing, whatever it is, out of your mouth, don't you understand?'

She nodded, blinking rapidly and, encouraged, Marlon moved in to try again, but once more she tried to retreat. Again he paused, showing her open palms in a gesture of pacifism. But this time when he drew close to her again he heard a gentle 'plop' sound, slightly muffled, and by the time he smelled the small cloud of gas that mushroomed up from Clarissa's cleavage, it was too late.

The smithy proved to be a ramshackle building that was halfway between a cottage and a barn, open at one end to reveal an antique-looking forge, various workbenches and racks and an assortment of unworked metal bars and rods stacked against one wall. In the midst of it all stood the blacksmith himself, and immense fellow of at least six and a half feet in height and weighing probably three hundred pounds, none of which was fat nor flab.

'Good morning, William,' he hailed the lad as they approached, his face lighting up at the sight of the new pony girl trailing helplessly behind him. 'Got yourself the new filly, I see?'

'Indeed I have, Master Gregor,' William laughed. 'And you shall now have the pleasure of shoeing and ringing her.'

'And the other pleasure?' the smith smirked. The stable lad shrugged.

'No one's said any different, so I suppose it'll be okay,' he said. Gregor's mouth twisted into a grin.

'Ye've not tupped her yerself, then?'

William shook his head. 'Never tup 'em till they're shod and ringed,' he said, knowingly. 'Gives 'em the wrong ideas, sometimes. Besides, she ain't even got her tail yet and y'can't tup a tail-less filly, t'wouldn't be right, would it?'

'As y'say, lad… as y'say,' the smith nodded. 'Now, let's have the filly over to the frame.' He nodded towards a curious assemblage of iron piping that stood in the centre of the space, and William indicated with a slight tug for Lianne to move forward. Still unsure of her footing in the towering hooves, she stumbled on the uneven surface and, unable to use her arms to regain her balance, pitched headlong, just managing to twist herself sideways as she fell, avoiding striking her face, but nevertheless jarring her left arm and elbow painfully.

Neither man made any effort, either to break her fall or help her to her feet again. Instead, they just stood to either side of Lianne, grinning at her plight and guffawing as she struggled to regain an upright stance. Only when she had finally done so did William once again pull her towards the frame.

The pipe work comprised two tall uprights, embedded immovably into the ground about four feet apart and standing perhaps eight feet high, supporting a cross-member of the same ironwork, from which dangled a pair of widespread manacles, plus a length of finer chain which hung from the centre point and reached down to a little below the average person's head.

There were two further crossbeams, one at ankle height, to which were rigidly attached a series of fetters that would enable the victims legs to be held in various positions of splay, and another at waist level, the height of this adjustable by means of clamps and the centre of which was bent back into a small semicircle. A further hinged semicircular piece stood open, but as soon as Lianne had been positioned with the small of her back against the rigid half and her arm sleeves released out of the way, the second was swung closed and she found her waist held within the thus completed circle.

Kneeling down, William grasped her left ankle and forced it outwards, locking it into the penultimate fetter on that side, and repeated the process on the other ankle, so that Lianne's feet were approximately three feet apart, an uncomfortable position given the height of her heels within the hooves.

While the stable lad completed this task, the smithy took her helplessly sheathed upper limbs, drew them above her head and locked them snugly into the hanging cuffs. Raising her bridled head, Lianne peered up at the manacles and could not suppress a small shudder when she saw how heavy and unyielding they were.

'Y'may as well get off for some breakfast while I attend her,' Gregor grunted, stepping back as William straightened up. 'T'whole process from scratch takes a good half-hour, and she ain't goin' nowhere now. Not that I'd ever have any trouble from a dumb nag like this anyway,' he added.

The youth nodded, muttered his thanks, and sauntered out of the forge with only a brief backward glance. Watching him go, the sun glinting on his tanned skin, Lianne shuddered, her eyes drawn hypnotically to where the smith was now pumping a bellows under embers that magically changed from dull red, through orange, to almost white.

And then he was no longer the smith, no longer Gregor.

'Surprised?'

Lianne gave a little whinny of horror as Christina, hands on hips, white leather thigh boots, brief skirt and halter top, stood before her. The blonde Dane, hair cropped as short as when Lianne had last encountered her, grinned maliciously.

'Oh, of course,' she smirked, 'I'd forgotten. Nags like you can't speak, can they, horsy girl?' A crop appeared in her right hand as if by magic and she struck Lianne a vicious cut across her right breast. The loud neighing this elicited rose almost to a human scream.

'And that's just the start, bitch!' Christina snarled. Lianne tried to draw back - an impossible feat given the heavy frame to which she was secured - expecting a further assault, but for the moment it appeared her tormentor was content merely to gloat.

'I've waited a long time for this,' she said. She tapped her leg with the crop. 'Out there in the real world this bloody thing still reminds me of you. That break never quite healed as it should have. Of course in VESTA's world there's no pain - not for me, anyway,' she added, her smile widening.

'Of course, for you and the likes there is pain aplenty, should I choose, which of course I shall. But first a small explanation, as I should hate for you not to realise exactly what our positions now are.

'Naturally, we all know this is not the real world we are in, but it is real enough and there is no escaping from it without help from outside, help which will not, I need scarcely add, be forthcoming. Therefore, my poor little helpless filly, to all intents and purposes, this painworld of VESTA's has now become your world for as long as you can possibly imagine.

'They tell me there is no practical limit to the time a person can remain here, assuming their physical body is fed and attended to in the other world. There may be psychological limits, but of course nobody knows, so you're breaking new ground, as it were.

'I, meantime, shall enjoy breaking you, and this is simply a beginning.' Christina waved a gloved hand around the smithy and then jabbed a finger towards Lianne's face. 'All this is my own little idea,' she continued, grinning even more when Lianne recoiled from the gesture.

'Thanks to Marlon's enforced co-operation, our German friend has had access to VESTA even before we arrived here to take complete control, so I had him devise a programme to my own specifications. This new body of yours, whilst an impossibility in reality - though for how much longer who can say? - represents my idea of genetic engineering at its most fascinating.

'I thought of actually giving you a completely equine body and may still do so, as a diversion later on, but came up with this compromise. Nice horsy features and mane, lovely long shanks and massive tits for us all to enjoy.' She reached out with the crop and prodded the welt that had appeared on Lianne's stinging right breast.

'You'll have noticed that your nipple rings and piercings have gone, which is deliberate, as I intend to have the pleasure of ringing you again myself. I also intend a few other pleasures denied me in that other world.'

She reached down, seized the hem of her ridiculously brief leather skirt and lifted it. Lianne gasped, a sort of nasally rattle through her elongated nostrils, for instead of the full sex lips she remembered from before, Christina now boasted a full set of male genitalia and her new organ, though still flaccid, was enormous. The Dane chuckled.

'Curious feeling,' she said, 'fucking like a man. I had a little trial run an hour or so ago and I must say it was different, though I had to ask Jurgen to make a few adjustments. The male orgasm is a pale thing in comparison to its female counterpart, but now I shall have the best of both worlds.

'But enough talk, you whore, we have work to do to make you fit for your new role.' She turned away again and pumped at the bellows once more. Lianne could merely stand and watch her, eyes wide in horror-struck disbelief.

That the woman was mad she already knew, and that she was dangerous. But she surely could not seriously be intending to keep Lianne like this permanently? Except that Lianne knew only too well that that was exactly what she meant and Christina, of all people, was perfectly capable of even greater atrocities.

'You tricked me!' Marlon snarled accusingly. 'There was no need. Like I said, you'd have had it all. I'd have kept my part of the bargain.' He had regained consciousness several minutes since, waking to find himself strapped securely to a wheeled gurney trolley, naked but for what appeared to be a small and very tight

74

pair of rubber briefs. Above him, looming large to fill his field of vision, the blonde amazon grinned cruelly down.

'Your problem, my little genius friend,' she replied smoothly, 'is that you don't live in the real world, even outside of this VESTA of yours. Maybe you would have kept your word. Yes, probably you would, I believe that, but then you would have been out there on the loose and our time here would have been very limited indeed.

'Moreover,' she added, stooping so that her face was very close to his, 'you would have taken your sweet little sister with you, and I just couldn't bear the thought of being parted from her, not when she was already shaping up so well as my new pony girl.'

'Pony girl?' Marlon was confused. 'You're going to use her as a pony in VESTA?'

Christina chuckled. 'Well, maybe that too, yes,' she agreed, 'but I already have a pony girl lined up for that role. The delightful Clarissa, however, will get to play the role for real, though I regret that reality brings with it a few necessary constraints that Koenig assures me are not necessary inside your amazing creation.'

She straightened up again and made as if to turn for the door, but hesitated, apparently considering something.

'On the other hand,' she went on, at last, 'there is no reason why you should not be added to your VESTA's company, perhaps as a dog boy, or maybe as a little piggy slave?'

Naylor thumbed the microphone key and spoke directly into it.

'Everything's secure here,' he said curtly. 'What's the machine status?'

'All normal.' The German's guttural tones echoed around the small control room. 'I should have reported anything to the contrary immediately.'

'Then it's time for you to make your way here,' Naylor said, ignoring the implied rebuke. 'The chopper has already started back for you, so I'll expect you before dusk.'

'You sound impatient, Herr Naylor,' Koenig chuckled. 'But there is no need. Our lady friend has complete instructions, plus a small disc which will take care of everything until I arrive, so you can play quite happily and safely in the meantime. Just don't try anything that is outside of those instructions.'

'Are you sure it's safe, though?'

'Perfectly, so long as you stick to what I told Christina. I'd have preferred for you all to wait, but the lady was most persistent. It appears there is someone there with whom she is most anxious to renew old acquaintances.'

Lianne hung limply in the frame, tears of pain anger and frustration running down her equine cheeks, blurring her vision and her view of the new rings that now adorned her distended nipples, from where tongues of fire speared through her very nervous system.

Unlike the pretty gold rings that had decorated her own much smaller teats in real life, these were made of steel nearly half an inch thick, with an overall diameter of at least three inches, their weight dragging down on the ends of Lianne's inflated mammaries. And this time, instead of piercing the flesh with a needle the vicious Dane had used a heated rod, pushing it slowly through the tissue.

'Of course, normally such an ordeal would cause you to pass out,' Christina sneered, when she had finished brazing the second ring immovably into position, 'but I instructed Jurgen to incorporate an automatic threshold cut out, just short of that level. Thus,' she added, stepping back, 'you will suffer the utmost agony short of losing consciousness. I should so hate you to miss even a single second of your new life.'

The rod came out of the furnace a third time, its tip once again a yellowish white. And this time it seared through Lianne's septum with ease, throwing her into a vortex of purple and green explosions, yet, as Christina had promised, no black velvet curtain descended to ease the torture.

On the contrary, with unnatural speed the worst of the agony receded immediately the rod was removed, and even the tears in her eyes miraculously dried, so that she was afforded a clear view of the heavy nose ring Christina eased through the freshly cauterised wound.

'Horses don't usually wear rings through their noses, I know,' the Dane laughed, picking up the brazing rod to seal the two ends of the ring, 'but I want you to remember just what a little cow you really are underneath everything.' She finished the task and gave the ring an experimental tug, jerking Lianne's head forward in helpless compliance.

'Very pretty, I don't think,' she said, tossing aside the still glowing rod. 'And now for some rings for your cunt, though I think they'll have to be smaller, or else they'll just get in the way.'

Ten minutes and much shrill protesting later, she was as good as her word. Although Lianne could not bend forward to view the finished effect, she was only too well aware of the five rings, two each in her outer labial lips and the fifth piercing that most tender bud, which was now held stiffly and proudly outside its usual dark hiding place.

'Splendid,' Christina enthused, clapping her gloved hands together. 'And of course, thanks to VESTA we can always do this over again, should I feel bored. Yes, I can have you returned to your normal state and then fit all your rings anew. Would you like that, horsy-whore?'

Dismally, Lianne shook her head, though she knew that what she wanted or liked would count for nothing with this demented witch. There was little doubt in her mind that the amazon blonde would indeed repeat the scenario and at frequent intervals and, at this sudden realisation of her true helplessness, Lianne began to weep silently. This seemed to please her torturess greatly.

'Blub-blub!' Christina teased mercilessly. 'That's the way I like you, I think. Where's the haughty little cow gone now, heh? Surely she can't really be this useless big-titted filly with rings in her nose, tits and cunt?' She laughed uproariously, slapping her thighs with unconstrained glee.

'But what shall we call our little dobbin?' she sniggered, eventually regaining some sort of composure. 'Let's see, what would be an appropriate name for a horse-faced, big-titted, whore slave?' She paced up and down for a few moments, apparently considering various choices.

'Ah, I have it,' she suddenly cried. 'Amber! Excellent choice, for so many things are preserved in amber. It's very fitting that the toity little bitch you once were should be preserved inside Amber the filly. And you shall have a proper name brass.' Whether Christina had intended the name all along, or whether it was just another display of VESTA at work, a brief visit to the nearest bench produced the brass; five ornate letters about two inches high and cleverly welded into one oval whole, with small hooks at either end that fitted into small rings set into Lianne's bridle, so the nameplate sat neatly across her forehead strap.

'And now we must shoe you, Amber,' Christina said smugly. 'You'll be pleased to know that, unfortunately from my point of view, there is no pain associated with the operation. Your hooves, like those of a real horse, have almost no sensitivity.'

She released each of Lianne's ankles in turn and, though the hammering in of the nails produced a mild sensation underfoot, there was indeed no actual pain. However, if walking in the hooves had been a problem before, the weight of the iron footwear would, Lianne immediately realised, make it an even greater effort from now on.

'And just so you don't try to repeat your kicking efforts of the last time,' Christina said, refastening the second ankle, 'I have a little present for you.' Again to the bench, this time returning with a short metal bar, at the end of each was fixed a steel cuff, fashioned to encircle the lower thigh just above the level of each knee. Locked in place it served two purposes, Lianne realised. One, she would no longer be able to close her legs completely together and two, it would prevent any forward kicking movement.

And when Christina finally released her from the frame, secured her sleeved arms to the corset girth and pushed her towards the doorway, walking was a matter of a curious shuffling progress, if progress could indeed be used to describe Lianne's shambling efforts.

'Time to prepare you for your tail, bitch filly,' the giant blonde growled, steering Lianne around to the left when they were outside once more. Jerking the lead rein and forcing the flanged bit plate to bite painfully into the roof of Lianne's mouth, she grinned widely, clearly enjoying her prisoner's total helplessness.

'But first,' she added, 'we need to warm you up a bit. Ah, I see everything is ready.'

'Everything' turned out to be a curious pillory-like stand, though one designed for a victim whose hands were already secured otherwise, for there was a single aperture through which the neck could be locked and the upright which held the device was adjustable for height. Forcing Lianne's head down and slamming the upper half of the mechanism into place, Christina lost no time in availing herself of this facility, until Lianne was forced to bend with her back parallel to the ground, her naked rump thrust high into the air by a horizontal bar that swung out on a pivoting extension pole.

It was a humiliating position, as if everything else that had been done to her already were not humiliation enough, and as she peered back along her body Lianne was greeted by the sight of her massive breasts swinging pendulously, their heavy rings adding to the already distorting effect of gravity.

To one side of the pillory stood a barrel, from the top of which protruded the handles of several implements whose purpose was only too clear to the hapless Lianne and, as Christina stepped over to select one of the canes, she closed her eyes and gave out a futile little whinny. This pleased the big woman greatly.

'Get used to it, horse girl,' she taunted, swishing the long bamboo through the air, close to Lianne's face. 'From now on I shall see to it that you get a good thrashing at least once every day.' She stepped around to one side, extended the rod and tapped Lianne's buttocks. Lianne jerked at the contact, but she knew far worse was to come.

The long cane hissed like an angry snake, cracking against the unprotected flesh with a report like a gunshot. Lianne tried to scream, but all that came out was a high-pitched neighing sound. Dimly, she heard Christina let out a short exclamation of satisfaction, but then the cane was whistling down again and the second line of fire exploded a mere quarter of an inch from the first.

Lianne bucked and twisted, but her bondage held her firm and all she could do was to stand there, bent over, a perfect target for the sadistic amazon who, unhurriedly now, began to beat her steadily and methodically. She had lost none of her skill, Lianne realised through the pain and tears. Every cut landed on previously unblemished flesh, each stripe, though Lianne could not see for herself, separate from the rest, until her buttocks and upper thighs became one complete red mass.

'And now you're about ready for your tail, bitch,' Christina growled, dropping the cane back into the barrel. 'Brown and white, I think.'

From somewhere - Lianne could not see where - she produced the article, a truly splendid confection of long horsehair, pale and dark brown strands blending with brilliant white, the whole bound together where they came to meet the method by which they were to be attached; a slender rod which swelled out into a bulbous tip, the purpose needing no explanation to the sobbing Lianne.

'In we go, horsy,' Christina smirked, presenting the tip of the rod to Lianne's rear orifice. Lianne tried to clench her buttocks, even though she knew resistance was ultimately a waste of effort. But a sharp smack from Christina's gloved hand across already throbbing flesh was all that was required to make her muscles relax. And before she could recover the thick rubber was inside, sliding home until her sphincter closed about the narrow band at the base of the tail, impossible for her to eject without aid, or at the very least, a great deal of effort and further pain.

'Excellent, my little Amber,' Christina said, walking around Lianne in a leisurely fashion, nodding as she examined the finished effect. 'And now, before the boy returns, I think I shall enjoy this thing between my legs.' She reached beneath her skirt and Lianne realised she was grasping the male shaft that hid there in this world.

'Of course, the boy will only see me as Gregor,' Christina laughed. 'Not that it'd matter anyway as he's only a hologram, or whatever, and he won't come back till

I'm ready for him,' she added, her left hand fumbling at the belt buckle. 'That's the beauty of this painworld, don't you agree? Those of us in control are truly in control.

'Now, what do you think of this for a pizzle, horsy cunt?' The skirt fell away, revealing a huge erect phallus, a member larger than Lianne would ever have believed possible to exist. 'The stuff of dreams, eh? How many men would give there all for even half of this?' Christina threw back her head and laughed outrageously.

'Well, my little slut whore pony girl, you're going to get all of it. Every last fucking inch, you bitch!' She moved around to stand behind Lianne, slapping her tenderised buttocks as she did so and drawing another series of pained snorts.

'Feel this, cunt!' she hissed, presenting the bulbous tip to its target. Lianne's stomach jerked convulsively as she felt the hot pressure against her gaping sex lips, felt the throbbing flesh pushing aside, the spreader bar preventing any semblance of resistance, other than that provided by the reluctance of the musculature to yield to such an invasion.

'Of course,' Christina breathed, steadying herself by grasping Lianne's hips, 'in the real world one good fucking from a cock this size and you'd be useless for ever more. And just for good measure I've added another little touch.

'From now on every time anyone fucks you you'll be a virgin at the beginning. Think of that, pony-whore, you get to lose your maidenhead a thousand times a year, at least!' She sniggered and Lianne gasped as the first inch of her gained entry, for what she said was true and already Lianne's hymen was beginning to stretch and tear.

'Now buck, you bitch!' Christina screamed, slapping hard at both thighs and thrusting her own hips forward. Lianne let out a high pitched squeal and dutifully bucked, for as the hot shaft pressed and tore its way home, the waves of abandoned lust were already washing over the rocks of her natural resistance.

The fight did not last very long at all and indeed, Ellen thought wryly as she was turned forcibly onto her stomach, hardly justified the description of a fight at all. For whoever - or whatever - was inside that male catsuit was fit, strong, quick and cunning, even if that combination was only as a result of VESTA's intervention.

Two, three, four times she leapt forward, her deadly talons raking at her opponent, only for the wicked claws to scythe through empty air as a nerve-numbing blow thumped into her unprotected kidneys or back, sending her sprawling in an undignified and helpless heap from which the male cat could easily have extracted her and brought proceedings to an even quicker end.

He, however, seemed content to play with her, as a real cat might have played with a mouse, circling her prone form each time in a predatory crouch, his movements so feline it was even more unnerving than the power of his strikes and the speed of his reactions. Finally, seeing the futility of continuing the charade, Ellen conceded to the inevitable.

As her breath returned slowly yet again she rolled onto her back, spread her legs wide and issued a plaintive mewling through the gag mask that was an unmistakable invitation to her conqueror. The victorious male, however, was unwilling, if indeed he were even able, to slip out of his cat role.

Stalking over to where she lay, he bent, inserted one clawed hand beneath the small of her back and flipped her easily onto her side, reaching down for one ankle to pull it out and wide, while the other hand forced her shoulder further over until she was laying face down in the grass. Still not satisfied, he jammed a foot under her crotch and lifted, until his message was unmistakably clear.

Grunting through her gag, Ellen steadied herself on all fours, then lowered her upper body onto her horizontal forearms, forcing her rump high into the air and spreading her legs again as she did so. Her opponent needed no further encouragement, dropping onto her with a cry somewhere between a squeal and a snarl, his rampant organ finding her defenceless sex with unerring precision.

For a brief instant Ellen tensed against the assault, but it was only an instinctive reaction and she quickly forced herself to relax again, so that the distended knob of his huge shaft met no resistance as it began to probe inside her hot, moist tunnel.

'Aaaahheoowww!' she squawked, as he continued to penetrate her, thrusting forward until she was impaled on the longest, hardest penis she could ever remember. She felt him rise up behind her, his fists grasping her hips so that his claws penetrated her catsuit and dug painfully into the flesh beneath, but by this time Ellen was oblivious to pain. Pain now was just another facet of pleasure and, as her conqueror began to pump in and out of her, she found herself reacting in rhythm and pleasure.

Degrading as it was, William's pony cart at least offered Lianne a respite from Christina's frenzied attentions. Seeming to change in appearance from her own blonde amazonian form to that of Gregor, the muscular smith, the Dane was plainly hell bent on exacting every ounce of revenge for what had happened between the two women on their last encounter, when Lianne's steel shod foot had broken her shinbone so sickeningly.

If there were any traces of that injury in the real outside world, here in this cybernetic painworld there were none. And if anything the woman was even more powerful than Lianne remembered from before, though dimly she understood that VESTA was capable of producing things that were as far from reality as most of her scenarios were so horribly realistic in their initial basis.

Finally, however, Christina appeared sated, though her virtual self showed no signs of the strenuous mauling she had inflicted upon her helpless prisoner. The steady rise and fall of her breasts could well have been no more than a reflection of her mental state as she stepped back from Lianne's limp form and turned away towards the back of the smithy.

When she returned she carried a coiled whip of heavily braided leather, tiny metal points glinting at intervals along its length. Lianne's heart sank yet again, for she could easily imagine the suffering such an evil implement could inflict, especially in the practised hands of a sadist such as Christina.

However, to Lianne's relief, William the stable lad chose precisely this moment to reappear, apparently quite unconcerned by Christina's now indisputably female appearance and seeing only Gregor before him. Christina held the whip at arm's length, proffering it to the youth.

'I want this hung on the wall of her stall,' she instructed. 'I want it where she can see it day or night, and I want you to give her one stroke with it every night before she sleeps. The marks will be gone again by next morning.'

William eyed the viciously toothed braid with not a little amount of scepticism. 'S'cuse my sayin', master Gregor,' he said, shaking his head, 'but I don't reckon any marks this bugger inflicts will be gone in a twenty-four hour.'

By way of reply Christina let out a bellowing guffaw and suddenly even Lianne was seeing her once more as the blacksmith. 'Take my word for it, lad,' Gregor rumbled, 'the marks will be gone by morning, for this is no whip like you've ever seen before.'

William's eyes widened. 'Ah, 'tis a magic whip?' he almost whispered, awe in his voice.

Again the smith let out a roar of laughter. 'Let's just say it ain't of my normal world,' came the cryptic reply.

Finally and, apparently satisfied, William stepped forward, unlocked Lianne's neck from the pillory post, clipped on a new lead rein and led her, unresistingly, away.

Back at the stable block Lianne was introduced to the cart she was expected to draw, a lightweight single-seater buggy with huge wheels on a single axle, a long central shaft projecting forward so that its weight, combined with that of the pony would more than stabilise the weight of even the heaviest driver.

It was this shaft, however, that Lianne realised was to be the source of her greatest discomfort and humiliation, for whichever mind had been responsible for its design and conception had plumbed the very depths of degradation.

At its front end a short spar rose vertically, supporting a lockable steel collar. And just ahead of this a horizontal bar carried two similar wrist cuffs, ensuring that the unfortunate pony would be forced to walk or run with her spine kept all but parallel with the ground. However, not content with this simple torture, other refinements had been added.

Not far behind this assembly a broader band, plainly intended to encircle the waist, rode on a metal collar that permitted front and rear movement along the shaft, whilst ensuring that the wearer's stomach was kept close to the heavy pole. But even this was not the worst feature, for just to the rear of this device sat another, also mounted on a movable collar, but refusing any latitude that would permit the victim to dismount the thick phallus once it had been inserted into her sex.

Realising its purpose Lianne could not stifle a neigh of terror. But William, as ever, appeared completely unmoved. Sensing her reluctance, he used the coiled whip to slap her resoundingly across her buttocks, laughing as he did so.

'Sooner you gets to learn, sooner it gets easier,' he chuckled, 'for all of us, as happens. Now, walk on, gel, and lets get you hitched up proper. Hup now, Amber, easy on.'

A second blow from the coiled whip, much harder than the first, convinced

Lianne that resistance was futile, for even though the blow was still considerably lighter than it would have been from the whip used in its intended fashion, it was still more than enough to allow the tiny barbs to jag into her flesh with painful results. She whinnied, bucked, but walked forward as instructed, making no attempt to resist as William positioned her astride the shaft on the ground.

'Stand still and I'll make this easier for you,' William said, turning back to take something from under the buggy's seat. As he opened it Lianne saw it was a crude jar and that it appeared to contain a jelly-like substance; a substance William scooped out using two fingers and proceeded to apply liberally to the phallus that reared up just a few feet below Lianne's quivering sex lips.

'No point in being over cruel, I reckons,' the stable lad said, and Lianne wondered if he was being ironic, before realising that was decidedly unlikely, given that he was, supposedly, nothing more than a computer generated entity. On the other hand, given that the vindictive Christina now appeared to be running things anything was possible, she reflected, as William lifted the shaft and presented the massive dildo to her gaping opening.

Thanks to the grease he'd applied and also to the fact that her pulsating tunnel was still wet from its encounter at the smithy, the phallus slid easily into Lianne, although its sheer length made her gasp as it was pressed fully home. Then, before she had time to react, William bent her forward and locked the waist band about her, following this by locking her neck and then her wrists, so she stood bent forward, the shaft held up between her thighs, her breasts dangling heavily to either side of it.

Still not satisfied, William attached a short strap to the top of Lianne's head harness, slipped it through a ring in the top of the neck collar and tightened it without ceremony, forcing her head up and back and depriving her of all but the slightest movement of it.

'Needs to see where we're going, don't we?' William said, fastening the buckle end off. 'You'll soon get used to it, same as all our fillies do. Now, let's add your tit chains and then we can go for a little practice trot.'

The chains in question were silvery in colour, but definitely not delicate in construction, for each link was at least two inches long and forged from metal more than a quarter of an inch in thickness. When clipped from either end to the heavy nipple rings they dragged Lianne's already distended breasts into an even more elongated shape, though the strap between head and neck prevented her from seeing this for herself.

William gave her a playful slap across her rump as he straightened up and then patted her between her shoulder blades.

'You're an 'andsome beast and no mistakin',' he said, stepping back to admire her. 'T'will be a treat to school you an' then, if you do well, I'll see to you properly in your stall later.' As he spoke his right hand went to the front of his breeches and, as he walked past her field of vision, Lianne could not help but see the unmistakable bulge beneath the rough fabric.

Strapped securely once again to another version of Christina's mounting frame,

Clarissa regained consciousness in the real world with a small gasp. The blonde amazon stood at the sub control console to one side, flicking up switches that cut the circuits to the assorted probes that surrounded the heavy cap that encircled Clarissa's head; probes that had taken Christina deep inside the painworld of VESTA as an invisible observer.

'And the bitch will stay like that for the rest of her life,' Christina growled, locking off the final breaker. 'They assure me there is absolutely no reason why that should not be for another fifty or sixty years,' she added. 'Half a century as a dumb nag, never ageing, never able to speak, never able to escape.

'Of course,' she continued, a wistful tone entering her voice, 'out here in reality the ageing process will continue for all of us, so I may well not be around that long, but I have decided that I shall last long enough to see her end. Maybe a visit to the slaughterhouse and have her turned into virtual dog meat and glue, eh?

'And then, who knows what strides science might make in the coming decades?' She stepped closer to Clarissa, reached out and grasped her jaw between fingers and thumb, pinching and squeezing most painfully. 'We might even be able to get some geneticist to alter these pretty features,' she laughed.

'Because, my little pretty, you are going to live a life out here almost identical to the one poor little Amber is living in there, and I think a nice horsy face would look good on you, too!'

'You're fucking insane!' Clarissa's Australian accent was even harsher than usual as her words echoed around the plain walls, but all her outburst earned was a hard slap across her face which brought tears streaming to her eyes. However, she had now arrived at a state of near madness herself, both from what she had already suffered and from what she had seen being done to the poor blonde girl in the scenario she had been made to witness, and mere pain was not going to deflect her.

'You're sick!' she screeched blindly. 'Hitting me ain't going to change that, you great cowardly bitch. Oh yeah,' she moaned, shaking her head in an effort to clear her vision, 'you can do what you want when you've got your victims all trussed up and helpless. But I doubt you'd be so fucking brave if I was free to defend myself, big as you are, you perverted filth!'

Christina's vague outline drew closer again and Clarissa flinched, steeling herself for the anticipated blow. However, the Dane did not hit her again.

'I may just give you the chance to prove those brave words,' she hissed through clenched teeth. 'It might be an interesting diversion and, when I've beaten you into a pulp, maybe I'll just circumcise you, like some of the African countries do to their women. That way I'd be sure you didn't come to like being used as a little sex toy - you'd just be a hole for men to fuck.'

'Only if you beat me,' Clarissa sobbed. 'But then, you're not going to give me the chance in a fair fight, are you?'

'That, my dear little firebrand redhead,' Christina retorted, stepping back once more, 'is where you could be so very wrong. So very wrong!'

Lianne was beginning to lose touch with what vestiges of reality remained to her in this unreal world, the snaking caress of William's driving whip keeping her up to a steady trotting pace around an oval circuit that was devoid of any feature, save its unending monotony.

At first, progress in the hideously awkward hoof boots was slow and ungainly, though even without them the presence of the main shaft between her legs, together with its uncompromising appendage, would have been a serious handicap to style and grace. However, the stable lad was uncompromising, the thin braid slapping across Lianne's upraised rump at any sign of her flagging. And after some time she found she was growing used to the extreme footwear and was able to establish and maintain a respectable progress of sorts.

Unfortunately, all the while the natural bobbing motion of the cart was causing the trace shaft to rise and fall slightly with every step, so that the huge dildo was now sliding in and out of Lianne's moist tunnel at a precipitous rate. And the steady tugging of the heavy chains at her distended nipples combined to lift her into a state of sexual tension and awareness that she at once both hated and yet was forever on the brink of yielding to.

Determined as she was not to submit to the indignities of her torturers, Lianne was only too well aware of her physical limitations. And by the time she had completed the fifth lap of the training circuit she knew she was on the verge of orgasm. And the severity of her bondage, the degradation of her appearance and the causally off-handed manner of her treatment all served only to increase the pressure upon her to surrender to her most inner urgings completely.

William, though, did not appear to be aiming for this outcome, for at the very moment when Lianne was preparing to concede defeat, he reined her to a complete halt with a cursory jerk on the reins that sent the bit flange rearing painfully into the roof of her mouth.

'Stand!' he commanded, leaping agilely down from his seat. He walked along her flank, one hand passing lightly over her dappled skin, wiping away little droplets of sweat that had succeeded in penetrating to the outside and nodding appreciatively to himself. Then, stooping down, he seized the rein where it joined the right side of Lianne's bit and jerked her head around towards him.

'Got to do these things by stages,' he chuckled. 'Can't use up all your energies in one go, can we? Needs to get these lovely legs fit and these big titties used to swingin' in the open. 'Sides, yer due a tuppin' shortly, so I don't want you plain tuckered first. I likes my fillies to explode on the end of my old todger.'

He stepped back and felt underneath her belly with his left hand, his fingers probing where the phallus penetrated her, then withdrew them and stared at the glistening film which now coated them.

'Ah!' he exclaimed. 'That's good, that is. A nice wet pony makes the best racer, it's a fact. An' a nice wet filly makes a good ride for her driver, too. But we don't want you comin' just yet, Amber, do we? So William will just let you stand a bit longer and then we'll 'ave another couple of circuits.

'Meantime, just so you knows what happens to fillies who lose control without permission, we'll 'ave a little sample session for you.' Wiping his hand on his breeches he walked back to the cart, rummaged behind the seat and produced a long flat leather paddle. Realising Lianne could not view his actions, he brought it around and held it out in front of her nose.

'This is what I calls Willie's warmer,' he laughed. 'Don't cut nor mark the skin like a whip or crop, but it certain stings, so I'm gonna warm up this lovely arse of yours before we carries on.'

Eyes wide, Lianne wished there was some way in which she could try to plead with him, for she knew only too well what the outcome of this would be, and it was not the prospect of the immediate pain from the paddle that worried her. Rather, her previous experiences left her in no doubt as to the ultimate effect the paddle would have on her treacherous body. For standing helplessly in the traces, her sex plugged with the monstrous rubber phallus, sweating and straining, the application of even a mild chastisement would undo all her efforts to hold herself in check.

Crack!

The noise as the leather exploded onto her flesh was far worse than the actual impact, but nevertheless Lianne bucked automatically, the dildo moving out and then plunging deeply back inside her as a result. She let out a helpless little whinny, but this served only to spur William on to greater efforts. Again his arm rose and fell.

Once more the leather slapped down onto exposed girl filly flesh. But Lianne scarcely heard the impact and felt it hardly even more, for already the trigger mechanisms within her were working, little relays of passion and lust tripping to open so many little lock gates that had striven to hold back the tidal wave for so long.

Slap! Slap!

Damn him! Lianne let out a high-pitched cry, biting into the bit in an effort - one final, doomed effort - to avoid the unavoidable, avert the inevitable. Damn him, her mind screeched, for there was no doubt he knew only too well what he was doing, despite what he'd said beforehand.

Crack!

'Atta girl!'

Lianne only dimly heard William's cry of triumph, neither did she see his hand grasping at the shaft to prevent her falling forward and her knees giving beneath her. With a surprising strength he supported the wooden pole with one hand, still using the other to wield the paddle and, with two more crisp slaps, brought her quivering, shuddering, mewling to a helpless, explosive climax, impaled there on the pole in all her harness finery, chains and brasses jingling in a musical mockery, a discordant witness to her ultimate humiliation.

Paul, now resigned to the role of Susie that Dolores was determined he/she should assume, was fairing a little better than Lianne, though he/she would not have believed that possible had anyone mentioned it. Initially, finding himself as Pauline had been an exciting development and Paul had regarded it as an excellent opportunity to discover what it was like to possess a truly feminine body, rather than just dressing in the relevant outfits to exploit his fantasies.

The reality, however, was proving to be far different from the anticipation.

In his role play with Lianne - and with other women before she had appeared in his life - it had always been a case of make-believe lesbianism, with the added advantage that Paul possessed one certain attribute that was denied a genetic woman. As Pauline, however, the contents of his panties were completely female and the Hazel lookalike VESTA had generated, or Dolores as she insisted on calling herself, was determined to exploit both that and Pauline's reduced physical stature and lack of inherent male body strength.

Within an hour of meeting the powerful dominatrix, Paul had long since ceased to think of himself as male, and now was beyond even trying to lose himself in his outer world alter ego of Pauline. For neither Paul nor Pauline would have succumbed so easily as did the silly, weak-limbed, quivering, tremulous Susie, who seemed to need little more than a cunningly manipulated stimulation of her huge nipples to reduce her to a gasping, helpless wreck.

Even that would not have been so bad, but Dolores was unwilling to allow pleasure without pain. Indeed, so far she had concentrated mostly on the pain, and the pleasure had been merely an incidental side-effect of the process at odd and unexpected moments. Hanging in the woman's sturdy whipping frame, arms and shoulders aching from the stretched position, plump buttocks throbbing from the repeated assaults from both cane and crop, poor Susie was a beaten shell.

Worse still, she was a humiliated shell, for every fibre in her new being was screaming out for the release that only orgasm could bring, and she knew it. More to the point, so did the evil Dolores.

'Beg me!' she taunted, thrusting her face close. Susie shook the damp hair from her face and stared defiantly up at her, battling to retrieve even some small measure of self-respect.

'No,' she croaked. 'You can beat me all you like, it won't make any difference.'

Dolores laughed and shook her head in mockery. 'That's not what I'm talking about, as we both know,' she said, softly this time. She reached down and one hand probed between Susie's outstretched thighs, pressing aside the soft flesh of her outer lips and seeking the swollen bud that throbbed within. At her touch, Susie's back arched as if from an electrical charge and a hoarse shriek ripped from her throat.

'No-ooo!' she wailed, twisting and turning in an effort to break the contact, but it was to no avail. Again Dolores massaged and again little fingers of fire rushed through every vein and muscle.

'Fuck you!' Susie shrieked, but was rewarded by a stinging slap across her unprotected breasts that served only to heighten her state of helpless agitation.

'No,' Dolores said, stepping back and thrusting her hands on her hips. 'Fuck you is what this is all about, if we're honest. Look at you, you little slut. You dance to the whip so prettily, tits a-bouncing and yelling and screaming, yet you're wet through and helpless to the slightest touch. What you need is a good stiff cock inside you, and maybe another one to suck on.' She turned away briefly and clapped her hands.

The effect was like magic. From out of the shadows, materialising like two spirits, stepped two strapping young men, dark-haired, dark-eyed and tall. Both, Susie guessed, in their mid-twenties. A groan of despair slipped from between her trembling lips as she stared at their naked bodies. Oiled to gleam in the harsh spotlights, the pale skin was a stark contrast to the heavily studded black wrist and ankle bands that were their only adornments, save for a similar, though much thinner strap that tightly encircled the bases of their rigidly erect penises.

'My little present for you,' Dolores sniggered. Susie closed her eyes, but another slap, this time across her face, made her quickly reopen them. 'Close your eyes again without permission and you'll live to regret it!' Dolores snarled. 'I expect my slaves to show proper gratitude for all the trouble I go to over them.'

From somewhere deep within, what remained of Paul seemed to watch as a detached observer. The Susie personality appeared to have taken over completely now, and yet he wasn't an observer at all, he knew, for he was Susie, Susie was him, and this was their body that was being so dreadfully abused. A body that, despite what the brain tried to say, persisted on being a willing participant, responding to each new torture or maltreatment by becoming more and more excited, and it was becoming rapidly more difficult for its owner or owners to exercise any cogent, logical thinking.

'Meet Grant and Devon,' Dolores said, convinced her warning had been heeded. 'Grant is the one with the slightly longer hair, but telling one from another needn't concern you. For that matter, you don't even need to know their names, but we must remember our manners, I suppose.' She stepped away and nodded to the waiting men.

Moving as one, they glided in at either side of their helpless victim, hands reaching out, touching, massaging, kneading, twisting. Susie gave a strangled scream and bucked wildly in her bondage, but there was no escaping this new onslaught and, as a mouth closed firmly over each of her nipples, she felt the huge wave of her first orgasm beginning to peak over the shores of her lust.

'You're certain you don't need the little creep any more?' Naylor persisted, staring hard at the impassive features of Jurgen Koenig.

The German shrugged. 'If I should need him I can always pull him back out for a while,' he pointed out. 'And meantime, the safest place for him is in his little world with the rest of his little friends.'

'And you've cleaned out any safe words or passwords?'

'Everything. VESTA is as clean as the proverbial whistle, you have my total assurance on that.'

'You seem very confident,' James Naylor almost sneered. 'Especially given that we are dealing with an absolute genius here. This work of his is so much more advanced than even we guessed.'

'And is a perfect illustration of what money can achieve. Had I had but...'

'Yes, yes, we've heard it all before,' Naylor cut him short with a wave of his hand. 'The fact that I did not have that sort of money at my disposal rather negates any argument. In any case,' he continued, a smile returning to his face, 'we now have all the money we could possibly wish for, courtesy of my dear friend Nadia.

Plus we have VESTA herself.'

'Together with a captive set of guinea pigs,' Koenig added, but Naylor merely shrugged.

'I'm quite happy to let Christina play with them for the moment,' he said dismissively. 'As far as she's concerned the VESTA painworld is the ultimate goal, both as a toy for her and as a means of making money from rich clients who share either her tastes or those at the other end of the spectrum.

'However,' he went on, pacing across the deep pile carpet to stand looking out of the huge bay window to the grounds beyond. 'Whilst that will undoubtedly bring in considerable revenue - certainly Nadia expected to recoup even her massive investment quite quickly - that is but the merest tip of the iceberg.

'Tell me, Jurgen, how quickly could you construct a replica of VESTA?'

'Depending upon my budget...'

'I thought I'd made it clear on that score,' Naylor snapped. 'Money is no longer a factor in this; you may have whatever budget it takes. So, how long?'

Koenig thought for a few moments.

'A month,' he said at length. 'Maybe a little less.'

Naylor waved a hand without turning to look back at him. 'One month will do perfectly,' he said. 'Plus a week, let's say, to move all the duplicate set-up up to Scotland once it's finished.'

'Scotland?'

'Yes, to the island house,' Naylor said. 'A completely separate site and a completely separate entity. Then the VESTA here can continue to run in something near to its original intention, but the new VESTA can be our demonstration model for even more worthwhile clients.'

'Ah, you mean the military!' Koenig's eyes lit up. 'Yes, I wondered whether you had recognised VESTA's potential in that direction. With just a few minor alterations...'

'I know,' Naylor chuckled, finally turning back from the view. 'And you, my little Bavarian friend, are just the man to make them. How soon can you start work?'

'That depends upon the woman,' Koenig said, a small smile playing at the corners of his mouth. 'If she persists in keeping VESTA as her personal plaything, my downtime for analysis and copying will be somewhat restricted. On the other hand, if I could have five days clear...?'

'Do you want to be the one to tell Christina she's going to have to take five days off from her fun and games?' Naylor exclaimed in mock horror. 'No, me neither. So I'm afraid you'll have to work around her. Even Christina needs to sleep sometimes.'

'A very interesting female,' Koenig nodded, his eyes losing focus as he mused on the possibilities, but Naylor was quick to interrupt his daydreaming.

'Forget it,' he warned. 'She's far more than you could ever hope to handle. Her tastes are even more extreme than my worst fantasies.'

'So I have already seen,' Koenig said. 'Very extreme indeed and, if I might say so, most wasteful. Tell me, why should she want to have the pretty blonde girl looking more like a horse than a woman?'

'Ah well, that's a long story,' Naylor said, grinning. 'Our Christina is a little bit miffed over her. It all happened a while ago, but it's the reason why Christina has that limp. Our little blonde fluff-head caught Madame Sin with her guard down, smashed her shin and legged it out of here with her boyfriend. He's the one now finding out what it's really like to be a woman in a cruel world, by the way, and I wouldn't put it past our blonde she-wolf to even let him find out for real. I certainly wouldn't want to offer odds on him staying in physical contact with his balls for too much longer.'

Pain and pleasure.

That was what Dolores had promised poor Susie and now, after the interlude of pleasure was to come the pain, for she had still, somehow, managed to hold back from actually begging for Grant and Devon to actually penetrate her. In truth, she truly would have, but by the time she had been ready to surrender she was past uttering the words in any intelligible form.

Instead she had writhed beneath the frame as their skilled hands went about their work, reducing her to a moaning shambles of abandoned gratification, the evidence of their success running down her thighs in mute testimony to her abject surrender.

At last they stepped away, but it was several minutes before Susie's senses returned to anything vaguely approaching normality. When they did she saw the three of them were already making preparations for the next stage in her subjugation, the two men selecting items under Dolores' watchful eyes.

It didn't take them long and very soon they came back to Susie, stooping to release her ankle bonds, though for the moment leaving her wrists secure, high above her head. Through misty eyes she stared down at the boots they presented to her feet, calf length creations in vivid crimson leather, tight laced and with heels that Susie recognised only too well, for they featured prominently in the scenarios she had created in another world, as another person.

The heels looked impossible. Indeed, Susie knew they would prove to be so for all but the best trained dancers, for they forced the wearer's foot into such an extreme position that she could stand in them only on the tops of her toes. And although the heels themselves would lend a little stability, all of the weight would bear down upon those tortured digits and the strain upon the calf muscles would be unbearable after even a few seconds.

However, as the duo tightened the boots onto her, Susie was amazed to find that she was actually able to stand in them. True her balance was aided by the fact that much of her weight was being taken on her wrists and arms, but to her surprise, neither toes nor leg muscles seemed to be complaining overly.

Dimly, she understood.

VESTA.

Here in this virtual painworld, whilst everything looked, sounded, smelled, felt so real, things were possible that would never have been so in the outside world, things that no sane person would have considered even trying.

So, when they finally released her wrists and guided her out from beneath the whipping frame, it came as no surprise at all to Susie that she found herself mincing into the centre of the floor like a bizarre ballerina, the huge heels and elongated feet making her legs look impossibly long. Instinctively she spread her arms sideways to help with her balance as she moved, but her captors had other ideas about this.

Grasping her wrists they bent her arms across her back and, as they held them there, Dolores took up a curious leather pouch, with which she sheathed Susie's upper limbs to the level of her shoulders. Thin straps, passing over those shoulders, were buckled tightly, preventing the pouch from sliding down again and, when the three stood back, although there were no manacles about either wrist or arm, they were held as immovably as if in a vice.

'Collar her,' Dolores said. Grant bent and retrieved the necessary device, a broad leather strap, beset with spiky studs and buckling at the back of the neck, the front widening out so as to force Susie's chin high and rising to a stiff point of leather that pressed into the soft flesh beneath it. She was left standing, face tilted towards the ceiling, only able to see in front of her through lowering her eyes.

'Now we'll give you some exercise,' the dominatrix said. 'I think we'll all enjoy seeing those tits bounce about for a while, but maybe we should be able to hear them, too. Devon, bell her please.'

A minute or so later it was done; two circular golden clips, serrated teeth gleaming from their inner circumferences, had been locked firmly around Susie's nipples, small golden bells hung from little hooks on their undersides. Now every slightest movement was transmitted, via her oversized breasts, to these distended teats and their ornaments, sending a mocking tinkling sound about the chamber.

'And now to the dance,' Dolores declared. The two men took up heavy tawses and positioned themselves to either side of Susie's exposed posterior. 'Around the room, around the obstacles, around and around we go.'

As Dolores finished speaking the room was suddenly filled with the sound of deeply pulsating music, vaguely familiar, yet at the same time alien, the persistent beat set to urge even the most reluctant dancer onto the floor. Except that this reluctant dancer was to be urged in another, even more insistent fashion.

In time to the bass the tawses rose and fell, landing in turn across Susie's buttocks with resounding cracks, forcing her to jump forward in most ungainly fashion, almost toppling despite her artificially enhanced ability to balance in the ballerina boots, so that once moving, her best chance of remaining upright was to continue forward, prancing on tiptoe in a degrading way, the two bells seeming to mock her predicament with every step.

Susie howled her pain and frustration into the darkened vaults overhead, but there was nothing else she could do except dance to their vicious tune, round and around, pursued by the two naked men, black leather flailing after her until everything became a blur of exploding red and violet lights. As if from afar, she heard Dolores' taunting voice.

'You know what you want, Susie dear... know what you need... only to ask... beg them, slut, beg them... you know how to stop it... know what you want...'

'Ye-e-essss!' Susie screamed. 'Yes! Stop it, please! Yes!'

'And what do you want?'

The pain was becoming unreal now. Nothing around her seemed to hold any substance. Light turned to darkness, darkness into brilliant dancing lasers, mists of all hues rose up to engulf her. Susie was past caring about anything, save the burning need...

'I... want...' Yet still she hesitated. The straps rose and fell again and she blundered on into a crazed half world, hearing the voice that was her own.

'I... want them... to... to... take me!'

Everything became still and silent and the picture cleared. Before her the two men stood, arms folded across muscular chests. Behind them Dolores' face, smiling and triumphant. It was she who spoke first.

'Both of them, Susie?'

Susie tried to nod, but the wickedly pointed collar precluded such a movement. Instead, she was forced to voice her reply.

'Yes,' she heard herself rasp. 'Both of them.'

'And at the same time, I think,' Dolores grinned. 'Grant!'

The figure of Grant loomed tall before her, taller than Susie still, despite the extra inches lent her by the extreme height of her heels. She eyed him mistily, eyes downcast and riveted upon the thrusting shaft that reared up before him, automatically moving her feet just a little further apart. But ignoring her thrusting sex he moved behind her, pressed gently against her pouched arms, supporting her firmly, the tip of his organ resting against the cleft in her buttocks.

She felt now its massive dimensions and, for a brief moment that part of her, deep within that was not Susie, threatened to rebel. But the burning lust fuelled by the heat from her beaten buttocks, thrust rebellion aside and she felt herself relaxing back against him.

'Devon.' The second man moved forward, confronting their helpless and now willing victim face to face, his own erection resting against her lower stomach, his huge hands reaching to grasp her hips. Then between them they lifted her from the floor, pointed toes flailing against thin air, manoeuvring, positioning her, so that two weapons pressed against the gates of their respective targets.

'Oh god!' The words came out without volition as they lowered her, impaling her upon their twin manhoods until she was filled to the hilt and Susie, slut creation of the bizarre painworld, whore beyond salvation, was swept aside by a tumultuous orgasm even before they began their slow, rhythmic pistoning.

'I thought you were going to keep this Clarissa outside VESTA,' Naylor said, looking puzzled.

Christina, resplendent in a gold bodysuit, gave him a half smile.

'That's the general notion,' she agreed, 'but something she said gave me an idea. She wants to fight me.'

'Fight you?' Christina nodded.

'That's right,' she said. 'Actually, I admire her spirit in a way, but I intend knocking it out of her.'

'Then why not just take her down to the basement and do it for real?' Naylor suggested. 'Why bother hooking up to a machine?'

Christina threw him a withering look. 'Because,' she said, 'I could end up killing the silly bitch. I'd certainly cause her a lot more damage than I intend for the moment, and she'd be no good to me laid up in her sickbed.

'Besides,' she added, 'it'd be no contest out here. I can give her five or six inches and seventy pounds, not to mention a few years of intensive training. That wouldn't stop her trying, at least, which is why I said I admire her spirit. But afterwards she'd always have plenty of excuses.'

'And it would be different inside VESTA?'

'You obviously need to try out our new toy first hand,' Christina said, a note of exasperation creeping into her tone. 'Of course it would be different - as different as I choose. I can let our little Clarissa have back some of the physical disadvantages by having my virtual self nearer her size, and tap into VESTA's inexhaustible creative banks to devise some sort of handicapping system which will make the thing a bit more of an even contest.

'And there's another benefit,' she went on. 'When I beat her - and I surely will, no matter how much natural advantage I forfeit - I can beat her really thoroughly, far more thoroughly than she could stand out here. In that way, even though she can recover at the flick of a switch, or the press of a button, the memory of that thrashing will remain with her forever and I'll bend her to my will so much more easily.'

'I don't understand why you're bothering,' Naylor said, leaning back in his seat and picking at his teeth. 'Why not just go for one of your usual routines? We could have an isolation tank put in here within a few days. Forty-eight hours as a floating rubber dolly sorts out most of them.'

'I wouldn't expect you to understand,' Christina retorted, turning towards the door. 'Things like the tank work, yes, but they're too impersonal. Anyway,' she added, turning to look back over her shoulder, 'I get the feeling even the tank might not work on this one. There's something almost spooky about her - and I thought I'd met just about all types, till now.'

If Lianne had entertained any hopes of being released from the cart, they were quickly dashed. Having proved his complete mastery over her and also, if it had been needed, proved to Lianne how much a slave she was to her own deep desires, he simply proceeded to climb back into the driver's seat, flick her rump with his long whip and continue trotting her around the oval track for another two circuits, whistling tunelessly to himself as they went.

For some reason his apparent detachment and lack of concern or interest was far worse for Lianne than anything the youth had inflicted upon her so far. Being thrashed so she virtually raped herself on the shaft phallus had been humiliating enough, but at least he had shown involvement with her, had had a purpose in his actions. Now, it seemed, he had returned her to the status of unthinking beast, exercising her as a groom might exercise any four-legged equine charge, and yet still the insistent up and down motion of the dildo was threatening to throw all the wrong switches again.

Desperately Lianne fought to push her mind beyond that, to think of things other than the fact that she was being treated as nothing more than a beast, and concentrate on other matters. Ellen had told her that she was a natural submissive and Lianne had not thought to disagree with her, for there had been too many illustrated proofs of that, but this was something else again and she was grimly determined to hold some sort of charge over her rawest emotions.

Ellen.

Lianne wondered how she was faring right now. Probably coping better than she was, for Ellen had a steel core that very few people appreciated until the chips were down. She also had a sense of humour that was warped worse than a barn door in a rainstorm, and very little ever seemed to throw her. Lianne wondered if her friend was yet aware of what was happening outside; realised that they were all prisoners and that the game had become serious.

This thought reminded her again and for several minutes she trotted on blindly, the track just a vague outline through the mist of her tears, seeming to symbolise the fate that Christina had promised her; a captive at the mercy of the merest whims of a sadistic monster. And that was before James Naylor was taken into consideration.

The blonde sadistic Dane was bad enough, but Naylor, in his own way, was potentially worse. Christina was brutal, violent and a bully, using her sheer physical size to terrify her victims, but with Naylor there was something else, something deeper, more psychological and far far more sinister.

Lianne tried not to think about Naylor, turning her thoughts instead to Paul and trying to imagine what he might be doing now. Of course she knew exactly what he was doing: he was out there, lying in his own pod dressed in that damned rubber maid's uniform, hooked up to VESTA, the same as they all were in reality.

Except that this wasn't reality.

Just the only reality they had right now...

...And possibly the only reality left to any of them if Naylor and Christina had their way, and that was a reality too grim to contemplate. Shaking her head again, Lianne whinnied plaintively and trotted on, ignoring the regular cuts of William's driving whip.

Two attendants awaited Melissa within the small chamber in which she made her entry into VESTA. She came round laying flat on a narrow raised palette, the hard surface pressing against her naked body like so many cold fingers. For several seconds she made no attempt to rise, allowing her eyes to do the work, wondering if her half brother's marvel of science had perhaps failed to operate, for everything seemed so real about her, if she ignored the bizarre costumes of the two lurking females.

Those costumes, however, had not been designed not to be taken notice of, and the same could be said of their wearers. The pair were tall, olive-skinned, their dark hair cut into matching styles that immediately triggered memories of Cleopatra, and their slim height was emphasised further by the high heels of the brown, thigh length boots that sheathed their legs.

Above the tops of these boots only a slim band of brown flesh was visible beneath the hem of the matching brief pleated leather skirts. Then, further above the bare midriffs, skeletal halter tops, strapped assemblages supporting but not covering their breasts, studded leather chokers circling the slim necks and hawkishly beautiful visages with piercing green eyes.

Carefully, Clarissa eased herself into a sitting position and swung her legs over the side of the plinth, resting her feet lightly on the tiled floor beneath. To her surprise she did not feel nauseous or shaky. But then her mind quickly seized on the reason, for this awakening was not like coming out of an anaesthetic at all, there being no chemical agents involved, simply a transfer of brain awareness via VESTA's probes and sensors, the brief sense of unconsciousness being nothing more than a necessity of the transition.

'Yer dress sense is a bit old fashioned and predictable.' Clarissa's Australian twang sounded echoey around the bare walls, but it was as if neither attendant had heard her. However, as she made to stand up they swayed forward in unison. Immediately Clarissa tensed, hands coming up before her in the defensive posture she had learned so many years ago in her self defence classes at college.

'First one to try it gets her tits shoved up her nostrils,' Clarissa snarled, trying to sound more confident than she felt. The women stopped and one - the one to Clarissa's left - spoke.

'We are not here to harm you, mistress,' she said, 'merely to prepare you for your coming battle.' She looked sideways to her companion, who nodded, sagely.

'Yes, you must be armoured and prepared, for your opponent is a worthy one.'

Clarissa straightened up, hands dropping to her hips. 'What the blazes are you two on about?' she demanded. Again the two women looked at each other. Again the one to the left spoke first.

'You are to fight the fair-haired one?' she said, half statement, half question. Clarissa blinked, trying to concentrate, half recalling.

'If you mean that hulking great blonde bitch,' she said, 'then I offered her, but she said bugger all to me about actually accepting.' She wrinkled her nose, scratching the side of her jaw.

'You mean I'm actually going to get a chance to fight her?' she asked at length. The two women nodded and Clarissa let out a low whistle.

'Fuck me,' she breathed. 'Well, in that case you'd better get stuck in finding me this armour stuff. With her, you'd better make it steel plate, preferably tungsten plated, 'cause I reckon I'm gonna need every bit of help going.'

'You are both to wear the same,' the one on the left said. 'There will be no advantage to either combatant - those are the rules.'

'Is that so?' Clarissa laughed harshly. She jabbed a finger at the speaker. 'What's your name, mongoose.'

The woman allowed herself the vestige of a smile. 'I am called Alma,' she said, and indicated her companion. 'This is Tara. We are your seconds.'

'So when's this bloody fight supposed to be happening?'

Tara stepped forward. 'It will be soon enough, mistress,' she said, 'but there is time aplenty to prepare you.' She nodded towards the wall on the left, where Clarissa saw a doorway she was certain had not been there a moment earlier. 'Perhaps you will follow me?' Tara suggested, turning and walking towards the opening. 'Everything is ready.'

It took Ellen several minutes to recover her senses and strength sufficiently to wriggle herself off the boy-cat's still rigid penis and slide out from beneath him. He hadn't looked particularly heavy, but as a dead weight it required all the effort she could muster, and he made no attempt to lift himself clear.

Scrambling unsteadily to her feet, Ellen stood over him studying the unmoving form, and then prodded his midriff with one paw-booted foot. There was absolutely no reaction. She dropped to her knees again and placed her ear as close to the side of his face as she could manage, but either the latex head mask was blotting out too much sound, or...

Standing up she kicked him again, much harder this time, but with the same lack of result. Puzzled, she scratched her head, but stopped when one of the claws dug into her.

She turned slowly, her gaze travelling around the trees and bushes, looking for inspiration as much as anything else. But everything still seemed as it had appeared before the now lifeless form at her feet had first appeared.

The mysteriously materialising portal led into another chamber, a little larger than the one in which Clarissa had first arrived. But unlike the first, this room was cluttered with a bewildering array of racks, stands and chests, and immediately upon entering Clarissa's senses were filled with the now familiar aromas of rubber and leather. Alma and Tara lost no time in getting things started.

'Please raise your arms, mistress,' Tara said, as her companion lifted a complicated looking piece of leatherwear from the nearest rail. Clarissa eyed the thing suspiciously. Alma held it out for inspection.

'It is part of your armour,' she said. 'You must be dressed correctly, as must your opponent. It is the rules.'

'Fuck the rules,' Clarissa growled. 'That thing doesn't look that much different from the bloody harness contraption that spiky bitch had me in before.'

'But it is to protect your vital organs,' Tara persisted. She placed a hand against her own side, moving it about and then across her stomach. 'Liver, kidneys, the solar plexus - the leather is thick and stiff and will deflect much force.'

'And your opponent will be wearing the same,' Alma intoned, as if that were the end of any possible argument. Clarissa hesitated, considering the situation. It could easily be a trick, she knew. But then given what she understood of this VESTA world, there was no need for the blonde dyke to resort to such measures. If she wanted Clarissa to wear this paraphernalia for any reasons other than those currently being given, it surely would have been a simple enough matter to have her wake up already attired.

So why, she asked herself, whatever the reasons anyway, was it necessary to go through this rigmarole, this ritual?

Ritual?

Yes, that was it. The ritual, that all-important aspect of all human sexuality, whatever the proclivity or preference involved, was always paramount, an integral part of it and, in some cases, the major part of it, more important than the final act itself. In all probability, the Christina woman was somehow tuned in to this scene, watching, enjoying, probably controlling it overall.

Just observing, slut. The programme is self-generating now and, for the moment at least, will react to you.

'Where are you?' The voice seemed at once inside and outside of Clarissa's head, though neither of the attendants seemed to have heard it and nor did they show any reaction to this last question. In fact, as she turned her head from side to side, trying to identify the source, Clarissa saw that Tara and Alma had frozen like statues, just a flickering aura about them in the manner of a video player on freeze frame.

At the moment I am out here, simply monitoring and waiting.

'Bitch! Have the bottle to come in here and face me!'

All in good time, slut! You'll have plenty of opportunity to regret it when I do. Meanwhile, let me explain.

You should understand that you are now inside VESTA, although, more accurately, VESTA is inside you, inside your head, as it is inside the head of everyone who enters it. But no matter. Enough of semantics.

What is important is that I intend to give you the chance to meet me face-to-face as you appeared to desire and, furthermore, I am prepared to concede certain of my natural physical advantages, to make the contest more interesting.

To that end and to all intents and purposes we shall start equal - equal stature, equal weight, equal armour and identical resources, as you shall see shortly.

'Why should I believe you?' Clarissa demanded. She heard a hollow laugh.

What alternative is there? Should I just return you as you were, my little pony bitch, put you in the stables with your bit and harness and trot and whip you once a day? That will come soon enough, believe me, so what have you to lose in the meantime?

'And what happens if I beat you?'

Again the laugh.

You won't.

'Just supposing I did. Will you free me? And Marlon?'

More laughter.

I could hardly do that, could I? I think maybe you know too much for that to be a feasible option.

'Then why should I play along with your games?'

My games? Need I remind you that it was you who issued this challenge? I need not have given you even this opportunity.

'So why have you?'

Because it amuses me - and appeals to me. Now, have you changed your mind? If you like you can join the other slut here for a while, as the sort of pony girl I cannot yet create outside VESTA. See for yourself. Look!

Clarissa saw, as the rest of the room faded out around her and she was suddenly looking into a swirling mirror, to where a lone figure stood before a curious cart affair, stooped, beaten, humiliated, the traces laying across her supine back, bit and bells buckled tightly to the rigid harness, dull eyes staring ahead over a...

'No!' The picture faded and the room came back. 'No, I'll fight you, you twisted shit! But if you're that bloody confident there should be something more in it for me. C'mon, blondie, put your money where your mouth is!'

Very well, let me think. Ah yes, I have it. Should you beat me, then I will allow you and your brother to remain here as prisoners in the manner that aristocrats and royalty were prisoners centuries ago. In other words, although you will still be prisoners, you will be given comfortable quarters and left largely without interference.

'Is that the best you can do?' It was something at least, Clarissa thought. But she was prepared to try for more while the opportunity existed.

Take it or leave it. You are hardly in a position to bargain. Besides, you will not win.

'Because you've fixed it?'

Not at all. There would be no satisfaction in that. I shall rely on my training and experience, plus the strength of my inner self. Now, let the ladies prepare you and remember, everything they give you I shall also have. There will be no tricks.

There was no actual sound, but Clarissa felt as if there had been an audible click, as if a switch had been thrown and she knew that Christina had gone again. Before her the two attendants were animated again.

'Please, mistress,' Alma said, holding the leather garment out again. 'If you would raise your arms.' With a sigh Clarissa complied and the girl stepped closer, wrapping the main section around her middle, hooking something at the rear to hold it temporarily in place.

Meantime, Tara had stepped behind her and quickly began fastening the heavy straps and buckles that not only effected a more permanent fit, but also drew the leather hourglass inexorably tight, drawing in Clarissa's waist to a seemingly impossible degree. However, to her astonishment although it felt constricting, it was not especially painful, nor did she have any trouble with her breathing, as she knew she would have done outside of this world.

As the two women fussed with the adjustments, Clarissa considered this and came to a rapid conclusion. This VESTA world might seem realistic, but it was only based on reality and anything that might have proved inconvenient in the real world was carefully doctored here, so that fantasies could be enacted to the full without the restrictions that normal human frailties might have imposed. That was an interesting concept, she thought, and carefully filed it away for future reference.

However, not every inconvenience had been removed, as Clarissa discovered when she made to move, for the tight bodice precluded any chance of her bending at the waist, regardless of how little it impeded her respiration. Evidently the removal of the human frailty factor was a selective business.

Having secured the corset-like section of the garment, which left Clarissa's breasts bared but supported with two narrow sections that came somewhat short of quarter cup dimensions, a baffling series of straps and cuffs followed, which Clarissa suspected might have proved a lot more difficult to sort out in any other existence. Her two attendants, though, moving like the automatons they so very nearly were, handled the intricate harness without hesitation.

Long straps were passed over Clarissa's shoulders, crossed between her shoulder blades and drawn tightly to the top of the main corset at the rear. Where these straps passed over the shoulders, smaller, very short tags were affixed at right angles. These in turn were attached to a stiff collar, beset with wicked-looking two inch spikes, that encircled Clarissa's neck and fastened at the nape with a sharp click of some sort of locking mechanism.

Lower down at the front, the long straps also supported a web of thinner straps that were designed to fit around her breasts, tightening to mould them into an elongated and exaggerated profile that forced her nipples through heavy steel rings positioned strategically for that purpose.

The remainder of Clarissa's upper 'armour' followed swiftly; stiff shoulder length gloves that laced to fit every contour and, in doing so, efficiently deprived the elbow joints of all but the merest flexibility and the fingers of most of their normal dexterity. When Clarissa pointed this out, the two women merely nodded and assured her that Christina would be handicapped identically.

'What's the point?' She shook her head. 'Why not just scrap it out naked?' They looked at her uncomprehendingly.

'It is not done that way,' Tara said, and Alma nodded her agreement. Clarissa sighed, her caged breasts rising and falling in exaggerated fashion.

'I always thought I was a screwy cow,' she said, 'but this crowd take the bloody blue riband.'

Her comments were wasted on her companions, who continued with their task in silence, now producing long boots that were similar in design to their own, but with one notable difference. She was not to know it, but the ballerina styled footwear was identical in concept to that being worn by another unfortunate inmate of the painworld, although Susie's extended only as far as mid-calf.

Like Susie, however, Clarissa found she could stand and move about in the steepling boots with only a minor degree of difficulty, a feat she knew she could never hope to emulate under more worldly circumstances. She stared down at herself with some difficulty, the high collar preventing her from lowering her chin more than a few millimetres, marvelling at how the boots made her legs seem endless.

'Y'know,' she said, as much to herself as to the two women, 'there are certain things here I could almost get to appreciate, if only the place wasn't crawling with so many weirdoes. Hey, what now?'

She had been so engrossed in admiring her lower limbs that Alma and Tara had taken her completely off guard with their next move, grasping her gloved arms and snapping spring links between rings set inside the elbows and the top hem of the main corset. Now Clarissa was deprived of yet more use of those limbs.

She could still use her lower arms, though raising them more than a few inches was still rendered impossible by the tightness of the leather in which they were sheathed, but there was no way in which she could reach with either hand to release the opposite elbow.

'How'm I supposed to have a bloody fight like this?' she protested, demonstrating the effectiveness of this latest bondage. The two women gave her identically wan smiles.

'You will see, when the time comes,' Tara said, simply. 'The rules will be explained. But now we must shave your hair.'

'What?' Clarissa screeched, stumbling back as she pulled away from them. 'You're not touching my bloody hair and that's final!' They regarded her impassively, not making the expected move on her, and then Clarissa realised. Proud as she was of her unruly mane of red hair, losing it here meant nothing, for afterwards when it was all over her real body, which doubtless still lay in the pod contraption where they had earlier strapped her, would remain untouched.

'Oh shit!' she said, a grin forcing itself onto her face. 'Go ahead then, do your worst. I suppose it let's out hair-pulling as well as scratching, so it'll be a decent scrap.'

They performed the task swiftly and expertly, using manual clippers and shearing her locks to within a quarter of an inch of her scalp. After so many years it felt curious to be without her heavy tresses, and she wondered why the likes of Christina apparently preferred to go through their lives like this.

'Are we through now?' she asked, as the two of them collected up the fallen hair and placed it reverently in a neat pile on one of the chests against the wall. Clarissa wondered why they were bothering; after all, it wasn't real, was it? Unconsciously, she pressed her gloved hands into the naked flesh above the tops of her boots. But it felt real enough.

'We have to fit you with your weapons now and then your mask,' Alma said. She lifted something from the adjacent chest and brought it towards Clarissa, who stared at it in disbelief.

'What the fucking hell is that?' she demanded. It looked like another glove, though only designed to fit as far as the wrist. But it was like no glove Clarissa had ever seen, nor even imagined, for each finger tapered into a gleaming, claw-like chrome fingernail, honed to a razor-sharp tip that could almost certainly slice through flesh like a butcher's knife through a Sunday roast.

'It fits over your left hand,' Alma said, unmoved. 'There is a whip for the other hand.'

Stunned, Clarissa stood rooted while the claw glove was fitted to her and buckled securely in position and waited similarly while her other hand was dealt with in the same fashion. Except this time there were no nails, simply the stubby handle of a whip stitched to the leather in such a way that it required no holding, yet suddenly Clarissa discovered she could once again clench her fingers, which seemed to grasp the shaft of their own volition.

She tried to release her grip again and was only half surprised when she discovered she could not. Experimentally, she flexed her left hand, the claws gleaming menacingly under the lights.

'Jeez!' she breathed. 'Am I glad this isn't for real.'

Real enough. You'll feel every cut of my whip and every slice of my claws, when the time comes.

'But will you feel mine?'

Oh yes, if you're as good as you seem to think you are.

'How do I know you're playing this straight?' Clarissa demanded, but once again the contact had been broken. She raised her right hand as far as the restrictive gloves and elbow links would permit and studied the whip properly for the first time, letting out a low whistle as she took in the multiple braided thongs, their tips set with what appeared to be small pellets of lead. It was a fearsome instrument, designed to inflict damage as well as pain on an opponent, an opponent who would be equipped with an identical whip and who would have no compunction about exploiting its awful potential.

For the first time Clarissa began to have serious doubts about the coming contest, but she thrust them aside, determined not to give the dyke woman the satisfaction of hearing her cry off. Besides, she reasoned, none of this was real and no permanent harm could come to anyone inside VESTA - that much she had learned from her captors.

'Ye gods!' she exclaimed when she saw the next item Alma produced, and then burst out laughing, despite herself. 'You want to fit me with a bloody cock!' She stared at the huge appendage that rose from the middle of the collection of straps that Alma was deftly shaking out, gaping at the thought of being impaled on such a monstrous appendage.

'What am I supposed to do with that? It better hadn't be going inside me,' she added. 'That'd rip me apart.'

'No, it goes outside,' Tara assured her. 'You're supposed to put it inside your opponent.'

'What? I'm not a fucking lezzie!'

'If you can,' Alma added, ignoring her. 'It's how you win,' she went on. 'Once your opponent is penetrated she cannot fight on and you must finish her while she lays helpless.'

'Even if I managed it,' Clarissa retorted, 'I can't see that big bitch laying down all helpless like and just letting me fuck her.'

'There will be no choice,' Tara replied, enigmatically. 'It is the way.'

'But if we're both wearing those things, how the hell - oh, I see,' she finished, as Alma presented the harness to her loins. She saw the things had been cunningly designed so that, whilst the straps held the massive shaft like an erection before her, they were cut away and adjusted so that her denuded sex was left open and unprotected, an easy target for Christina's own phallus.

Clarissa shook her head. 'This gets worse and worse,' she grunted, as the straps were pulled tightly about her. 'Me and my big mouth. Why didn't I just shut up and ride it out. Someone's bound to find us eventually.'

Eventually could be a long time, but I shouldn't even count on that ever happening.

'Back again? Well, let me tell you, no one ever gets away with anything forever. They'll be onto you in the end.'

Don't hold your breath, slut. Save it for something worthwhile.
'Bitch!'
You better believe that!

Slowly Susie dissolved, the personality that had established the total lack of control of Paul's female virtual body beginning to fade back almost as soon as Dolores and her two henchmen departed, leaving the ballet-toed form lying limply on the floor in the centre of the halo created by the spotlights overhead.

Susie's bondage, however, remained, as did all her exaggerated femininity, and Paul lay motionless, eyes screwed tightly closed, unwilling and unable to look at the evidence of what he had been reduced to.

'Very fetching.' The voice cut through his befuddled thoughts, his eyes opening wide as he recognised the accented tone. Rolling further onto his side, he stared up at the towering blonde figure.

'You!' he gasped, wishing his arms were free of the cramping pouch at his back. Christina laughed, but without real mirth.

'I'm touched to see you haven't forgotten me,' she sneered. She extended one booted foot and pressed it against his naked left breast. 'Suits you,' she said, deliberately making the fleshy globe wobble beneath her sole. 'And no male bits either, I see. Let's have a closer look.'

She kicked him onto his back and, still using her boot, forced his thighs apart, exposing the evidence of his virtual feminisation.

'Inviting,' she said, her tongue tracing a track across her upper lip, 'but plenty of time for such things later - plenty of time.'

'What do you want?' Paul croaked, staring up at her through saucer-like eyes. 'How did you get here...?'

I got here,' Christina said, stepping back, 'the same way you did, through Marlon's clever little boxes of tricks. However, unlike you, I was not prepared to trust myself to one of his so-called "passive" portals. No, I am here via one of the active portals, which gives me control over you and your friends in the same way that we have now taken over control of VESTA in its entirety.'

'But how?'

'Oh, you don't need to know the details,' Christina said, 'just that we do have absolute control now, not only of the machine, but of the building in which it stands and the entire estate around it. Your old friend, Mr Naylor, went to a lot of trouble to see to it.'

'What about the others?'

Christina raised her eyebrows. 'By that, I assume you're referring to your little girlfriend, the blonde slut who showed such scant respect for my hospitality at our last meeting,' she said. 'Well, she is safe and secure, I can assure you - very secure as it happens, and you shall see her in time, though not just yet.'

'What are you going to do to us?' Paul said, wishing his voice would return to its usual male sound.

Again the eyebrows went up. 'Anything that takes my fancy, I expect,' Christina said. She aimed an idle kick at his right boot, but the contact was not heavy, simply a symbol of her power over him.

'I've already done plenty,' she continued. 'For instance, it was my idea to create those two studs and have them screw your pretty brains out, though I didn't expect you to enjoy it quite as much as it appeared you did. I must say that was quite a floorshow. Oh yes, I was watching the whole thing. Quite the slut, little Susie, aren't you?'

'You're warped!' Paul cried, but turned his face away from her steely eyes.

Christina shrugged. 'I am constantly amazed at how you people keep accusing me of being warped, sick and many other things, and yet here you are...' She paused to let her words sink in. 'Was it my idea for you to come in here as a big-titted whore, eh? No, I don't think so. That was already underway before I was able to take a hand - an extension of your little secret longings, I believe - and then I merely took things to what I assumed would be a natural conclusion. If you take on the body of a slut, you must expect to take on everything else that goes with it.

'The same goes for your subservient little girlfriend, except I'm not so sure she likes it now she's found out once more what it's really like to be helpless and completely under the control of someone else.'

'Hardly surprising when that someone else is you,' Paul pouted. The facial expression was not missed by Christina.

'Oh, how delightfully pretty you are when you sulk, Susie dear,' she taunted. 'And such a pretty mouth, too. We shall have to find other uses for those full lips, though. It would be a shame to waste them on such sullen expressions.'

'I reckons you should be just about ready for a damned good tupping now,' William said, unfastening the last of the straps that kept Lianne bent over the shaft of the cart. He lowered it and the attached dildo slipped easily from her. Lianne stood motionless, unable to look down, though she would not have done so even had she been able, for she did not need reminding of the evidence of her surrender.

'C'mon, pretty Amber,' William said, grasping the reins and flicking them to encourage Lianne forward. 'You can come upright now.' Unresisting, she allowed herself to be led back into the stables, her shod hooves clattering her shame as they reached the hard flagstone surface, her bells and chains rattling at every step.

'Seems they don't need you for a bit yet,' William said, guiding her towards the curious frame that now sat between the facing double row of stalls, 'so you and me got plenty of time to get proper aquatinted, like, 'specially now you're a proper filly.' He shortened the reins until he was holding them in his fist just a few inches from Lianne's elongated face, and stared into her eyes.

'See, I can't be doing with gals that gives 'emselves airs and graces,' he said. 'Me bein' only a country boy, they don't wanna know, see. No, they don't fancy shaggin' the likes of poor William, that'd never do, would it? But my ponies, now that's different, innit?

'My ponies gets to be dead grateful, 'cause if they shows me a bit of love an' affection, then I shows it back. Y'see, Amber, I kin make things a lot easier for you around here,' he continued. 'Or a lot worse,' he added, grinning unevenly. 'D'y'unnerstand that, horsy gal?'

Miserably, Lianne nodded, for William had left little room for misinterpretation. She looked at him through heavily lidded eyes, wondering what was so fascinating about a girl whose face looked like a horse's, and then she remembered. This wasn't the real world, after all, just something that had been created - was still being created - by an inanimate machine that was trawling between the heights and depths of all human sexual experience. She shuddered, setting her bells and brasses to tinkling once again.

'Now, I'm gonna take the bit out of yer mouth,' William said, reaching out to detach the necessary clips, 'and then you gonna use that tongue of yours just exactly like I shows you. An' don' you go gerrin' any silly ideas about using them teeth of yours, pony girl, else I'll have the vet pull 'em all and afterwards I'll take the crop to yer rump like there's no tomorrow.'

Except, Lianne reflected forlornly, as the bit came away and she allowed herself to be forced down onto her knees, there would be a tomorrow. And another tomorrow and the day after that and the day after that...

Nadia was beginning to get worried - seriously worried, and was also angry with herself that she had not realised earlier that something was wrong. And now that the 'safe' phrase was refusing to have the desired effect she had no idea of what she should do next.

She tried to console herself with the thought that it was probably only a temporary hitch. Marlon would soon realise something in VESTA appeared to be failing to make the desired connections and either put it to rights, or else just pull her out of the virtual world while he sorted the problem. After all, she reasoned, in reality he was only a few feet away from all of them, operating and monitoring his master console in the same room where Nadia's 'sleeping' physical body lay in its pod.

Damn it, she thought fiercely. At first it had all seemed to be going so splendidly, even better than her first experience inside VESTA, for this time she was in control, which was generally how Nadia liked her world. She furrowed her brow and tried to think back.

How long ago had it been? One hour? Two? Five? Marlon had warned them all that time inside VESTA might not always coincide with time in the outside world, and that a scenario that appeared to have filled ten hours inside might turn out to have occupied only two hours of the outside world's clock. So maybe she'd only been in here less than half an hour, in which case it might still be a while before she could reasonably expect Marlon to discover they had a problem.

She strode across the empty chamber, heels clacking hollowly, perched herself on the narrow bench that ran the length of the far wall, and tried to clear her mind of all thoughts save the safe phrase; perhaps it required more concentration than she had been led to believe.

'Bag and baggage,' she said out loud, enunciating the three words very carefully. Nothing. She tried again, speaking much faster, but the result was the same. Automatically, she lifted her left wrist, but of course, even in the real world she never wore her watch when in costume.

'Shit!' she hissed, standing up again. She walked over to the blank door and tried the handle for the fifth time in as many minutes, but still it refused to budge. She swore again and tried to remember where and when it was that events had started to go wrong...

Resplendent in her high boots, catsuit and studded collar, switch grasped in her gloved right hand, Nadia opened the door and entered the larger chamber, not in the least surprised to see the circle of spotlights illuminating the area at the far end of the space, nor the three figures kneeling, heads bowed, hands behind their backs.

One male and two females, she saw as she approached - a good balance for most circumstances and a good mix of ages, for the male was somewhere in his early thirties and the females were aged about five years older and ten years younger respectively. All had golden yellow hair and lightly tanned skins, which contrasted beautifully with the crimson leather of their bondage.

All were secured identically, broad collars about their necks, their arms secured high up their backs by means of leather mittens that tapered into D-rings that were, in turn, locked to the backs of their collars. Their feet were clad in matching strappy sandals, all with heels, though those of the male were much lower and chunkier than the needle thin points upon which the females would have to balance when Nadia ordered them to stand again.

Apart from their footwear and their bondage, all three were naked, their bodies clean shaven and lightly oiled, so that they glinted and shimmered beneath the slowly changing coloured lights. Nadia nodded and grinned to herself, wondering if any of them were connected to the real people outside, or if they were just VESTA creations.

She stopped short of them, slapped the switch against her right boot and ordered them to their feet. They obeyed with a languid grace and turned upon her next command to stand facing her. She studied their features, but the result was inconclusive: the younger girl could have been related to Lianne and the older woman bore a vague resemblance to the girl Lianne had replaced a year or so earlier. But the similarities were very superficial and the heavy eye makeup and mascara that both wore had an almost cloning effect in many ways.

Even the male had a bland face - attractive enough, but as though a machine had taken all the acceptably handsome or attractive attributes and blended them in a mixer; which was, Nadia reflected, precisely how VESTA was programmed to work.

'Names!' she snapped, slapping her boot again and raising the switch to point it to the older woman, who stood on the left of the line. Dull-eyed, she replied.

'Gina, mistress.'

'Troy, mistress.'

'Becky, mistress.'

Nadia nodded, running her eyes up and down each figure in turn. Both females were long-legged and had firm high breasts, the older, Gina slightly wider hipped and heavier limbed, whilst Troy's body was muscular without being overly so, with an exaggeratedly slim waist and almost girlish hips, an impression immediately countered by the size of his thighs. He also boasted a rigid erection and Nadia shook her head at this.

'No, Marlon,' she whispered, wondering if he could hear her, or whether her words would be recorded somewhere for later analysis. 'It's too bloody blatant.' She decided to experiment.

'Can you get rid of that?' she demanded, flicking the switch at the bulbous head of his stiff organ. Troy looked baffled.

'Get rid of it, mistress?'

Nadia sighed. 'No, maybe not,' she conceded. 'Oh well, that's one job you two sluts have been saved.' It was not going as she would have liked; slaves, after all, were supposed to be more cowed and scared, whereas this trio were too docile and accepting. She decided to try something different.

Behind the three of them, at the far edge of the circle of light, stood a simple whipping horse, four legged, padded top and cuffs waiting for wrists and ankles. The legs appeared to be adjustable and Nadia immediately saw some potential.

'You,' she said, indicating Gina. 'Get over there, against the horse. No,' she cried, as the woman tried to drape herself face down over it, 'facing away from it, standing at one end. Right, wait there. You, Becky,' she said, crooking a finger for the younger girl to approach her. 'Turn around and let's get these things off you.' Using the key that hung from her belt she released the locks on the girl's mittens, drew her arms to the front of her and released her right hand from the leather pouch completely, before passing her the switch.

'Just keep hold of that,' Nadia said. For a second or so the girl looked almost confused, but the blank expression returned almost immediately. 'Now, let's see to you first,' Nadia said, striding across to Gina.

'Enjoying your new lifestyle, slut?' Lianne looked up miserably from the narrow trough at the front of her stall, a trough which she kept feeling compelled to drink from, even though reason told her she should not - could not - feel thirsty here.

Christina towered over her, their height difference emphasised by the fact that Lianne could no longer stand upright, the taut leather lines from the thick collar down to her ankles forcing her to remain in a stooped position.

'Not so much to say for yourself nowadays, have you?' Christina sneered. She reached out and grasped the ring that held the left-hand side of Lianne's bit and twisted her head over viciously. 'Maybe I'll get Koenig to let you have a working tongue again, at least for a while,' she grated. 'I think I'd like to hear you beg now and then.

'Meantime,' she continued, dragging Lianne sideways along the front barrier until she was level with the stall gate, 'maybe a few whinnies and neighs will have to suffice. Out here, pony bitch!' She released the gate catch and hauled Lianne out into the central concourse.

'I think you've had enough rest for the moment,' she said, turning the hapless girl towards the outer door, 'and ponies get lazy if they're not exercised regularly. Of course this,' she said, suddenly reaching down between Lianne's legs and grasping her bare mound in one large hand, 'has had plenty of exercise. We made sure of that with William. He's a big lad, isn't he?'

She broke the rough contact and jerked hard on the bridle harness again, almost sending Lianne headlong, but steadied her again with another tug before setting her towards the paddock outside.

The sun did not appear to be any lower than when William had last taken Lianne inside, but now there were a few changes in the way the small field was set out. In the centre stood a tall pole, a sturdy timber of perhaps four inches in diameter and some ten feet tall. Near its top, Lianne saw, a thick iron collar had been nailed around its circumference and this held up a heavy metal ring, from which dangled a long slender chain.

The pole formed the centre of a circle of short stakes, the radius of which was a good thirty metres and around this circle, at intervals of no more than ten metres, was set a series of low fences, obstacles ranging from simple grass banks to more complex structures of twigs and leaves, including one which had on its one side a narrow trench filled with water. It did not take Lianne very long to understand the significance of all this.

'Your training circuit,' Christina said, as if reading her thoughts. 'Of course, most of the time there will be either William or one of the new stable girls I'm working on, but I thought I'd like to make the introductions in person. Friend James likes to think he can conquer whole worlds, but I prefer the personal touch. Now, stand!'

She brought Lianne to a halt between two of the fences, facing in a clockwise direction, and stepped through the perimeter stakes to walk over to the high central pole. Stooping, she gathered up the coils of chain that lay at its foot and began making her way back, paying out the links as she came. By the time she stood before Lianne once again, she had reached its limit and clipped the spring catch from the final link to the ring at the right side of Lianne's bit.

'Just in case you get any thoughts about wandering off,' she laughed. 'Of course, I'll stay with you for a while - it would be too much not to take the opportunity of whipping this delightful rump you now have.' She slapped Lianne hard across the buttocks to underline her point. 'However, I do have other calls upon my time, so I'll be forced to leave you from time to time.

'But that will not mean you can slack off in my absence. Of course, VESTA's memory banks could monitor your efforts anyway, but I have thought of something even better, something you can see for yourself. Look!' She jerked a forefinger towards the first obstacle, a low brush fence.

'On the far side of that is a wooden plate on which you will have to land. Every time you do, the counter there...' she pointed to a small shed-like structure that stood alongside the fence on the inside of the stake perimeter and Lianne saw there was a round aperture, through which a painted figure zero was visible '...will advance by one.

'For every hour I am absent, I shall expect to see an average of thirty circuits recorded there and for every circuit under that, you will receive a dozen lashes with a weighted whip. You will only stop when instructed either by myself, or by William. And I tell you now, William will appear within minutes of you failing to

106

maintain your targets.

'Of course,' she said, looking down at Lianne's legs, 'you cannot sensibly be expected to jump even these little fences like that; those tethers will only snag your ankles. So, we must first change them.'

To one side stood a small cart, a tarpaulin covering it, and from this Christina produced another set of straps and chains. Before removing the ankle to collar set, however, she began putting these in position to take their place.

The two cuff sections were designed to fit about the thighs, more like sleeves than cuffs, lacing tightly to compress the muscles so there was no danger of them slipping below the knees. From their lower edge, thin chains extended to clip to the same collar ring that held the tethers from the ankles and these Christina now exchanged, thus ensuring that Lianne maintained her stooped posture without giving her the chance to straighten up, even for a few seconds.

'That's much better,' Christina pronounced, finally removing the ankle cuffs themselves and coiling the chains in her hands. 'And now, off you go my little pony. Plenty of time for mindless exercise, plenty of time to reflect upon your sins. Just think, poor little Amber, you'll be spending the rest of your life like this, running, jumping, dancing to the whip and having your hot little cunt serviced by anyone who fancies it.

'I think you'll actually be something of a net asset to friend Naylor's overall operation, but meantime, pony girl slut, just remember you're my filly from now on and when I tell you to jump, all you think of is how high. So - jump!'

Without warning she lashed out with the coiled chains, which bit deeply into Lianne's taut flesh, sending her stumbling forward on her awkward hooves so that she was forced to break into a trot in order to keep her balance, her arms still being pinioned uselessly to her sides.

Within a few short, faltering strides, she was at the first fence and had no option but to jump over it, barely clearing the top with an awkward half hop. Behind her she heard Christina break into a guffaw of delighted laughter, but already, with the second fence looming ahead, she was forced to concentrate on things nearer at hand.

Even before she had realised that something was wrong, Nadia was beginning to think Marlon still had quite a lot of work to do before VESTA would meet the standards she was seeking. True, the surroundings were realistic in every detail and the characters were indistinguishable from real people in every way, except that perhaps there was one way in which they differed, and that was the all-important one, so far as she was concerned.

All three of her current 'victims', whilst presenting a variety of choice that opened up any number of possible combinations, lacked one vital element - spirit. In the real world, Nadia knew only too well, even the best trained and most docile submissive would at least betray some sort of reluctance, whereas this trio did exactly what she told them and the chains and cuffs, let alone Nadia's switch, were totally surplus to requirements.

There probably were dominants who would welcome such passivity, she thought, but as yet Nadia was still to meet them and certainly she could not think of a single one of her current extensive client list who would not pick up on this and probably complain vehemently about it. Still, she reflected, these were still early days and Marlon had explained that these scenarios worked better when the characters in opposition were all hooked into real 'players'.

'You three are pathetic,' Nadia said, smiling sadly at her charges. 'Not an ounce of go in any you.'

She had already fastened Gina over one end of the whipping horse, face up, her arms linked beneath the padded top with a length of fine chain, her ankles cuffed to the two supporting legs so that her thighs were widespread and her shaven sex gaped open. Troy had then been led forward, arms still cuffed behind his back, erection bobbing obscenely before him, and Nadia had released Becky's wrists and given her instructions, passing her the switch as she did so.

The younger girl had obediently stepped up, grasped Troy's burgeoning shaft and pulled it towards Gina's waiting sex, positioning the head between the glistening lips and then pushing against his buttocks so that he entered her. Then, stepping back and to the side, she had brought the leather braids whistling around in an arc, so that as they slashed across his firm buttocks, he thrust in and out of her in an involuntary lunging action, a sharp gasp accompanying his reaction.

Again the switch rose and fell, but Nadia shook her head and held up her hand.

'No, no, no!' she cried. Becky stopped, but did not turn to face her and Nadia let out a deep sigh of frustration.

'Can't you at least try to put something into this?' she said, at the same time aware that she was addressing what were only electronic images, but hoping her intervention might trigger some response deep within VESTA's data banks. She decided that maybe it was best to lead by example.

'Troy,' she ordered, 'pull out of her and turn around.' With calm deliberation, Troy withdrew and pivoted to face her, his organ still glistening from Gina's juices. VESTA had got that much right, at least. She reached down and swiftly detached the studs that held the triangular leather crotch piece over her own sex.

'Stand still,' she said, and moved up to him, raising herself even taller on her toes, gripping his penis and straddling it. 'Now,' she said, as she sank down over his length, pleasantly surprised by the pure physical contact, 'this is what I mean by putting something into it.'

Gripping his shoulders she swung her legs up and around, crossing them behind the small of his back, and quickly began to raise and lower herself on him, astonished at how good it felt.

'Now,' she breathed, 'this is more like - oh shit!' She swung her legs back around and dropped her feet to the floor, lifted herself clear of him and stepped back, slapping him hard across the face as she did so. He flinched and his cheek reddened immediately, but he scarcely took a backward step.

'This is a waste of time,' Nadia rasped. 'I'd be better employed seeing how some of the others are getting on and I just hope they're having better luck than I am. Now, what's the phrase? Oh yes.'

She uttered the failsafe words and waited. Nothing happened.

'Bag and baggage,' she repeated. There was a slight shimmering in the air and the image of Troy blinked out, but Nadia remained in the room with the two women. She tried again. This time the women dematerialised, but everything else remained the same. A third try brought no further change, so Nadia turned back towards the door, hand extended towards the handle. It turned, but the door itself refused to open.

'Bag and baggage!' Nadia shouted, but to no avail, and that was when she began to realise that something might be seriously wrong.

'I hope this so-called problem isn't going to cause any serious delays,' Christina said. Jurgen Koenig smiled and shook his head.

'No problem at all,' he assured her. 'I was just telling Mr Naylor all about it. What appears to have happened is that a small executive file somewhere has crashed and that has caused some minor malfunctions to a couple of the terminal ports, that is all.'

'Who's connected to the ports in question?' Naylor asked, his eyes narrowing. 'It wouldn't be our little genius friend, by any chance?'

'No,' Koenig assured him. 'His port is functioning normally. I believe he is currently spending his time hanging in an isolation suit - based on your original design, I believe?' he added, turning back to Christina.

'He was when I last looked in on his circuit,' Christina confirmed. 'I have a few other ideas for him, but they will have to wait. Right at the moment I have other more pressing matters to deal with. So who are the two?'

'Ah - Miss Muirhead and the Sanderson girl.'

'And they don't present any sort of threat?' Christina demanded, suspiciously. Koenig waved his hands in the air.

'Threat? What threat could they possible pose? They cannot disconnect themselves from the complex, neither are they on ports that could in any way be made active. In the meantime, I'm afraid they may become a little bored, as VESTA is unable to input any new data into their particular scenarios.'

'So, you didn't finish telling me what you were doing about these faults,' Naylor said. 'I presume you don't just intend to sit back and do nothing?'

The German smiled. 'For the moment,' he replied, 'that is precisely all I can do. You see, this VESTA is a very complicated lady, as indeed is the brain of her creator, and he is even better than I anticipated. The system is almost foolproof and, if I wore a hat, I should take it off to him.

'VESTA is possessed of her very own fault diagnosing and correcting programmes. If I were to interfere at the present time I should risk crashing the entire system.'

'You mean the bloody computer fixes itself?' Naylor said, eyes opening wider.

Koenig nodded. 'Mostly, yes,' he said.

'And if this isn't a "mostly" situation?' Christina interjected. For a second or so, Koenig appeared confused by this, but then his English grasped her meaning.

'Ah, I see,' he said. 'Well, if VESTA cannot cure her own ills, then naturally I shall take over and sort out the glitches, but I have a feeling it will not come to that.'

'How long before you'll know, either way?' Naylor said.

'Difficult to be as precise as I should like,' Koenig admitted. 'It is possible, you see, that the diagnostics and repair packages will find the faults within a matter of minutes, but it is also possible that they will have to run through their full repertoire of tricks. In some ways, it is almost a matter of luck.'

'I thought computers didn't rely on such human weaknesses as emotions and luck?' Naylor snapped. The German shook his head again.

'As such,' he agreed, 'they do not. However, we mere mortals who are responsible for their initial programming are not fortune-tellers and even the little Marlon has to trust to his instincts concerning the way in which he structured these packages. Of course, logic dictates a certain running order, but as I have said, this is not a pocket calculator we are dealing with here and, since the original programming, VESTA has been adding things at a rate well beyond any human ability to keep pace with.'

'But if this machine is so bloody perfect and powerful,' Christina pointed out, 'how come it's developed a fault in the first place?'

'That, my dear lady,' Koenig said, patiently, 'is the way of these things. I could sit here all day and bore you to sleep with theories and explanations, but I fear you would be little wiser for the tedium of the experience and I say that without intending any insult upon your undoubted intelligence. Suffice it to say that, as the English say, these things will happen and are sent to try us.'

'But it can be fixed, one way or the other?' Naylor said.

'Oh yes,' Koenig confirmed. 'The very worse scenario would mean two ports down for maybe twelve to fifteen hours, and that is only if VESTA does not heal herself, as it were.'

'What about the rest of the system?' Christina demanded. 'I have plans that I would rather not postpone.'

'The remainder of the system is functioning perfectly,' Koenig replied. 'I have run extensive checks.'

'And what if something else goes wrong, while we're all in there?' Christina suggested. Naylor looked round at her.

'All of us in there?' he echoed. 'Who said anything about all of us being in there?'

'I assumed,' Christina said blandly, 'that you would all like to watch my little show with the firebrand artist?'

'But it would be risky if we were all under and something else went wrong,' Naylor pointed out. 'Then we'd all be stuck.'

'Not at all,' Koenig said confidently. 'If any of the active portals become corrupted they immediately deactivate and the subject regains consciousness. In fact, the same would happen with the passive portals after two hours, but I have over-ridden that facility in the case of our two current subjects. I assumed it would be less troublesome to leave them safely in their limbo for the time being.'

'It would,' Naylor agreed. 'But I'm still not sure...'

'And I should not want any of you to miss out on this,' Christina said firmly. 'There are still two spare portals, apart from the one I've been using, and both are designated as active at the moment, so what are you worrying about? You wouldn't be just a little scared, would you?'

'Not scared,' Naylor growled, 'just careful.' He paused, thinking. 'So, what's so special about this little side-show of yours? Still keen to give this slag an even break?'

'Let us just say more even than if we met out here in the real world,' Christina replied. 'Jurgen here has carried out a few adjustments at my request, so the loudmouthed Australian girl and I will be of equal physical stature and dressed and equipped in identical fashion. Beyond that, she certainly has none of my training and experience.'

'So you're confident of winning?'

'Totally, as I told you before. But it will make the fight far more interesting,' Christina added, turning towards the door. 'Far more interesting indeed.'

Even before she had realised that something was wrong, Nadia was beginning to think Marlon still had quite a lot of work to do before VESTA would meet the standards she was seeking. True, the surroundings were realistic in every detail and the characters were indistinguishable from real people in every way, except that perhaps there was one way in which they differed and that was the all-important one, so far as she was concerned.

All three of her current "victims", whilst presenting a variety of choice that opened up any number of possible combinations, lacked one vital element - spirit. In the real world, Nadia knew only too well, even the best trained and most docile submissive would at least betray some sort of reluctance, whereas this trio did exactly what she told them and the chains and cuffs, let alone Nadia's switch, were totally surplus to requirements.

There probably were dominants who would welcome such passivity, she thought, but as yet Nadia was still to meet them and certainly she could not think of a single one of her current extensive client list who would not pick up on this and probably complain vehemently about it. Still, she reflected, these were still early days and Marlon had explained that these scenarios worked better when the characters in opposition were all hooked into real "players".

'You three are pathetic,' Nadia said, smiling sadly at her charges. 'Not an ounce of go in you.'

She had already fastened Gina over one end of the whipping horse, face up, her arms linked beneath the padded top with a length of fine chain, her ankles cuffed to the two supporting legs so that her thighs were widespread and her shaven sex gaped open. Troy had then been led forward, arms still cuffed behind his back, erection bobbing obscenely before him and Nadia had released Becky's wrists and given her her instructions, passing her the switch as she did so.

The younger girl had obediently stepped up, grasped Troy's burgeoning shaft and pulled it towards Gina's waiting sex, positioning the head between the glistening lips and then pushing against his buttocks so that he entered her. Then, stepping back and to the side, she had brought the leather braids whistling around in an arc, so that, as they slashed across his firm buttocks, he thrust in and out of her in an involuntary lunging action, a sharp gasp accompanying his reaction.

Again the switch rose and fell, but Nadia shook her head and held up her hand.

'No, no, no!' she cried. Becky stopped, but did not turn to face her and Nadia let out a deep sigh of frustration.

'Can't you at least try to put something into this?' she said, at the same time aware that she was addressing what were only electronic images, but hoping that her intervention might trigger some response deep within VESTA's data banks. She decided that maybe it was best to lead by example.

'Troy,' she ordered, 'pull out of her and turn around.' With calm deliberation, Troy withdrew and pivoted to face her, his organ still glistening from Gina's juices. VESTA had got that much right, at least, Nadia grimaced. She reached down and swiftly detached the studs that held the triangular leather crotch piece over her own sex.

'Stand still,' she said and moved up to him, raising herself even taller on her toes, gripping his penis and straddling it. 'Now,' she said, as she sank down over his length, pleasantly surprised by the pure physical contact, 'this is what I mean by putting something into it.'

Gripping his shoulders, she swung her legs up and around, crossing them behind the small of his back and quickly began to raise and lower herself on him, astonished at how good it felt.

'Now,' she breathed, 'this is more like - oh shit!' She swung her legs back around and dropped her feet to the floor, lifted herself clear of him and stepped back, slapping him hard across the face as she did so. He flinched and his cheek reddened immediately, but he scarcely took a backward step.

'This is a waste of time,' Nadia rasped. 'I'd be better employed seeing how some of the others are getting on and I just hope they're having better luck than I am. Now, what's the phrase? Oh yes.'

She uttered the failsafe words and waited. Nothing happened.

'Bag and baggage,' she repeated. There was a slight shimmering in the air and the image of Troy blinked out, but Nadia remained in the room with the two women. She tried again. This time the women dematerialised, but everything else remained the same. A third try brought no further change, so Nadia turned back towards the door, hand extended towards the handle. It turned, but the door itself refused to open.

'Bag and baggage!' Nadia shouted, but to no avail and that was when she began to realise that something might be seriously wrong.

Once again, the woods seemed totally deserted and as endless as before. Pausing every now and then, Ellen strained to listen through the latex cat helmet, but as far as she could discern, everywhere was absolute silence, not even a breeze to stir the foliage overhead.

She stopped, squatted against a handy tree and for at least the tenth time tried the mask helmet, padded fingers probing for any clue as to its means of removal and, for the tenth time, drew a blank. Exasperated, she lowered herself even further, settling on her buttocks, legs stretched out before her, and considered her situation.

Further walking was almost certainly likely to prove a waste of time and effort. Not that there seemed to be that much effort involved, for the virtual reality set-up, whilst programmed for such things as pain and pleasure, did not seem to recognise more mundane symptoms and Ellen guessed she could probably walk another hundred miles without becoming physically tired.

The problem was, she reflected ruefully, that she could also probably walk another hundred miles and still not find the end of these interminable trees. Presumably because the environment was created from some sort of loop system, a theory which was borne out to a great degree by the regular reappearance of certain distinctive trees and bush clumps, a repetition that was not completely obvious to the casual observer, but one which, despite the subtlety of its various combinations and variations was nonetheless inescapable to someone who had walked through it with nothing to do but use her eyes.

So I wait, Ellen told herself. I sit here and I wait, stuck inside a giant sized pussycat skin, without a fag, without a drink, and without anything else to relieve the boredom.

She closed her eyes and wondered if it were possible to sleep in a world which largely existed inside her own brain...

Marlon had been inside VESTA's world many times before, but never as a passive participant, and his first hour had not been an enjoyable one; how Nadia thought people would ever pay good money for similar experiences was beyond him. It was one thing to put oneself into a position of absolute power, with a bevy of willing slaves conjured up out of his brainchild's massive memory banks, but quite another when one of the slaves was him and he had no way of telling which, if any, of the creatures that kept arriving to torment him were hooked up to real players and which were simply creations of the computer.

He looked down at himself and shook his head. The costume he was wearing - and costume was a word he selected only advisedly - was like hundreds of others he had seen during the programming and development stages of the VESTA project. But it was one thing to see illustrations and photographs of it, quite another to experience it first hand.

Basically, it was a body harness, fashioned from what appeared to be heavy rubber straps, all dependent upon a central body belt, or corset, which had been laced and buckled until Marlon's waist was as slim and tightly compressed as those of any of the females that populated this scenario.

From this, straps went up and down, over his shoulders to support another web that criss-crossed his upper torso and also fastened to a thick rubber collar, down his legs to connect to knee length boots, a series of transverse straps biting into the flesh of his thighs en route and a final series of straps performing a similar duty down the length of his arms, to where they fastened to padded mittens that held his hands clenched into useless fists.

Thus attired, and hampered by the fact that his boots perched upon outlandishly elevated wedged heels, Marlon was a helpless puppet in the hands of a series of tormentors, the latest of which was a willowy brunette who, in her own high heels, towered over him by several inches. She was dressed - surprise, surprise, he thought - in dark red leather, the boots thigh length, the studded skirt barely reaching the top of her thighs and the matching halter-top plunging to reveal most of what was an inordinately large cleavage for so slim a woman.

The long gloves had an open-work design throughout, a pattern which was repeated in the leather choker, and the fingers were cut away to reveal long, black lacquered nails. With her severely styled hair, heavy eye makeup and black lip-gloss, the woman was an imposing and intimidating sight, an effect not lessened by the multi-thonged whip she carried clipped to her waistband.

She had lost no time in arranging Marlon beneath the suspension frame, cuffing his wrists to either side of his collar and attaching chains to various parts of his body harness, where sturdy rings had been strategically positioned. Then, using the winch mechanism at one side, she had quickly hoisted his feet clear of the ground, bent his legs back and up at the knees and kept them in that position by clipping short chains between his ankles and the corset belt.

Stalking around him, she reached out one hand and cupped his scrotum with surprising gentleness, but Marlon's organ steadfastly refused to stir.

'The little man is reluctant, little man,' she smiled. Marlon tried not to look into those green eyes, but it was a losing battle. With her other hand, she took hold of his limp penis and began to massage it.

'Perhaps we should have a little slave come in and suck it for you,' the woman suggested, her eyes twinkling. 'We appear to have tried everything else and you don't seem to respond to all the usual methods, so whipping you would be a waste of time, I suppose?'

'Unless you just want to cause me pain and suffering,' Marlon said quietly. 'I'm afraid I don't really get off on that stuff.'

'It is a predilection not shared by everyone, I agree,' she replied. 'However, it is what I generally specialise in.' She continued to play with him all the while and, to his chagrin, Marlon realised that her ministrations were beginning to have some effect at last. She peered down, saw the evidence for herself, and smiled.

'The problem is,' she continued, 'that my instructions are that you are to be prepared and trained as a slave, which means you must quickly accustom yourself to all this.' She nodded to include the frame, chains, and Marlon's own attire.

'And you must also learn to respond at the behest of your superiors, master or mistress. This thing,' she said, squeezing his slowly thickening shaft harder, 'must learn to serve and obey.' She looked down again and nodded once more.

'That's better,' she said, her voice dropping almost to a whisper, 'nearly there. And, when we have you good and hard, do you know what we're going to do next?'

'I can't imagine,' Marlon replied, through gritted teeth. The smell of her perfume, mixed with the twin odours of her leatherwear and the rubber about his own warm body, was beginning to have a strange, heady effect on him.

'Well, let's see now,' she said, smiling enigmatically and looking up into the air above his head, 'should we maybe have a couple of girls in here to keep this thing nice and hard for a few hours? After all my efforts to make it stand up, it would be a great shame to waste it all immediately.'

'Then why don't you put it to use yourself?' Marlon groaned. 'Or do you prefer just to tease?'

The woman looked horrified. 'Good heavens!' she exclaimed. 'How could you possibly suggest such a thing? You don't for one moment suppose this miserable object is worthy enough for me, do you? I can see you need a severe lesson in humility.' She stepped back and released her hold on Marlon. 'I think now I know exactly what to do with you next,' she said, turning away. 'Just you wait there a moment and don't go wandering off.'

Hanging helplessly clear of the floor, Marlon did not appreciate her attempt at humour, nor the sight of the object she drew out of the trunk that stood against the wall. She brought it back over to him and held it up in front of his face, giving him a good close-up view so there could be no mistaking what was about to happen.

'This,' she said, 'is one of my favourite adornments for my slaves, especially those who get ideas above their station. See this?' she asked, pointing to the curiously shaped leather spheroid and probing for something with her long nails. 'This fits nice and snugly around your balls.'

She finally found what she had been looking for and the spheroid suddenly hinged apart in two sections, revealing a lining of dozens of short steel spikes, the needle-sharp points gleaming against the black of the leather.

'And then this,' she added, turning over the attached strap to reveal a further band of the same spikes, 'buckles around the base of your cock. Even a partial erection becomes very painful after a time, but then you have to get hard before you can come, and coming is the only way to take some of the pressure off your poor balls - at least, for a little while.

'So you see, this is quite an interesting little game. If you don't come, the needles play havoc with your balls. If you get hard they also play havoc with your cock stem, so the sooner you manage to come, the better. The skill in this is to see just how long we can keep you nice and hard without actually letting you come.'

She stooped down and began fitting the leather sac about his testicles, and the first touch of the devilish barbs brought a gasp of anguish from Marlon. There was no doubt that she heard this, but she did not deign to look up and acknowledge the fact.

'I think I shall send Penny and Patsy in to play with you for a while,' she murmured, tugging the various adjustments into place. 'And I think they will amaze you with the different ways they have of keeping a man on the verge. Hours at a time is nothing to them.'

She buckled the spiked strap about the base of his now tumescent shaft, dragging another gasping cry from his lips as she pulled it tight.

'Comfortable?' she enquired, standing up again, an evil smile on her lips. 'I sincerely hope not.' She patted his cheek and made a moue with her mouth. 'Feel free to scream,' she said. 'Of course, if you scream too loudly we'll have to gag you, but then maybe we'll do that anyway. I do so hate to hear grown men grovelling.'

'Christina insists they should all be able to watch this idiotic contest affair,' Naylor said. Jurgen Koenig nodded.

'So I understand,' he confirmed. 'Actually, I do not share your opinion of what she intends. I think this could be very interesting indeed and will also serve as a salutary lesson to the others.'

'I doubt they'll need any extra lessons,' Naylor grunted. 'In any case, all the time they're safely wired up to VESTA they have little alternative. They do, after all, have no control over events whatsoever.'

'Quite so,' Koenig agreed, 'but there is yet another factor you appear not to have considered.'

'Oh yes?' Naylor raised on eyebrow, almost a challenge, but the German remained unperturbed. He eased himself down into the armchair opposite, crossed his legs and leaned back, making himself comfortable.

'Yes indeed,' he said, 'for there is a very interesting possibility here. You see,' he continued, placing his fingers together and making a steeple of them, 'it is your idea to keep them all inside VESTA's world indefinitely, yes?'

Naylor nodded. 'Yes,' he said. 'Indefinitely. They will make interesting slave characters for our future clients.'

'Of course,' Koenig said, 'but would they not perhaps make even better slaves out here, in the real world? After all, we can generate slave clones electronically and, whilst it would no doubt suit your sense of retribution to have them all suffer for as long as possible, why waste them so?'

'Because they'd be unmanageable out here,' Naylor said. 'One or two of them might be trainable, but I can't see the likes of Nadia Muirhead kow-towing as a humble sex slave.'

'Maybe not the Nadia you know now,' Koenig said, sagely. 'But who's to say any of them will be the same people after a few weeks in VESTA?'

'You think this machine might break their spirits? That's an interesting thought.'

'Fascinating,' Koenig concurred. 'But it is a little more than just breaking their spirits that we are talking about.' He leaned forward again. 'I cannot be sure - not one hundred percent sure, anyway - but I have a theory that, if they remain in there for long enough and if everything is handled carefully, we may find that they become... well, brainwashed, I suppose is the best way I can put it.

'You see, after a while the human body is pushed to its limits. In the real world overexposure to pain causes certain parts of the brain to close down in an automated defence or self-preservation move. The victim faints, passes out, whatever you wish to call it, and only regains consciousness again when the system has had a little time to recover.

'However, inside VESTA they are deprived of this safety valve. Our little friend has carefully ensured that there is a pain threshold - for instance, you could place a welding torch to their most sensitive parts and the pain experienced would be no greater, nor less, than that of a sound whipping.'

'But you could reprogramme to alter that, I assume?' Naylor demanded.

Koenig gave him a patronising look. 'Of course,' he replied, casually, 'but it would not be a wise move. You see, although they are not actually experiencing genuine physical pain stimulus inside VESTA, the effect upon their brains is just the same. After all, the various stimulating electrodes are designed and positioned for just that result.

'Because of that, if you push any of them too hard or too far, it is quite possible that the shock could kill them. Much better to leave that buffer effect as it is.'

'Point taken,' Naylor conceded. 'But I still don't get what you're driving at.'

'Then let me finish explaining,' Koenig said patiently. 'Even with the buffer effect in place, they are all still capable of experiencing quite a high degree of pain, but after a while they can grow accustomed to this. Even in the real world this has been known to happen.

'However, it is a curious fact that the one thing the human mind cannot condition itself to accept is the pain and suffering of others, especially when those others are near and dear to them. Of course, only Marlon has any direct condition with the artist woman, but to see her suffer a bad beating at Christina's hands would be a salutary first lesson for them all.

'But even that is only the smaller part of what I am trying to explain. You see, if they remain inside VESTA for long enough, especially if they are all made to witness the punishments and humiliations of their friends, they will eventually come to a stage when the brain has to resort to different failsafe measures.

'It is quite possible - highly likely in fact - that they will ultimately become quite mad; in the strictest sense of the word, that is. Eventually they will be so conditioned to their new existence that they will be totally unable to distinguish reality from virtual reality.'

'Are you saying what I think you're saying?' Naylor asked, his eyes narrowing.

His own eyes still closed, Koenig smiled. 'It depends upon what you think I am saying, Herr Naylor,' he replied, quietly. 'But to save an extended guessing game, let me make it clear.

'If I am right, and I have every reason to believe I am, then eventually you should be able to remove the subjects from VESTA and they will continue to act as if they were still inside its world. They will have become so accustomed to the maxim that resistance is futile that they will lose any ability to do so.

'In other words,' he ended, opening his eyes again at last, 'you will have yourself a crop of perfect, mindless, docile and obedient slaves - and that includes Ms Muirhead.'

At Christina's command, Lianne stumbled to a halt and stood panting, sweat running down the bridge of her nose and sideways along her lip to dribble onto the straps of her bridle. The powerful blonde looked across to where the lap counter board stood, noted the number showing and gave a grudging nod.

'You've done much better than I expected,' she said, 'but then there is a stubborn streak in you, slut. Not that it will remain there for much longer, I can assure you. I have a way of knocking streaks out of my slaves, believe me.' She walked across, detached the long check rein from Lianne's bridle and jerked her head sideways.

'Come,' she said, 'it's time for William to groom you and then there will be some entertainment for you and all your friends to enjoy. The stupid red-headed slut, Marlon's sister, seems to think she might be some sort of match for me, so I intend to give her the opportunity to find out that she is not.

'I am even going to concede certain of my natural physical advantages, which I think is extremely generous of me, under the circumstances. Then, when I have beaten her, I think we shall have her join you in the stables for a while. A week or two with a horse face should teach her due humility.' She stopped, dragging Lianne to a halt, and peered down into her eyes.

'I am sure you understand what I mean,' she said. 'It must be so frustrating not to be able to talk, even if the bit were removed, and also to know that you look more beast than human. Maybe I can arrange for VESTA to handle a few more improvements.' She slapped Lianne across her rump.

'This arse and these legs are still far too human,' she said. 'Maybe we can give you a proper pony body from the waist down. I wonder what it will feel like to have knees that work back to front - interesting, do you think, Amber?'

She laughed, jerked the lead rein again and they continued back towards the stable buildings.

'This really is most remarkable,' James Naylor said, as much to himself as to Christina. He stood in the centre of the room, turning slowly, studying every tiny detail of the cupboards, racks, stands and their contents. He stepped over to the nearest rail, selected one of the long boots that hung from it and turned it over slowly in his hands.

'Quite incredible,' he whispered. 'It's impossible to tell, isn't it?'

Across the room, Christina was putting the finishing touches to her outfit, aided by the lithesome Marika, whose brown form was being displayed to its best advantage by the brief cut of the white leather skirt and halter she now wore. Naylor smiled to himself as he tried to accustom himself to the sight of a Marika who was now taller than Christina. Or to put it more accurately, he reminded himself, a Christina who was now shorter than the Asian girl.

'There are a few anomalies,' Christina said, as Marika finished tightening the dildo harness about her hips, 'but they're not that important and Koenig reckons they can all be taken care of in time.'

'But even this is far more realistic than I ever expected,' Naylor said, replacing the boot and taking up in its place a complex head harness. 'I mean, when I came to here, for a moment or two I thought the machine had failed. It's hard to believe I'm still laying out there in that coffin-like thing.'

'It takes some getting used to,' Christina agreed, holding out a hand for Marika to begin fixing the whip to it. 'But you'll be surprised how quickly it happens. What about you, Marika? This is also your first time inside VESTA.'

'I am trying not to think of this as anything but the real world,' Marika replied, her features expressionless as ever. 'And in a way that is all it is; an extension of one reality taken into another, a form of reincarnation without the intervention of the death mechanism.'

'Don't get her started,' Naylor laughed harshly. 'When she starts banging on about karma and levels and all that other religious bullshit, I start falling asleep.'

Marika did not appear to react to the insult, but her words were carefully measured. 'You may dismiss many things simply because you choose not to understand or believe them,' she said, 'but be careful they do not ultimately dismiss you. We tamper with the natural laws at our own risk and should not forget that for every cause there is an effect and for every effect a cause.'

'Well, I've got my cause all nicely mapped out, thank you girl,' Naylor said. He was working his way along the rail and had discovered a very lifelike rubber face mask, complete with attached wig. In its unstretched state the features were very distorted, but even so, there was no mistaking the identity of the woman's face it was meant to replicate.

'I can't understand why the machine has gone to all this bother,' he said, pulling the rubber this way and that. 'After all, if we want to make someone look like someone else, why not just programme the computer to do it anyway? It'd be a lot quicker than fitting this over someone's head.'

'But not so symbolic, I think,' Marika said. She took up the claw-nailed glove for Christina's other hand. Naylor shook his head.

'I've never been able to understand all this so-called symbolism,' he said. 'You want to bring someone to heel, give 'em a dose of pain and promise 'em more of the same and they soon come around to your way of thinking, I reckon.'

'Some understand and some don't,' Christina retorted. 'I long ago gave up trying to re-educate you, James.'

'Is that so?' Naylor snapped. 'Well, bully for you, but you've been able to enjoy your little games thanks to me and don't you ever forget it, so don't get on your high horse.'

'I wouldn't dream of it,' Christina replied, sweetly. 'Not when I can have all the horses I want right here, but then...' She did not bother to finish the sentence and the room fell silent, while Marika continued to prepare her for the coming duel.

A huge mirrored wall had been added at one end of her stall and Lianne studied her reflection in it in dismay, for it had taken almost no time at all for Christina's latest whim to be put into action. Presumably her computer expert had now mastered Marlon's creation, for the transition had taken place without Lianne realising it, and it was only when she'd raised her head from the drinking trough and turned to move to the back of the wooden cubicle that she'd suddenly become aware of the changes in her lower body.

The mirror had appeared at the same time and now, as she stood before it she saw, instead of just the parody of a pony girl, a creature that might have come straight from the pages of mythology. A centaur or centauress, with the hind legs and flanks of a horse and the torso of a well-endowed human female. Above which, unlike the beast of ancient legend, sat a head that was more equine than human, yet still retained enough of its original features not to hide her true identity.

She looked down at her hands, or rather to where her hands should have been, for her arms now ended in useless hoof-shaped stumps, on the underside of which were glittering horseshoes that matched the ones upon which she now stood.

Fighting back tears of horror and helpless frustration, she turned slightly, noting dully how her new tail swirled with the movement and wondering just how much further the perverted amazon bitch would be prepared to go in her crusade of revenge.

The rattle of the stall door disturbed these thoughts before Lianne had time to dwell on them and she turned to find William standing there, lead rein in hand, clip held up ready to attach it to Lianne's bridle. He showed no surprise at her unexpected metamorphosis, simply made a clicking noise with his tongue that indicated he expected her to come to him.

'Got a special little surprise for you, Amber,' he whispered, patting her muzzle. 'Going to drive you down to the new arena. There's going to be special games today - cart races and a big gladiator contest to start with. After that there'll be a new pony girl to keep you company; name of Flame, so they tells me.

'Now, you walk on steady like and we'll get you hitched up to your nice new racing buggy. Don't know who's going to drive you for the races, but just you remember I'll be watchin' you.'

Nadia, try the door again.

The voice inside her head brought Nadia out of her dozing state instantly. For a few seconds, not understanding its source, she looked around the empty room in bewilderment.

I'm not there with you.

'Marlon? Where the fuck are you?'

That's not important now. Just listen to me and do what I say.

'But there appears to be some sort of malfunction going on here,' Nadia protested, rising to her feet.

It's not a malfunction. I haven't got time to explain. You have to trust me.

'Why? What's going on? What's wrong?'

It's your friend Naylor and, from what I can tell, the woman whose leg young Lianne broke back last year.

'What about them?'

If you'll just listen, I'm trying to tell you. They're here, them and some others and they've taken over control of VESTA. I can tell you, that big dyke is in her element with all this. She ought to be locked up and the key thrown away.

'But how...?'

I'll tell you later - no time now. For the moment they can't monitor the circuit you're on. They think it's gone down but it hasn't; it just went into a sort of limbo for a while. The same with Ellen's circuit. The German bloke has checked that the self-diagnosing modules have activated, which they have and he'll know something is up before long, so we have to rely on speed here.

'Can't you do anything out there?'

I'm not out there. At the moment I'm - well, it doesn't matter, but I'm sort of able to be in two places at once, at least for a few minutes. I daren't push it, though. I need to check out a lot of things in a very short time, but I've already activated a few things they don't know about as yet.

In a few minutes your pod will disengage, but be very careful. At the moment Naylor, the Christina woman and some Indian girl are all hooked up to VESTA via active terminals, but there are at least a couple of gorillas wandering around the house - sort of minders, I guess you'd call them. So when you come to out there, take it very easy. Don't jump up and start pulling wires off you until you're sure there's nobody in the room with you.

Before you unhook you'll be linked to Ellen's circuit. Tell her what I've told you and then see what you can do to take the goons out of the equation.

'Shouldn't I just switch off the power to VESTA?' Nadia asked. 'That'd put a stop to all this straight away, wouldn't it?'

Except that VESTA has back-up supplies, because we don't know what damage a sudden power failure might cause to the participants. In any case, that'd mean the people on the active terminals coming out of it several seconds ahead of all of us and they have guns with them out there. No, I have a better plan. Just trust me.

You and Ellen should be able to deal with the heavies. There are only two of them, or there were last time I saw. They're probably outside patrolling the grounds anyway. I'm sure the pair of you will think of something.

'And what will you be doing in the meantime?'

Like I said, trust me. I'm a great believer in an eye for an eye... poetic justice, if you prefer. There's a little scene about to go down, involving my sister.

'Your sister? But...'

I repeat, it's a long story. Just do as I say, okay?

'Okay.'

Fine. See you soon. Go find Ellen.

The racing buggy was not that much different from the one she'd been harnessed to earlier, although Lianne saw that its black and gold design gave it a much flashier appearance than its training counterpart, and she also thought its construction appeared much lighter.

The shaft to which she was harnessed was also contoured so that the length over which she was impaled and chained was able to remain parallel to the ground, but several inches higher than before, compensating for the increased length of her new hind legs. Miserably, she stood passively while William finished buckling and chaining her, and then dutifully began to walk forward when he climbed into the seat and flicked the whip across her back.

However, William was not satisfied with this pace and very soon she found herself trotting along at an astonishing trot, moving much faster than she could have imagined before her latest metamorphosis. She looked down at her useless arms, which hung just a few inches clear of the ground, and wondered how long it would be before Christina decided that they, too, should be altered, so that she would be able to canter and gallop on four hooves, instead of just two...

Alma and Tara stood quietly to one side, watching Clarissa as she studied her reflection in the long mirror Tara had wheeled in.

The mask had been the final addition, a carefully contoured creation of thick toughened leather, that covered her face entirely whilst leaving her cropped hair in clear view. Over the eyes were clear plastic lenses, which although they did nothing to hamper her vision, gave her eyes a peculiarly enlarged appearance when she looked at them in the glass.

'The mask is for protection,' Alma had explained, as she finished buckling it into place, ensuring the lenses were correctly aligned with Clarissa's eyes. 'Without it the eyes would be an obvious target for your opponent to concentrate on, which would ruin the spectacle.'

'And we wouldn't want that, would we?' Clarissa retorted. 'And does my opponent get to wear a mask too?' Both women nodded in unison.

'It is always the same for both contestants,' Tara told her. 'You are evenly matched and it becomes a test of skill.'

'Except this bitch is a head taller than me and several kilos heavier,' Clarissa said sourly. They shook their heads as one.

'Not at all,' Alma assured her. 'You and your opponent are the same height and the same weight.'

'But...' Clarissa's mouth remained open for several seconds, before she understood the significance of this. Finally, behind her mask she grinned.

'Oh, I get it,' she said. 'In here we can all be anything or anybody, so the bitch-dyke thinks she'll lull me into a false sense of security. Well, maybe I'll have a few surprises for her before she finally beats me.'

'Beats you, mistress?' Alma looked genuinely surprised. 'Surely that is defeatist of you?'

'You must fight to win,' Tara added.

Clarissa flicked her forearm through its restricted arc, drawing a satisfying crack from the multiple thongs. 'I don't quite know how to put this, girls,' she drawled, 'mainly because you're basically a pair of unthinking electronic bimbos, but then that's not your fault, is it?' She stared at the two faces, neither of which registered any reaction to this challenge.

'However,' she went on after a short pause, 'let's get one thing straight, especially as I've got no way of knowing just who might be listening in to this little *tete-a-tete*. If you, the blonde cow, this bloody machine, or anybody else thinks for one minute that I'm going to believe I'm getting into a fair fight, you can bloody well think again.

'She may have had me looking like some sort of perverted bimbo, but that's one thing I ain't, right? So I'm not daft enough to think I'm going to get a fair crack here. Okay, she might spin it out for effect and I might just get a couple of good 'uns in as a result, but ultimately this fight is what is known as a fix.

'Come the end, I'm gonna end up flat on my back with her rubber cock in me. What happens then I don't know, but if that's what decides the winner, that's what's going to happen to me.' She reached down and encircled the thick dildo with her clawed hand.

'You might as well not have bothered strapping this thing on me,' she continued. 'She and I both know I ain't gonna get the chance to use it - mores the fucking pity!'

'But you must fight!' For the first time Alma appeared concerned, and her companion likewise.

Clarissa pursed her lips, cracked the whip again and nodded grimly. 'Oh, I'll fight all right,' she promised. 'Where I was brought up it goes against the grain to lay down and give up without giving it a real go, even when you knew the other drongo was going to beat the living crap out of you eventually.' She turned back to the mirror for one final look at herself.

'Jeez!' she whistled. 'If ma could see me now, she'd have a blue bloody fit!' She tilted her head, first to one side and then to the other, and then stood up straight, thrusting out her breasts.

'Right,' she snapped, turning back to face the two women again. 'Let's do it!'

Whatever was going on, VESTA had really excelled in creating the backdrop, Lianne thought, as she trotted into the arena beneath a high arched gateway and came obediently to a standstill at William's signal.

The stadium was a large oval, with tiers of seating banked up all around, seats that were packed to capacity with what appeared to be a very expectant and eager crowd. Underfoot and across all of what Lianne thought of as the playing field area, for want of a better description, the ground was firm but covered with a layer of white sand. All that was missing, she reflected, was a bunch of cowering Christians and a pride of hungry lions behind a metal gate, waiting to be turned loose for their lunch.

Approaching from the outside, her first thought had been that she was going to be raced against other pony girls, but now they were inside there was no sign of any sort of racetrack, nor any posts or ropes that could be used for marking out such a course. There were posts - six of them in fact - but they were being put to a different use altogether and it did not take Lianne long to work out the identities of at least some of the figures bound to them, despite VESTA's alterations to their physical appearances.

Carla Wayne and Hazel O'Dee did not look at all out of place in their skimpy rubber outfits; it was, after all, fairly normal daily attire for the pair of them, both in and out of role, though it was the first time Lianne had ever seen them so helpless. Normally they played the dominant roles and it was others who found themselves chained and bound by their expert hands.

Likewise with Gavin Cross, whose facial expression betrayed both his anger and his frustration at finding himself in the role of slave. And Simon Prescott, who never ventured out from behind his cameras, was clearly both embarrassed and terrified at being exposed almost naked to so many prying eyes. The fact that most of those eyes had to be nothing more than computer generated images did not seem to have registered with his confused brain.

Next to Simon stood Marlon, looking almost completely blank, his rounded eyes hardly seeming to notice what was going on around him.

But the figure strapped to the final post was far more animated and only the gag in her mouth was preventing her from voicing her disquiet as she struggled fruitlessly against the thick straps that held her.

Except, Lianne realised with a sudden start, it wasn't a 'her' at all. True the body, complete with exposed breasts and heavily ringed nipples, shaven sex and shapely legs was female, as were the heavily made-up features at first glance. But VESTA - whether deliberately or otherwise Lianne could only guess - had made very few modifications to the face structure, apart from a slight raising of the cheekbones and softening of the jaw line, and there was no doubting the true identity of the man with whom she'd been sharing her bed for more than a year.

She saw Paul turn his head in her direction, but if he recognised her at all, he did not show it. But, as he continued to stare at her in the goggle-eyed fashion peculiar to all who were forced to wear a ball gag, Lianne knew he'd guessed and she lowered her gaze, hating for him to have to see her like this.

Ready to enjoy the show, horsy girl?

Go fuck yourself, Lianne thought.

Not while there are others to fuck instead. But I haven't got time to bandy words with a slave slut, especially not one with a horse face and hooves.

I'd rather have this face than yours.

Of course you would. Now, shut up and listen. You may hear something to your liking.

Like you've contracted terminal guilt complex?

I hardly think so. One needs a conscience for that and I long since decided I couldn't afford such a luxury. However, you may just get to get out of here.

Oh?

Yes, but I'm afraid your fate is not in your hands. It's going to be up to Marlon's dear sister, who's issued me with a personal challenge. If she wins I have agreed to free you all from VESTA. The stupid bitch thinks I meant you'd be free altogether, but we both know that couldn't happen.

However, at least your continuing misery could take place in the real world, with the limitations that would impose upon my ingenuity.

Such generosity seems a bit out of character, blondie, if you'll pardon my bluntness.

From your tone I assume you believe things couldn't get any worse for you? Don't count on it. I've got plans for you to spend a while on a racing stud farm - very realistic, complete with stallions to cover you and get you into foal.

You're sick!

And you're in no position to do anything about it, so I would advise you to keep your clever comments to yourself.

You're not going to release me anyway, not even from this bloody awful world, so what's the difference?

Oh, I'll let you out of VESTA if the girl wins, I give you my word on it, whether you think my word is worth anything or not.

Assuming it might be, that makes me think she isn't going to win. It'd take a Sumo wrestler to knock you off your feet.

Under normal circumstances, maybe. But these circumstances are far from normal, aren't they? Just take a look straight ahead across the arena. See that pair of small gates beneath the lower seating level? Keep your eyes fixed on them. Any minute now...

'Makes me feel like a Roman emperor,' Naylor said smugly, settling back into the ornately padded seat. Beside him, Jurgen Koenig sat in a similar chair, the two of them surrounded by a collection of very beautiful and scantily clad young women, whose sole purpose, apart from being decorative, appeared to be to waft the air above them with large fans made from palm leaves. The box in which they were preparing to view the coming contest sat apart from the main terracing, offering the perfect view.

'The entire place is modelled on a coliseum,' Koenig confirmed. 'And yes, this is exactly where and how the likes of Nero and Julius Caesar would have viewed the games.'

'The idea has great possibilities,' Naylor said, craning his neck to look back and up at the sea of faces. 'Given enough portals, I guess we could recreate this crowd using real people. I assume this lot are just put together by the computer?' he added, turning back to the German.

Koenig nodded and smiled. 'Of course,' he said. 'Mind you, I've dulled down the smells just a little. All that leather and rubber crowded together in the sunshine would be a bit overpowering otherwise.'

'Very thorough, as ever,' Naylor said, straight-faced. 'So, how long before the so-called action starts?'

'Any moment now,' Koenig replied. He produced a small pair of binoculars from his pocket, almost as though he had plucked them from thin air. 'Use yours,' he said, nodding downwards, and when Naylor followed the direction indicated he saw to his surprise that an identical pair was now resting in his own lap.

'As I said,' he muttered, raising the lenses to his eyes, 'very thorough. Why not just create us here with telescopic vision built in.'

'It's a thought,' the German smiled. 'I'll do some work on that, once our Danish friend has finished giving me her lists of tasks she wants me to do. Ah yes, look down there, on the far side.'

'Where? What am I looking for?'

'The pony cart. See? Unless I'm much mistaken that's the blonde girl, Lianne. Christina asked for certain modifications, but this is the first opportunity I've had to see the results. Curious, but most impressive.'

'Most bloody bizarre, you mean,' Naylor rasped, swinging his binoculars around until he found the desired target. 'Oh, fucking hell, that's a bit much, even by Christina's standards. Only she could think up something like that!'

'Not if we are to judge from some of the data VESTA has been drawing in from the Internet,' Koenig said. 'But I wonder just how the girl feels, standing there more horse than human. Of course, she knows it's only an illusion, but Christina has made it very plain to her that this is the only reality she will ever experience from now on. It must have a very dispiriting effect, I should imagine.'

'Serve the snotty little bitch right,' Naylor snapped. 'It couldn't happen to a nicer girl. Talking of which, who's the bimbo on the end post down there? I recognise all the others, but - ye gods! It can't be!'

'I believe it can,' Koenig chuckled. 'I've never met the chap in real life, of course, but apparently he has a certain penchant for wearing female costumes. When I first tapped into VESTA he was all set for a pleasant little outing as a 'real' woman, so

I just made a few alterations. I'm not so sure he's found the experience quite as pleasant as he might originally have hoped.'

'Another one with ideas above his station,' Naylor growled. 'I think we'll keep him like that and maybe put him to a few nice rough studs.'

'Christina was ahead of you on that one, I'm afraid,' Koenig said. 'Ah, wait - do I detect something starting to happen down below?'

'What the hell have they got strapped to them?' Naylor gasped. 'Christ, those claws look bloody lethal.'

'In the real world, they would be,' Koenig agreed. 'Here, well... let's just say they can't inflict a mortal injury, but they can certainly cause quite a degree of damage, as can the whips, if you study them closely.'

'But why the damned strap-on cocks?'

'Again, our blonde friend's idea. The aim of the contest is for each contestant to try to penetrate her opponent. Full penetration triggers a pre-programmed response which instantly disables the penetratee; her circuit will immediately lock up and she will be unable to move at all, let alone continue to fight.'

'Except that knowing Christina if the Aussie girl should, by any chance, manage to do it to her first, it just won't work like that?'

'Quite so, but our fearsome amazon assures me that is only a precaution. Despite surrendering physical advantage she seems very confident she cannot lose. I almost feel sorry for the other girl. She might be better off facing a wild animal.'

'She might at that,' Naylor agreed, but his reply was lost amidst the renewed cheering of the crowd.

It required all her powers of self-discipline for Ellen to keep her eyes closed and remain immobile once she knew she had emerged from VESTA, but Nadia had been very firm on this point...

'I'll move first,' she had said, 'and if the coast is clear I'll let you know. If I get caught, then you're the reserve, okay?'

'But what am I supposed to do against two bloody muscle men?' Ellen protested. Somehow, although the cats head mask remained in place, the gag had disappeared the moment Nadia had appeared through the trees ahead of her.

'Try and get to my bedroom,' Nadia replied. 'The mirror above my dressing table hides a small safe. The combination is zero-nine, one-three, seven-four, right, left and right, in that order. Then thirteen left for luck,' she added with a grin. Ellen looked at her in amazement.

'That first bit is my date of birth!' she exclaimed.

Nadia nodded. 'I know,' she said. 'I've got a terrible memory for numbers, but I have all your birthdays on your personnel files. It would be too obvious if I used my own birthday, wouldn't it?'

'I suppose so,' Ellen agreed. 'So, let's see.' She repeated the combination, complete with left and right directions. Nadia nodded.

'Good,' she said. 'Now, inside the safe are three handguns. Go careful; the one with the pearl inlay handle is a real gun. Only use it if you really have to. The others fire fast acting tranquilliser darts. You'll find a small tin box with six spare darts as well, but careful how you load them. Prick yourself and you'll get enough of the drug to make you feel very dizzy, even if you don't pass out.'

'How do I go about reloading?'

'You'll find it easy enough,' Nadia assured her. 'It's pretty much obvious. Each dart comes complete with a charge of compressed gas that propels it when you pull the trigger. But you need to be within about thirty metres at most, just to be safe. I don't know how accurate those things are over a greater distance than that.

'Anyway,' she said, 'hopefully I'll be okay, so I can show you myself.'

'Amen to that,' Ellen said. 'So what happens now?'

'We just sit here and wait. Shouldn't be long now.'

'I bloody hope not. This pussy cat outfit is starting to make me feel claustrophobic.'

'Okay, you can open your eyes now.' Ellen sighed, her eyelids flickering open against the light. Nadia was standing over her, already detaching the web of sensor connections.

'Nobody about?' Ellen asked, easing herself into a sitting position. To either side of her the line of coffin-like pods stood, a human form just about visible over the top of all except the one Nadia had so recently vacated. Ellen nodded towards the five on her right.

'Can't we release our crowd now?' she asked. Nadia pulled away the last connector and began fumbling with the chinstrap that held the curious looking helmet over Ellen's head.

'No, not yet,' she said. 'If we do that Jimmy Naylor and his buddies will know instantly that something is up. And from what Marlon told me they still have control to bring themselves straight out of VESTA. I don't know about you, but I don't fancy facing that one empty-handed.' She jerked a thumb to Ellen's left, to where the imposing leather clad form of Christina reposed, apparently slumbering.

'I take your point,' Ellen conceded. 'But we can't just go off and leave them. God alone knows what they're going through in there.'

'We have to,' Nadia urged her. 'We have to take care of the two guards and also make sure there aren't any more of them arrived since Marlon was put under. Besides, my little revolver and the two tranquilliser guns will cut madam over there down to size if she does wake up suddenly.'

'It's about the only thing that would,' Ellen retorted, lifting her legs over the side of her pod and levering herself upright. Nadia smiled as she turned to lead the way out.

'Not according to Marlon,' she replied.

Christina managed to sway away from Clarissa's first two passes with the whip, but when she tried to counterattack after the second she misjudged and the younger girl's third attempt caught her exposed left nipple, despite her desperate backward twist. Despite herself the blonde woman let out a small yelp, but was immediately back on her balance, her own weapon flicking out against a follow-up attack.

'Got blood on your tit, blondie!' Clarissa taunted, circling slowly, keeping just out of range. 'Hope it bloody well hurts.'

'You'll find out for yourself in a few seconds,' Christina rejoined. She flexed her clawed hand, considering whether to feint with the whip and then go in low for the other woman's exposed thigh and hip. It would be easy enough to land a lash across the lower legs, but both they and most of each arm were protected by a thick layer of leather, as was the face and most of the vital organs.

The targets, therefore, had to be the shoulders and upper chest, including the breasts in their leather cages, the hips and upper thighs and, of course, just behind where the rubber dildo thrust up and out, the unprotected sex lips. That, however, was not an easy mark, she decided.

Without further warning, Christina suddenly darted forward, whip thongs flailing before her like a demented propeller, her claws raking out in a low arc, only to find herself clutching at thin air and then a line of fire exploding across her shoulders. Twisting away she staggered backwards, moving out of range, wondering just how her opponent had been able to move that quickly.

'Surprised, drongo?' The eyes behind the redhead's mask gleamed maliciously. 'I was more dragged up than brought up, mostly with boys who had an idea they could use me as a sort of parking bay for their randy little cocks. It was a case of fuck them before they fucked me.'

'Very impressive,' Christina conceded. 'But I spent several years training in various combat techniques. I think you might find me a little more of a challenge than a couple of outback hooligans.'

'Who said anything about being brought up in the outback?' Clarissa laughed. 'That would have been a picnic. Most of the fellas out there are more interested in shagging sheep, haven't you heard the stories?'

'You won't find it so funny in a few minutes,' Christina warned, tensing for another attack. Clarissa merely laughed even louder.

'You talk a good fight,' she said, 'but so far the only blood is on you, in case you hadn't - whoa! Nearly!'

Christina had thrust forward with the whip again, hoping to catch her off guard. But Clarissa seemed to be made of rubber, not just wearing it, and it was as though she had springs in the heels of her long boots, for she pirouetted, leapt and was gone, though not without landing another stinging cut across the top of Christina's right arm.

The blonde let out a hiss of pain and annoyance as she staggered to regain her balance yet again, but Clarissa was already moving and twice her whip found unprotected flesh, before she was once more out of range. There were roars of approval and encouragement from the crowd, but neither combatant was hearing them now.

Christina bounded forward once more, twisting, jumping, her right boot lashing out in a vicious karate style kick, but her opponent was yet again too agile for her and this time her claws opened up four deep gashes in the back of Christina's airborne thigh.

'Five-nil to me, I think!' Clarissa kept circling, flicking her whip idly, deliberately trying to goad her former tormentor into lunging again. Breathing hard Christina resisted the temptation, knowing it was precisely what was expected of her.

'You're pretty good,' she rasped. 'Makes it all the more interesting. Maybe I should have kept an inch or two and a couple of pounds advantage.'

'Maybe you should,' Clarissa agreed. 'So why don't you get your computer boffin to - waheyyy!' She spun away as Christina attacked again, but this time her whip also missed its target and, with a backhanded flick, Christina landed her first scoring contact; two vivid welts across the back of her right shoulder. The Australian girl barely seemed to notice the blow.

'You're learning,' she sneered. 'Maybe you're not as stupid as you look.' She backed off a few steps, whip hanging limply. 'I'll give you one thing, only being able to use the forearms makes this pretty interesting.'

For several minutes they circled, feinted, lunged. Christina managed to land another whiplash across Clarissa's other shoulder and rake the top of her thigh with the tip of one claw. But in return she received another stinging lash, this time across both breasts and her opponent's claws opened up a deep gash along the top of her left arm. Drops of bright red blood splattered the sand about them and, to Christina's disgust, she realised that most of it was her own.

Her breathing was much harder now, as much a result of her frustration as from the efforts she was largely wasting. It was, she decided, time for serious methods.

She dived forward, hitting the ground on her side, rolling and kicking upwards, the thick soles of her boots driving into Clarissa's abdomen with a satisfying thud, knocking the other girl onto her back, though not before her whip had exacted another welt across her back. Ignoring the pain Christina rolled over, coming back to her feet in one movement, only to find herself hurtling backwards as Clarissa's right boot arced around and slammed into the side of her head.

Bright lights exploded before her eyes, but she retained enough presence of mind to keep rolling backwards, whip thrashing as a defensive screen until her head began to clear. When it did she saw that Clarissa remained several feet away, standing easily, legs slightly apart, whip hanging idly, her clawed hand gripping the rigid dildo and pointing it towards her dazed opponent.

'Come suck some cock, blondie!' The Australian accent was even harsher now and, for the first time Christina began to have serious doubts. She looked up towards the gallery where Naylor and Koenig were sitting and gestured with her whip hand, making the sign of an X at her feet. Koenig raised a hand in acknowledgement, but Christina could not afford to take her eyes off her opponent for any longer. Already she was moving in again, brandishing the thick shaft like a pennant.

'You made the rules, blondie,' she called out. 'Let's see you stick to 'em - or is your little mate up there going to fix things for you, eh? Well, he'd better be quick about it.'

Ignoring the jibe, Christina went in again with a flurry of kicks, landing one, two, three times, the final impact sending Clarissa sprawling onto her back, legs akimbo. In a trice, Christina was on top of her, landing with her knees driving into the other woman's midriff and driving the air from her lungs with a satisfying hiss. The claw raked out, ripping four bloody tracks across both undefended breasts, tearing apart one of the leather harness straps with its force.

'Now we'll see who's fixing who!' she snarled, thrusting her knees between Clarissa's thighs, her claw hand reaching to guide the black phallus to its target. She forced the swollen knob between the damp lips, pushing the shaft in an inch or so and then lowered herself over her vanquished opponent, who lay with eyes closed, face contorted with pain.

'You can suck my cock later,' Christina leered. 'But first I'm going to push it into you so far you'll think you're choking.' She wriggled her hips, feeling the phallus settling into the soaking tunnel and could not resist one final taunt.

'The next cock you feel inside you will be about fifteen inches long, slut,' she snarled. 'But you'll have a cunt big enough to take it. You'll be joining the other bitch in the stud farm. A nice pair of brood mares you'll make - Aaaahhh!'

Again lights exploded everywhere, this time accompanied by what felt like an explosion somewhere between her ears. Christina's entire body suddenly went rigid, her every sense numbed. When she came round again it was to find herself lying on her back, Clarissa poised with her own rubber phallus nestling between the tops of her thighs. Desperately Christina tried to wriggle aside, but her muscles were refusing to obey her brain's feverish commands.

Clarissa sat back slightly, the back of her whip hand glove wiping away the flecks of blood that had appeared in the centre of her forehead. Behind the mask she grinned triumphantly.

'Back home we call that the Botany Bay salute,' she said. 'In this country they call it the Liverpool handshake, and I believe the Jocks call it the Glasgow Kiss. Fuckin' hurts me almost as much as it hurts you,' she added, but the fact did not seem to bother her. 'Difference is, you're stunned silly and I've just got a lump on my head. However, it wears off a bit quick, so let's just make sure of you, shall we?' She grasped Christina's shoulders, arched her back, and thrust hard with her hips. Christina felt the long rubber penis penetrating deep within her, just as the strength began to return to her arms. She tensed her muscles, preparing to swing a round-arm blow into the back of the unsuspecting redhead's neck and...

...her entire body went completely limp and numb again, except this time it was not as the result of a stunning head butt between her eyes.

'No-oooo!' she cried. 'It shouldn't have...'

And then her vocal chords also stopped working. Only her eyes and ears remained normal. Above her Clarissa was lazily pumping back and forth, her black phallus sliding in and out of a helpless tunnel that its owner could no longer feel.

She stopped, holding herself up on extended arms. 'Shouldn't have worked, should it?' she said, giggling happily. 'So, I wonder what went wrong? Whatever it was,' she added, pulling herself clear and staggering to her feet, 'I'd say you were well and truly fucked - in all senses of the word!'

'The really clever part was, in all honesty, only clever because of its simplicity,' Marlon said, beaming from ear to ear. The rest of the company looked at him in a mixture of bewilderment and awe, for the little computer genius' definition of simplicity would have rendered Einstein's theory of relativity as the equivalent of the blurb on a cereal packet.

'Okay,' Ellen said, speaking for all of them, 'so tell us, brain-box, how you managed it. I'm no expert, but I thought the Kraut had searched for all the safe-words and stuff and erased them?'

'Oh, he did,' Marlon agreed, nodding enthusiastically. 'And he did remove them - all the ones that were there, including some very sophisticated failsafes I'd generated.' He sat back in the huge armchair and his smile, if it were at all possible, seemed to grow even wider.

'Some of those little programmes took me at least fifteen minutes to create, you know,' he said. 'In all I wrote five special ones on top of the original stuff, and buried them pretty deeply, though I was pretty certain he'd find them eventually.'

'So why bother at all?' Paul asked, leaning forward. 'If you knew he was good enough to dig them out, wasn't that just a waste of time and effort?'

'Au contraire, mon ami,' Marlon smirked. 'Our Bavarian friend - or is he Prussian? - would have been most suspicious if he'd searched and found nothing. After all, he knew I had those few hours and that I wouldn't waste them, so if his search software had unearthed a blank he'd have smelled the proverbial.'

'Now, just hang on a minute,' Lianne interrupted. 'I probably know less about computer stuff than anyone in this room, but even I see a flaw here. If this Koenig guy was good enough to write programmes that could search your programmes out even in the very depths of VESTA, how come he never found what you'd done?'

'That,' Marlon said, his chest puffing out visibly, 'was the really clever and simple bit about the entire thing.' He chuckled and looked around the eager eyes for a few seconds before continuing. 'Let me ask you all a question.' He was beginning to really enjoy himself and no one was prepared to spoil his fun; after all, whatever he'd done, whether any of them would ever understand it or not, he was the one who had proved to be their saviour. Only Nadia betrayed the slightest sign of impatience. She raised her glass in his direction.

'Marlon,' she said, smiling gently, 'my bloody wine is getting warm.'

'Of course,' Marlon nodded. 'You must forgive me.' However, he still milked the stage for a few more seconds before continuing.

'The thing is,' he said at last, 'friend Koenig was looking for something that wasn't actually there at the time. No,' he said, raising one hand, 'I'll explain, so don't all get on at me, but I am rather proud of this, you know.

'This was the simple bit I was talking about. All the various clever little bits and pieces I created were really nothing more than a smokescreen. There was always the slim chance he might miss one, in which case I could have sorted everything a few hours earlier than I did, but I never really thought he would. So, having set up a few decoys, I put the real failsafe somewhere he'd never be able to find it - on a small private website I've had for a few years now.'

'It's all beyond me,' Ellen said, uncrossing and re-crossing her legs. 'What bits of my brain VESTA hasn't already scrambled have just run up the white flag!'

'Bear with me,' Marlon persisted. 'It really is so simple. This site is not cached in VESTA - sorry, that means that there isn't a copy of it here. The files I created originally are in my own computer in a small cottage in Herefordshire, and the active site is on a very small commercial server based in Bali, I believe it is.

'Anyway, that's not important. What is important is that it's a long way away from VESTA herself, though distance, in this technological world of ours, is a relative thing.

'As you may know, VESTA was originally programmed to search the world wide web for data from which to carry on constructing a base from which to create the various scenarios which her subjects would experience. In order to do that in the shortest possible time, she is connected to fifty ISDN lines - Nadia happily underwrote that cost some weeks ago - and continually surfs the net via those lines.

'Now, given the nature of the data she needed, there were certain keywords for which she was programmed to search. One of these keywords was contained within my private website, which also contained an automatic download of a new failsafe programme. However, I didn't want VESTA downloading this failsafe until our friend had finished satisfying himself he'd found all my little devices.

'So, all I did was write in a time delay in my site, destroy the file at this end afterwards and then wait. Of course, I couldn't be completely sure how long it would be before it would be safe to activate the thing, so I had to put in four separate programmes, leaving twelve hour gaps between them. I'd figured they'd have me hooked up to VESTA in under forty-eight hours easily, and that Koenig would have finished his search patterns inside four or five hours tops.

'After that, once my own terminal had become active instead of passive, it was all quite simple. Of course, I had to delay long enough to get a couple of you back outside to deal with the two heavies - Nadia and Ellen did that quite efficiently, thanks to Nadia's stun guns.'

'But you didn't know I had those,' Nadia pointed out. Marlon's smile remained broad.

'My dear lady,' he said, 'I knew you'd find some way of putting those two thugs out of commission, especially with the redoubtable Ellen as your accomplice. I'd have liked to free up one of the chaps, but they were all occupied in active scenarios I couldn't risk interfering with. Anyway, I never doubted your resourcefulness for a moment.

'After that I was able to put a computer clone of myself into my own scenario and pop in and out making a few programming adjustments. Within minutes, if not less, they couldn't have taken back control if they'd wanted to, although none of them knew it. I let Koenig finish off getting the big blonde prepared for her fight with Clarissa, but their little ruse to prevent my dear sister winning was taken care of by myself.

'I also made a few other minor alterations. I knew Clarissa was a karate black belt and she'd told me about her somewhat unorthodox childhood games, but I confess I didn't want to take any chances, so I just hyped her reflexes and physical level a tad and dulled Christina's abilities a touch, just for good measure.'

'Why didn't you just freeze them all up before the fight anyway?' Clarissa demanded. Lianne couldn't help noticing how the girl kept running her fingers through her long auburn tresses, as if not quite able to believe that being shorn of them inside VESTA's painworld had only been an illusion.

Marlon gave a little shrug. 'Well, that was my initial reaction, I must admit,' he said. 'However, after they'd gone to so much trouble to set everything up, I thought I'd let them go through with it. You were never in any physical danger and I also dulled your pain responses quite a lot and, thanks to what I'd done, you were never going to lose.

'After what that hulking great bitch did to you to get to me,' he went on, his face darkening for an instant, 'I thought you might like to give her a taste of her own medicine.'

'Shame about the masks, though,' Clarissa laughed. 'I'd have liked a better view of her face when she realised what had happened. When that cock went into her it was like turning off a switch. She went like a rag dolly.'

'Well, she's going to get a lot more of that sort of treatment before she's through here,' Nadia said. 'Jimmy Naylor, too. By the time I'm finished with them they won't want to come within a thousand miles of VESTA.'

'Let me see if I've got this right,' Paul said, leaning forward. 'You set things up for VESTA to go get this failsafe thingy after Naylor and Koenig had taken control here, so that when they'd done their mine-sweeping bit, VESTA went and found a new bomb?'

'Yes,' Marlon nodded. 'That's a good way of putting it, I suppose. I had to let them think they'd succeeded and also that they'd outwitted me. I was also pretty damned certain they'd put me into VESTA with the rest of you, that being the surest way of keeping me out of trouble.

'Unfortunately for them, once my little surprise kicked in it was actually the one place where I could cause the most trouble for them, mainly because it was the last place they would look for trouble to come at them.'

'And you were a hundred percent confident it would work?' Paul said, amazement showing in his expression.

'Oh yes!' Marlon exclaimed. 'Never any doubt at all. After all, VESTA may be female, but she's programmed with male logic.'

He ducked the first cushion that was hurled at him, but there were too many women in the room for such a remark not to earn retribution and, a split second later, Marlon disappeared beneath a hail of airborne soft furnishings.

'No skirts this evening?' Lianne said, emerging from the bathroom to find Paul stretched out on their double bed, completely naked. He shrugged.

'You can have too much of a good thing,' he said, somewhat sheepishly. Lianne gave a little snort.

'So, your little adventure without balls has turned you off the idea,' she said, towelling her damp hair vigorously. He looked up at her, his expression suddenly quite serious.

'It did make me think a bit,' he admitted. 'Don't get me wrong, despite everything it was... well, quite interesting in some ways, and now we've got control of VESTA back I wouldn't mind continuing the, er, experiment, but I think my head needs a day or so to get itself round a few things.'

'Like the fact that when you're tied down, spread-eagled, some horny sweaty bastard just uses you as a receptacle?' Lianne suggested. He hesitated, but then nodded.

'Yeah, that's part of it,' he admitted. 'The thing is - was - there was no feeling involved, if you understand what I'm getting at? I was just, well, I was just fucked and that was it. Don't get me wrong, I could have handled that scenario if it had been created for the right reasons, but by that time I knew things had gone wrong and I was convinced I was stuck as a woman full time, stuck as some sort of animated sex doll and destined to spend the next fifty years as a repository for every cock in Europe.'

'Now there's sad,' Lianne said, her eyes twinkling. She tossed the towel to one side and flopped down on the bed alongside him, propping her chin up on cupped hands. 'It wouldn't be that you actually enjoyed some of that, would it?'

'No!' The protestation came too quickly, but she said nothing, just stared straight into his eyes. It took less than five seconds. 'Okay, so I did, until I thought I was stuck with it full time. No, to be honest, it wasn't even that that scared me.'

'No?'

'No,' he said, reaching out to touch her still damp shoulder. 'It was thinking I would never be able to be with you again, never be able to enjoy what we have together, not inside nor outside of VESTA. If you'd been one of those guys it'd have been fine, I could have handled that - at least, I think I could. But I knew Christina would never let us be together again in any sort of situation we might have mutually enjoyed. Sorry, I'm not explaining this too well.'

'I think I understand where you're coming from,' Lianne said softly. 'And I think I know what we both need. I'll get some clothes on and go see Marlon.'

'You, er, don't actually have to do this for real,' Marlon stammered, his cheeks reddening. 'I mean, this could all be done through VESTA, if you'd rather.'

Ellen, clad from head to toe in a silver latex catsuit, only her eyes, mouth and sex visible through strategically positioned apertures, shook her head.

'I don't think you understand, Marlon, sweetie,' she purred. 'The thought of you fucking some VESTA generated clone of me is a bit - well, a bit disgusting. It'd be like you wanking over pictures of me, I suppose.' She pirouetted on her steepling heels and came to a stop facing him again.

'No, this is for real, Marlon,' she went on, pulling open the towelling bathrobe and reaching down with rubber-sheathed fingers to grasp his already stiffening organ. 'This is because I want to show my appreciation for your talents, and also teach you an appreciation of mine.'

She guided his now almost complete erection towards her, rubbing the engorged head of his penis against her glistening sex lips. She saw and felt him shudder with anticipation.

'Steady,' she whispered. 'There's plenty of time.'

'But why?' he croaked, his voice breaking. 'There's no need.'

The featureless silver head bobbed eagerly.

'Oh yes there is,' she said. 'There's a very urgent need - mine.' She pursed her lips through the tight opening in the mask and planted a damp kiss on his forehead. 'Call me a silly tart if you like, but you turn me on something wicked.'

'Me? But...'

'But nothing,' she said, placing a silencing finger against his lips. 'And I'm only ever going to say this to you the once, so listen and take note.' She stepped back, but retained her grip on his organ, which was now swollen fit to burst.

'I've been involved here for some time now and I've done just about everything there is to be done. I've also enjoyed it totally and I'd be a liar if I tried to deny it. Some of us are just made that way. Me, Lianne, Hazel, all of us. But there's one difference between Lianne and me and I've only just figured it out.'

'There is?' Marlon could barely get the words out.

Again Ellen nodded. 'Yup,' she replied, massaging his shaft slowly. 'I've got a real brain. Don't get me wrong, I love Lianne to death and she's no dummy, but she also... well, it's hard to explain, but she was in a job that required brains, so she obviously isn't stupid, yet she arrived here - my fault - and seems to have parked her IQ in neutral. I'd done the same, I suppose, but now I understand.

'Which is why I fancy you, I guess. You're the smartest sod I've ever met and that really turns me on, for some reason. Maybe a little part of me thinks you could fuck some intelligence into me,' she added, unable to suppress a giggle.

'I don't think you do yourself justice,' Marlon protested, but Ellen was not in the mood for any further delays. She stepped forward again, raised herself up and guided his rampant phallus inside herself with practised ease. Marlon let out a strangled gasp and she had to grab his waist to prevent him from buckling at the knees.

'This,' she breathed, 'is reality, Marlon.' She raised and lowered herself once and he gasped out loud again. 'And it's also both your reward and your penance. From now on, professor, this cock belongs to me, both inside and outside of VESTA.

Marlon's reply was completely incoherent and his reaction was both sudden and expected. Ellen didn't mind at all, for she suddenly understood that she now had all the time in the world at her disposal. Somewhere inside VESTA there was now an electronic version of Ellen who would do all the routine chores, if routine were the correct word.

Meanwhile, out here in the real world, she was once more in full charge of things - including the thing that was convulsing so helplessly inside her.

Abandoning herself to her own orgasm, she idly reflected that it was going to be a long life from now on...

Pauline stood in the centre of the high vaulted chamber, the circle of spotlights reflecting off the tight thin rubber that adorned her voluptuous body, the changing colours highlighting her full red lips and the matching nipples that were bursting out of the tight cut-outs in the bodice of the brief latex dress.

A few feet from her stood her new master, a towering figure dressed in dull black leather; mask, cape, high boots and studded belt, swathed in a matching cape that gaped open to hide nothing of the impossible erection that awaited her. She closed her eyes briefly, opening them again to stare at her fate, painfully aware of the damp warmth that seeped onto the few inches of naked thigh above the rubber stockings.

'Kneel, Pauline,' the master commanded.

Perched on the high boots, her arms caught up behind her back in the tight rubber pouch, Pauline obeyed with some difficulty. She knelt, head bowed, her long blonde ringlets cascading about her face, partially obscuring her vision. The master stepped forward.

'Worship me, whore,' he ordered. Head still inclined downwards, Pauline extended her neck, parting her lips about the purple head of her master's organ. Gently she sucked the monster into her mouth, her tongue massaging its under surface.

'Deeper, my little slut slave,' the master said. Pauline obeyed, marvelling that the massive shaft did not cause her to choke.

'Enough!' The master stepped back, his burgeoning rod coming out of her mouth with an audible plop. Pauline remained kneeling in submission. The master gave a low chuckle.

'First we warm up that sexy little rump,' he said. 'And I have just the thing for you, my little whore. Look!'

Slowly, Pauline raised her eyes, gazing past her master to where the means of her re-education stood waiting, and sighed as she understood.

'Come,' said the master, extending a gloved hand, raising Pauline to a standing position with surprising ease. 'Come mount my new horse and let's prepare your saddle.'

Tottering unsteadily on the towering heels, Pauline allowed herself to be led forward without protest, stepping up onto the black velvet draped box and easing her right leg up over the pommel, feeling the thick phallus pressing against her dripping sex, shivering as the stubby head penetrated her, lowering herself until its length had sunk fully inside her and sighing loudly as she settled her weight upon it.

She did not demur as her ankles were taken in turn, lifted and buckled into the wide straps at each of the rear support legs. Did not resist as her master pressed her upper body down, passing the even broader strap over the small of her back and buckling it until she could scarcely breathe, had become one with the leather top of the horse, her full feminine buttocks pushed upwards by her position, the brief skirt riding high, revealing the pink nakedness beneath.

The master stepped away, reaching down for the first instrument, presenting it to her willing lips for worship and consummation, the soft kiss full submission to the fiery pleasure it would bring her in this wonderful painworld.

And as the first stroke fell, as the first scarlet welt sprung up across the quivering girl flesh, Pauline bucked, rose and fell upon the unforgiving dildo and shrieked her total abandonment into a world of virtual unreality that was, at this very moment, only too marvellously real...

For the first time since childhood, for the first time she could really remember, Christina Fredrickson knew what it was to feel afraid. Not the knife-edged fear that came complete with the thrill of anticipation when taking on some new challenge, but the sort that brings with it a dull ache in the stomach and a weakening of the knees, the fear that comes with knowing what it really means to be helpless.

And as she stared at her new reflection in the long mirrored wall. Christina saw helplessness personified staring back at her from the impersonalised rubber mask which now enclosed her entire head, hiding away even the new face VESTA had given her after the judgement had been handed down.

The ritual had taken place inside the painworld itself, for Christina, after the ill-fated contest with Clarissa, had not been permitted to return to the outside world. Instead, she recalled only a period of stasis - how long it lasted she had no way of telling - during which she seemed to be floating in a peculiarly coloured world that was at once gaseous and liquid, shapeless forms floating by her distorted field of vision, her ears filled with a mixture of meaningless noises.

And then she had found herself in the courtroom, standing in a dock, facing a high bench upon which sat not only Nadia, but all her friends and associates, including - and Christina had ground her teeth at the time - the little blonde bitch she had earlier turned into such a wonderful pony girl.

There were nearly a dozen of them in all, each figure dressed in simple black, catsuits of latex or leather, many of them hiding their features behind matching hoods and masks. But not the Muirhead woman, nor the blonde bitch and her friend. The former stared down at her impassively, the latter pair made no attempt to hide the triumph in their expressions.

It was a complete parody, but the outcome was no surprise, for Christina had not expected, nor hoped for mercy and the fact that her 'trial' had been conducted inside VESTA was a powerful clue as to what was intended by way of retribution.

'Take the prisoner down,' Nadia had intoned, finally. At either side of her powerfully built male warders moved in and Christina whirled around, prepared to go down fighting.

Except...

She came round again standing naked in the centre of a pool of lights, the areas beyond swathed in gloom. Looking down, Christina saw that heavy steel cuffs were locked about her ankles, the short chain that connected them locked in turn to a heavy ring set in the bare stone floor. She looked up again, blinking, trying to discern the movements from the shadows, but as she did so another movement caught her eye.

Reaching up she grasped at the pale red tresses in disbelief, running the thin strands through her fingers and drawing them down over her bare breasts, astonished at the length of them. For not since the age of fifteen had she had long hair, and then it had been the same white blonde as the stubble she had maintained ever since.

Then there were her breasts themselves, if breasts was an appropriate term for

137

the twin swellings with their pert pink nipples, a bosom that was hardly fit for a grown woman, the sort of thing one would expect to find on a schoolgirl who had only just acquired her first brassiere.

And the rest of her body appeared to be in keeping with that image, although in truth the slim legs would not have disgraced an eighteen year old, while the sparse triangle of wan auburn hair...

'Hiya, toots!'

Christina did not have to look up to identify the speaker, but she did nevertheless, and was barely able to suppress a gasp of astonishment at what she saw. Lianne was barely recognisable as the girl Christina had abused so badly, both a year ago and again so recently.

She appeared somehow much taller, much more powerfully built, the deep gold of her latex catsuit apparently stretched to its limits to contain shoulders, bosom and hips, the fabric rippling over fabulously developed thigh muscles as she strode forward in knee high platform boots, crop swinging from one gloved hand.

'Like the new bod?' Lianne asked, grinning briefly. 'We all had quite a discussion before we decided what would be best. Ellen fancied having you look like a racing whippet, but then she always has had peculiar ideas. In the end we decided to make you into a sweet little five foot two teenager - the proverbial nine stone weakling, except that you're about a stone lighter than that, at least.'

She stepped forward again and Christina could see that, even without the heels, she would have topped her by several inches; with them she had a height advantage of nearly a foot.

'Not so much to say for yourself now?' Lianne taunted, prodding at her with the end of the crop. 'Well, maybe it's about time you learned a few lessons, starting with what it feels like to be at the mercy of someone bigger and stronger than you. Actually,' she continued, walking slowly around her prisoner, 'there's a sort of poetic justice in what's going to happen now.

'No doubt you'll remember spending several sessions with your German friend, apparently some months ago, detailing for him all the various devious and nasty ideas you had for mistreating your unfortunate victims. Well he had, according to our Marlon, used all of that to create a programme he was originally hoping to incorporate in his own version of VESTA.

'Of course, when he arrived here he discovered that all his hard work had virtually been rendered obsolete by what Marlon had done. However, that programme was very interesting anyway, and is a sort of archive of all your little twists and turns, so Ellen thought it would be a good idea to let you be the first to test drive it, as it were.'

'Don't get too clever,' Christina said, but the intended threat was largely nullified by the curiously girlish sound her voice seemed to have taken on. Fighting to try to make herself sound more authoritative, she nevertheless struggled gamely on.

'You won't be able to keep me here forever,' she said, 'and I have a long memory.'

'As I've already found out,' Lianne reminded her. 'And maybe we won't keep you here forever,' she conceded. 'After all, we're not all as fucking evil as you, bitch.' She thrust the crop under Christina's chin and forced her head back. 'Don't think I don't know what you had in mind for me over the next few years, either,' she snarled. 'That's all in Koenig's little programme too, don't forget.

'But don't worry, we've cut some of the more repulsive stuff. There's plenty to occupy your time without that. Now, shall we get you ready?'

There were helpers - enough to have overpowered Christina even if she had retained her original size and power - and she struggled to no avail for only a few minutes before conceding to the inevitable. Apart from Lianne they all hid their identities behind full masks, but Christina recognised one or two voices and was in no doubt that all her tormentors were linked to real people and not just VESTA generated characters.

It took them an hour...

'Up on the horse, you know what to do!' Lianne's barked command was accompanied by the sharp overhead crack from the long bullwhip wielded by her companion. Miserably, the petite figure that was now Christina tottered on ballet-toed boots towards the huge black creature that waited, tethered to the post at the side of the field.

Beside the creature stood a simple wooden mounting block, built to resemble two steps, for there were no stirrups attached to the saddle that awaited her, just a huge phallus rearing from its centre, a shaft upon which she was expected to impale herself under pain of a further whipping if she even hesitated.

With a grunt Christina swung her right leg up and over, settling first behind the glistening member and then, using her arms as leverage, lifting herself up and forward. With a deep sigh she sank onto the shaft, letting it enter her through the cut-out in the pale green rubber catsuit and sat passively, hands crossed behind her back.

Lianne stepped quickly forward, snapping steel bracelets about her wrists and then passing securing straps from the sides of the saddle over Christina's now slim thighs, drawing them tight and buckling them securely to prevent her falling off. The beaten Dane ground her teeth into the gag that filled her mouth inside the rubber face that had been glued over her own, closing her eyes to blot out the sight of the twin ginger pigtails that hung forward over her shoulders.

'Will you look at that?' the faceless companion laughed and Christina did not need to see her features to know who she was. 'Anne of fucking Green Gables, in the flesh - well, rubber, anyway.'

Lianne laughed. 'Hardly Children's Hour,' she said. 'Mind you, it'll do her good, I reckon. Are you sitting comfortably, Chrissie dear?'

Unable to speak anyway, Christina maintained a rigid pose, staring straight ahead through the eye slits. She heard Lianne sigh, extravagantly.

'Oh well, suit yourself. A couple of hours on Black Beauty here and then a good thrashing will do for this afternoon. Then maybe the evening as a mermaid, or maybe as a pony girl? I seem to remember you have a liking for pony girls.'

'D'you know,' Ellen said, from behind her mask, 'I get the feeling our Chrissie here is going right off horses, full stop. I mean, I've heard of aversion therapy, but this is taking it to the limits.'

'The limits?' Lianne echoed, raising her eyebrows and smiling. 'I haven't even started with her properly yet. By the time I've finished with this bitch she won't even be able to open a racing paper without having an orgasm, and that's a racing certainty.'

She stepped forward and unhitched the rope that held the black stallion to the post. Then coiling her whip, brought it sharply down across the magnificent beast's flank. With a snort it half reared and then, in a blur of mane and hooves, it was off, cantering strongly across the meadow, its hapless rider bobbing up and down in the saddle. Satisfied, Lianne watched until horse and rider had disappeared into the trees at the far end of the field and then turned to her friend.

'Everything's set to keep her occupied for the next three hours,' she said, 'so time we were out of here. Unless I'm much mistaken, the Grand National is on telly in about half an hour.'

'Bitch,' Ellen said simply, and they both laughed as the world about them began to fade to black...

Also by Jennifer Jane Pope and available as paperbacks at AMAZON:

Assignment for Alison
Chain Reaction
Net Asset
Bridled Lust
Cauldron of Fear
The Bridle Path
The Devil's Advocate
Teena Thyme
Thyme II Thyme
Teena - A House of Ill Repute

www.ingramcontent.com/pod-product-compliance
Lightning Source LLC
Chambersburg PA
CBHW060937120626
46557CB00003B/1032